YESTERDAY'S SECRETS

KELLY ANN RILEY

Guideposts
New York, New York

Guideposts.org
(800) 932-2145
Guideposts Books & Inspirational Media

Cover design by Wendy Bass
Cover illustration by Joyce Patti
Interior design by Lorie Pagnozzi
Typeset by Aptara

Printed and bound in the United States of America
10 9 8 7 6 5 4 3 2

This book is dedicated to Ashlyn Riley who keeps me inspired with her creativity and enthusiasm. Thank you for being an awesome daughter and friend.

I also wish to thank my wonderful editors, Beth Adams and Andy Meisenheimer, for their many hours of editing and insightful suggestions. They have made the experience of working on this series an exciting adventure. And finally, a huge thank-you to my agent, Kelly Mortimer, who helps turn dreams into reality.

 CHAPTER ONE

May sunlight danced through the oak leaves and warmed Sarah Hart's back as she worked in the little garden behind her house. She relished the feel of the cool soil between her fingers as she yanked a weed encroaching on the perimeter of one of her heirloom tomato plants.

"Be gone, you dastardly villain!" she said with dramatic flair as she tossed the weed into a growing pile. The night before, she'd fallen asleep reading one of her favorite Agatha Christie mysteries, and this morning, melodrama peppered her speech.

She leaned back on her heels and surveyed her botanical kingdom. Green fruit dotted the leafy tomato plants. Several tomatoes had swelled to the size of golf balls, and she couldn't wait for the first tomato sandwich of the season. Lacy sprigs from her baby carrots waved in the breeze. Cucumber plants crept up the trellis, and her zucchini and pepper plants flourished on their mounds of soil.

Even though her back ached now, it had been worth coming out here and taking a break from her current quilting project. The birds singing in the trees and the soft spring air made it a perfect day to relax outdoors and enjoy the beginning of a new season. She sighed and stood, brushing the dirt off her knees. Even with obligations awaiting her, surely nothing could disturb the peace of such a glorious day.

She gathered up her tools and the basket of yanked weeds and strode to the backdoor of her cozy Queen Anne-style home. She kicked off her garden shoes and was reaching for the door handle when someone said, "Sarah?"

Sarah jumped and dropped her basket, the dirt, and weeds scattering across the porch.

"Oh, I'm sorry. I didn't mean to startle you." A petite woman with bright red hair bent down to help clean up the mess. The sound of amusement in her voice triggered the right memory.

"Suzy Carmichael!" Sarah exclaimed. Except for occasional photos with the yearly Christmas card, she hadn't seen her college roommate since graduation. "I'd give you a hug, but I'm covered in dirt."

Suzy laughed. "You're a sight for sore eyes. I can't believe how many years have passed."

"I can't either, and here you are," Sarah shook her head in amazement. "We have a lot of catching up to do. Would you like to come in? I have some strawberry iced tea in the refrigerator."

"That sounds great," Suzy said as Sarah opened the door. "I love strawberry season. Phoenix is nice, but I miss seeing the green fields this time of year. Does Maple Hill still have the Strawberry Festival?"

Sarah set her basket and tools by the sink. "In two weeks. Memorial Day weekend. The weather has been perfect, so there are plenty of strawberries this year. Then in June we're having a big festival to celebrate the quasquibicentennial."

"The quas— what?"

Sarah laughed. "The town's 225th anniversary. No doubt tourists will flock in. It's great for the town and my daughter-in-law's business. Have you been downtown yet? She owns Magpie's Antiques on the square."

"How fun! I read about your son moving back to Maple Hill in your Christmas letter. He's a lawyer, right? You must be so proud of him. How are they adjusting to life in a small town?"

Sarah set out the pitcher and tall ice-filled glasses on the kitchen table near Suzy. "Jason's doing well, but then of course he grew up here." She filled Suzy's glass with the pink-tinged tea. "It was a little rough in the beginning for their girls, since they left friends behind in California. The twins are turning thirteen this month, so you can imagine how important their social life is becoming to them. They seem to be settling in fine now. I'm so thrilled they're here."

Suzy tasted the tea and added sugar, her spoon clinking on the glass. "I know what you mean. Luckily two of my three have settled in Phoenix. My youngest is expecting her first baby any time now, which will be my third grandchild and the first girl."

"Congratulations!" Sarah beamed. "Babies are even more fun when you're the grandmother."

"Oh, I know! I'm a bit anxious to get back. I just wish..." She sighed and gazed out the window. "You have such a lovely place. So homey. It suits you. I just wish I hadn't stayed away all these years. And I wish I could've come back for Gerry's funeral. You were in my thoughts and prayers."

Suzy reached across the table and grasped Sarah's hand. "I really, really liked him and thought you two were the perfect couple, even back in college."

"Please don't feel bad." Sarah squeezed Suzy's hand. "Your note was very touching, and I knew if you could've been here, you would've come."

"I just feel like I've let so many people down in the past. I'm going to try extra hard to make sure my Uncle Carroll is taken care of right," she said, determination in her voice.

Sarah studied Suzy while she lifted her glass and took several long swallows. Time had deepened the lines around green eyes that had sparkled with continuous mischief in their college days. The dusting of silver highlights throughout her bright short locks lent a distinguished air, and if Sarah wasn't mistaken, they'd been artfully enhanced. Her petite frame, dressed in a purple pantsuit, had broadened slightly but was still athletic looking. Overall, the years seemed to have been good to her old friend.

Suzy set her tea down, drawing circles in the condensation with her finger. "I only wish it wasn't a sad occasion that brought me back. I don't know if you've heard, but my cousin was killed in a car accident a couple of days ago."

"Oh Suzy, I'm so sorry. I read about the car accident in the paper. I didn't realize the woman was your cousin. I don't think I ever met her."

"I don't think you did either. Her mother was my mom's sister. Dawn and I weren't close. Too much of an age difference. When you and I were in college, she was only six. And then, of course, I moved away afterwards. In fact, she was the only one of the cousins who stayed in Maple Hill. Wanted to be close to her parents. She was their only child.

"Her father is in his eighties now and he was really dependent on Dawn. His health has been steadily failing, but with Dawn's help and her preparing meals for him, he was able to stay in his home."

"This must be so hard for him."

"It is, and it's going to get worse. I'm afraid I need to get him into assisted living and arrange for his house to be sold. He hates the idea, but I don't see that we have a choice. Without Dawn, he has no assistance, and he says he doesn't have the funds to hire someone to come into his house."

"Change can be hard at any age," Sarah said, thinking of her own father living at Bradford Manor. "But he may like the social life and activities at a care facility. I know my father likes the company. There's always someone to talk to."

"I don't know," Suzy said. "He's a tough old guy. You'd understand if you met him. He served in World War II and then started his own car dealership. He did well, considering his snarly personality. I guess he knew how to hire the right people." She sighed. "This move is going to be a nightmare."

"Is there anything I can do to help?" Sarah asked.

"Just talking about it has helped, and I seem to have dominated the conversation with my troubles when I'd really like to talk about the good old days." She lifted her watch. "But, I need to stop by and check on Uncle Carroll and see what needs to be done in that house. I got here yesterday just in time for the funeral today. I hope I can wrap up things in a couple of days."

"It sounds like you're going to be busy. How about I treat you both to dinner at The Old Mill tonight? That way you won't have to cook."

"I'd love to, but I don't know about Uncle Carroll. Other than going to church occasionally, he's pretty much homebound from what I understand. But," Suzy clapped her hands together, "even if he doesn't want to go, a girls' night out sounds wonderful. Would you like to ride over with me to Uncle Carroll's? It should only take me a minute to check on things, and we can see if he'd like to go to dinner."

"Great! It's a date then." Sarah refilled Suzy's glass, then excused herself to change out of her jeans and into a soft blue spring skirt and white peasant blouse. When she returned downstairs, she found Suzy in the living room examining a quilt Sarah had left on the back of the sofa, where she'd been doing some hand-stitching the night before.

"Pretty." Suzy lifted the delicate rose and lace Fan bed quilt.

"It belongs to a client and is over fifty years old. Some of the lace and stitching had torn loose here." Sarah ran her fingers over the corner where the damage had been done.

"I can't even tell where the old stitching stops and where you repaired it."

"I had to yellow the thread using tea. The lace was a bit harder to match. If you look closely, the pattern is slightly off."

"I'm still impressed. You were always artsy even in school. Do you get much business?"

"I stay busy enough. Some projects take longer than others. I do it mostly because I enjoy restoring someone else's handicraft. I hate to see beauty and history lost."

"I've never had a knack for sewing and doubt I'd have the time to learn if I tried." Suzy sighed and set down the quilt. "Well, are we ready?"

Sarah grabbed her new paisley purse. Suzy insisted on driving, so she and Sarah hopped in the white Taurus sedan. Carroll Shepherd's house was located about twenty minutes across town.

Suzy parked in front of an old Victorian on Elm Street. "Funny how some things don't change. Although I was thinking when I dropped Carroll off after the funeral how the place looked smaller than I remembered, but maybe I'm just bigger." She laughed and set the parking brake.

They walked up the sidewalk to the spacious front porch that was bordered by a waist-high hedge. As they ascended the three wooden steps, Sarah caught a whiff of paint and sawdust before the breeze snatched it away.

"Is your uncle remodeling?" she asked as Suzy rang the doorbell.

"I have no idea. I don't keep in touch much with this side of the family," Suzy said, opening the screen door and trying the door handle. "Oh look, the door's cracked open." She pushed it open further.

"Uncle Carroll?" she called. "It's Suzy. Can we come in? I brought a friend."

When no answer came, Suzy glanced at Sarah, a wrinkle forming on her forehead. "He can't go far. He uses a walker and is confined to the first floor."

Suzy called his name again and entered the foyer. Her heels clicked on the hardwood floor as she walked down a hall and turned to the first opening on the right. She gasped.

"What is it?" Sarah rushed forward and skidded to a stop next to Suzy. She gazed into a large living room. A Tiffany lamp lay in the middle of the rug, glass shards from its broken shade fanned out across the room. An overturned end table rested beside it. Books lay tumbled on the floor beneath the shelves by the mantel, and the doors of a large china cabinet stood wide open.

"Uncle Carroll? Where are you?" Suzy called again, a panicked note in her voice. She darted down the hallway toward the back of the house. "The backdoor's open too," Suzy yelled from the depths of the house. "I think someone broke in!"

"Suzy, come back. Someone may still be here," Sarah called, her heart pounding. She dug through her purse for her cell phone.

A few moments later, Suzy reappeared with a broom in her hand. Her gaze turned to the wide staircase.

"Call the police! I'm checking upstairs," she said and charged up the staircase.

"Wait, Suzy!" Sarah yelled after her. But just as in their college days, Suzy hurtled into the situation, heedless of Sarah's cautionary advice. Though in college, she'd never wielded a broom like a sword.

Sarah dialed nine-one-one with shaking fingers. What was she supposed to do if Suzy actually found someone up there?

The operator answered, and Sarah reported that there'd been a possible break-in and gave the address. The woman instructed Sarah to wait outside, preferably at a neighbor's home.

Sarah explained to the operator that Suzy was still in the house. "Can the police please hurry?"

"They've dispatched a car. I'll hold on the line until they get there."

"Thank you," Sarah said and breathed a prayer. *Dear Lord, please protect us even though Suzy refuses to listen.*

Despite her fear, the thought that this wasn't the first time she'd uttered that prayer where Suzy was concerned tickled her lips, making her want to giggle.

How many times had she uttered that prayer when following Suzy about in college? Sarah always thought Suzy should have become an investigative reporter. Her Nancy Drew-like curiosity had her poking her nose into places where no "nice girls" should enter—all in the name of research. In college, Suzy had wanted to be a lawyer and she was accepted at Yale Law. Then she had surprised everyone by taking off to Florida to "find herself." Suzy had never offered any explanation in their brief notes to each other, and Sarah had never asked, figuring her friend would confide in her when she was ready. About a year later, Suzy moved to Phoenix and got married.

"Suzy!" Sarah called when the footsteps overhead stilled. Her heartbeat skittered to a higher rate until Suzy called down, "There's no one here. I'm going to check the attic."

"The police are on the way. The nine-one-one operator wants us to wait *outside*. Suzy?"

"I assume your friend is not listening," the operator commented. "Ma'am, I would suggest for your safety you need to wait outside."

"I will." Yet Sarah couldn't help inching toward the staircase, straining her ears for any sound. Maybe she should join Suzy. If anything happened to her while Sarah just stood there, why she'd never—Sarah's thoughts were interrupted when a deep voice barked behind her, "What are you doing in my house?"

Sarah whirled around, banging her elbow against the banister. Her cell phone flew through the air and landed at the feet of a large bear of a man hunched over a walker in the front doorway. His blue eyes glared at her from under shaggy white eyebrows, and his face was as red as a strawberry under a shock of snowy hair.

Sarah rubbed her elbow and took several deep breaths. "Mr. Shepherd?"

"Uncle Carroll!" Suzy called from the top of the stairs and rushed down. "You're all right."

"Of course I'm all right! What's the matter with you, woman?"

"Someone broke in. The police are on their way."

"Police! I don't want any police here. The neighbors will think I died or something. Bad enough people think I can't take care of myself." He jerked the walker forward, thumping across the hardwood floor. When he moved, Sarah and Suzy could see a woman standing just outside the doorway. She wore a white lab coat over blue scrub pants, and she gave them a little wave.

"I'm Nancy Ferguson, the neighbor next door. I saw Carroll down the street and offered him a ride home. Is something wrong?"

"When we got here the front and back doors were open, and it looks like someone vandalized the living room," Suzy said.

"That's terrible!" Nancy said. "This is usually such a safe neighborhood."

Carroll stopped in the living room entryway. "You're all overreacting."

"But Uncle Carroll, the doors were open and anyone could've come in here and stolen something. Don't you care?" Suzy asked.

He gazed around. "The only things I care about are my tools, and someone already took those."

"When did that happen?" Suzy asked, her voice rising. "Did you report it to the police?"

Carroll's face flushed to a deeper red. "The police can't do anything, the incompetent—"

"You have to be more careful, Uncle Carroll. You're here all alone. Bad people will see you as a target. Anyone could've walked in the house and hurt you," Suzy said, exasperation making her voice tremble. "Has this happened before? Have you wandered off and left the doors open?"

"Of course not!" he bellowed. "Do I look like a fool?"

"Maybe I should go," Nancy said, as a knock sounded on the door.

"Maple Hill police."

Sarah was relieved to see Officer Hopkins, one of the policemen she knew on the force. He gave her a smile. Nancy apparently changed her mind about leaving, and moved toward the staircase.

"Oh, great!" Carroll said. "It's you again. Didn't I tell you that I don't want you in my house?"

"I'm just trying to do my job, sir. I'm responding to a call about a possible intruder," Officer Hopkins said mildly. His gaze swept the scene.

"I'm the one who called it in," Sarah said. "Both downstairs doors were open and the living room is ransacked. Mr. Shepherd wasn't in the house and we assumed the worst."

Carroll blocked their path. "*I* broke the lamp. This is all a mistake. You can leave now."

"What about your missing tools?" Suzy asked.

"That's none of your business."

The officer paused with his pen poised over his notebook. "Mr. Shepherd, would you like to report a theft?"

The old man grunted. "Happened a few weeks ago. Dawn might've moved them. She sold a couple to that young whippersnapper she hired to do some carpentry work. Didn't even consult me until after the fact. She had no right to do that."

"So they weren't actually stolen?"

"I didn't say that. Dawn may have sold some, but I can't find the rest."

Officer Hopkins tapped his pen. "Do you want to make a report or is this going to be a repeat of what happened last time?"

"What happened last time?" Suzy asked.

"No, I don't want to make a report. Just go!" Carroll waved the officer away and stomped into the living room, giving his walker an extra thump each time he set it down.

Suzy went after him with Nancy following. "Uncle Carroll, what happened?"

"It's none of your business."

"I'm making it my business since someone has to take care of you."

"Who asked you?"

Their voices grew fainter and Sarah looked at Officer Hopkins. "I'm sorry."

"No problem. This isn't the first time we've been called out here. His daughter suspected someone had been in the house. We didn't find anyone. The old man called a week ago to report that things had been stolen, but that turned out to be nothing too."

"What happened?" Sarah asked, following the officer out onto the porch. Carroll and Suzy's arguing could still be heard from the living room.

"You better ask the old man," Officer Hopkins said and tapped his temple. "Though, I think he may be losing it."

When Sarah returned to the living room, Carroll's yelling had softened to muttering about people making decisions for him. He sprawled in a chair, his chest heaving and a bead of sweat glistening on his forehead. Nancy hovered over him, and Suzy had disappeared.

"Carroll, do you need your heart medication?" Nancy asked as she lifted his wrist and felt his pulse.

"No!"

"Maybe we should call your doctor."

"No doctors! I'll be fine if everyone just leaves me alone."

"But if you're having any pain you need to take them. Your pulse feels a bit erratic." Nancy released his arm. "Where do you keep your meds?"

"Here, his pills were in the kitchen," Suzy said, hurrying in with a water glass and two orange medication bottles. "These say take as needed."

"No pills! They make me sleepy, and I won't be able to watch the news."

Suzy leaned over Carroll. "It's either take the meds, or I call the paramedics." She placed two pills in his hand.

He made grumbling sounds and swallowed the medication. "Happy?"

"Not quite, but it's a start in the right direction," Suzy said.

Nancy stepped back to where Sarah stood in the entryway and whispered. "Don't let his behavior fool you. He's not that bad. Underneath all that blustering is a heart of gold. My son Jared really likes him. Carroll hired him to do yard work and odd jobs so Jared could buy a new bike. Now he buys all his own clothes and is saving for a car and college."

"What were you doing outside anyway?" Suzy asked Carroll, fetching a small couch pillow and placing it behind him.

He leaned his head back, closed his eyes, and muttered, "Eddie."

"Eddie? Who's Eddie?" Suzy looked at Nancy.

"There wasn't anyone around when I picked him up."

"Uncle Carroll—"

A wheezy whistle rose from the chair, followed by a deep exhalation. Carroll's eyes were shut tight.

"My money says he's pretending to be asleep," Suzy said. She stared at Carroll for a moment longer, then motioned for Sarah and Nancy to follow her though the doorway, down the hall to a sunny yellow kitchen. The appliances appeared at least thirty years old, and the countertops were worn and chipped. Dishes were piled in the sink, and the floor looked like it hadn't been mopped in weeks. Suzy leaned against the counter. "This doesn't make any sense. Why would anyone come in here and just steal his tools? There has to be more valuable stuff in this house. That cabinet in the living room alone looks like it's full of antiques."

"Do you know what kind of tools he lost?"

Suzy shrugged. "I have no idea. But not only did Uncle Carroll own a car dealership, he was a top-notch mechanic, and Dawn used to brag he was an inventor. The few times I visited—and it was years ago—it seemed like he had hundreds of tools lying around."

"Did you notice anything unusual when you dropped him off earlier?"

"No, but then I didn't get a good look around. Carroll insisted he wanted time alone. I helped him to the doorway and then went for a drive. I know he's grieving, even though he doesn't want to talk about Dawn. This whole situation really worries me."

"Does he have memory problems?" Sarah asked, thinking of her father's frequent forgetfulness.

"Not that I know of," Suzy said. "Like I said, I haven't stayed much in contact with this side of the family. This is the first time I've been here for thirty years. I guess I need to speak to his doctor." She looked at Nancy. "Do you know anything about his health?"

"Dawn used to come over once in a while and update me on what was going on. He has high blood pressure and suffered a small stroke two years ago, which is why he uses the walker," Nancy said. "They both had my number if he needed any help during the night."

"Where was Dawn living?" Suzy asked.

"In an apartment about a mile from here, but she said she was planning to move in here eventually. I guess she wanted some measure of independence for both of them until Carroll deteriorated enough to need live-in help. He seemed to do fine with her popping over here every evening to fix him dinner."

Sarah remembered how her father had refused to move in with her and Gerry when Sarah's mother died. He didn't want to be a bother. Maybe Carroll felt the same way.

Suzy latched the backdoor and threw the dead bolt. "We still don't know if anything valuable is missing. Why does Uncle Carroll have to be so uncooperative?"

Neither Sarah nor Nancy had an answer to that.

"I'm not sure how I'm going to handle this. Just from my quick look at the upstairs and attic, it's going to take weeks to go through all the junk," Suzy said. "I didn't plan to be here that long."

"I'd help, but I'm putting in double shifts at the hospital. I'm a lab tech, and one of our guys just quit without notice." Nancy glanced at her watch. "In fact, I better run and get a quick bite before I have to get back there."

"Thanks for getting Uncle Carroll home."

"No problem. I feel bad about the whole situation. The neighborhood isn't going to seem the same without him and Dawn." She paused in the doorway. "Jared should be home in a couple of hours, if you want to talk to him. My house and work phone numbers are next to the kitchen phone if you need me." She gave them a wave and hustled down the hall.

Suzy studied the numbers listed on the index card. "I'm going to give his doctor a call anyway. I don't like his color."

"Can't hurt," Sarah said. "I'll go check on him." She walked quietly down the hall. Carroll still snored softly, his breathing deep and even, and the crimson flush of his cheeks had faded.

She got a small wastebasket from the corner of the room and picked up the glass from the lamp. If Carroll hadn't been asleep, she'd have found a vacuum to pick up the remaining slivers.

"How's he doing?" Suzy asked, breezing into the room.

"His color is better."

"I finally got one of his doctors. He said Uncle Carroll can have episodes where his blood pressure spikes. It can cause forgetfulness and even blackouts, but as long as he takes his medication, he should be all right." She ran her hand through her short hair, tousling the red curls. "I'm sorry. We won't be able to go to The Old Mill. I need to watch him for a couple of hours."

"Of course, I understand," Sarah said. "Tell you what. How about I get some groceries and we eat here? Then maybe we can have a look around for those tools."

Tears glistened in Suzy's eyes. "Sarah, you're such a good friend. Why did I stay away so long?"

CHAPTER TWO

Sarah turned on the lamp by her sofa and pulled the rose and lace Fan quilt onto her lap. A few more inches of minute stitches and she would call the restoration done. She felt bone tired. After returning from the grocery store, she had made spaghetti and salad for their dinner, and then she and Suzy had conducted a quick search through the first two floors for Carroll's tools.

Carroll had eaten a few bites of supper before nodding off again, but not before he mentioned that Dawn had gradually moved all his tools up from the basement. They could be anywhere now, if they were even still in the house.

Suzy was correct in saying it would take weeks, if not a month, to pack up the house. Carroll was a pack rat. Every closet and bedroom was stuffed with items accumulated over fifty years. Suzy said the attic was even worse, but she had called it quits for the night before reaching that floor. She had gotten only four hours of sleep the previous night and wanted to get back to the motel.

The kitchen phone rang, and Sarah raced to grab it before the answering machine picked up.

"Sarah? Suzy here. I've had some disturbing news. My daughter's gone into early labor, but there are complications and..." Suzy hesitated, a catch in her voice. "There's a chance the baby might not make it."

"I'm so sorry, Suzy. I'll keep them in my prayers. Is there anything I can do for you?"

"Actually there is," Suzy said. "I'm going to take you up on your offer to help out with Carroll for a few days. If you could check on him and bring him lunch, I'd so appreciate it. I hate asking, but I got a flight out tomorrow morning at ten. I'll drop by with the key to the house."

"Of course. But will Carroll allow me to help? He didn't seem to like me."

"He doesn't like anyone. But I just had a chat with him, and don't worry, he'll cooperate."

Sarah wasn't so sure about that. "Would you like me to start organizing some of his things for the move? Maybe I can figure out where those tools ended up."

"That would be great, and while you're at it, can you keep an eye out for Dawn's will? Apparently it got misplaced. According to Uncle Carroll, when Aunt Betty passed away, she left her half of the house to Dawn, and if we can't find the will, it may take months of probate to get the house title cleared so we can sell it."

"If I come across it, I'll let you know."

"Carroll still hates the idea of going into assisted living, but pretty soon he'll be out of options. I took a gander at his finances and hiring live-in help or even a visiting nurse will drain the bank account before the year's out.

"Right now, if he sells his house, he can get a place in a retirement village where he'll get meals and people who'll look after him. He's going to have to get organized, regardless of the timetable we set up. I'm tempted to let him fend for himself for a few days, so he can see how difficult life is going to be now, but I don't have the heart to."

"Suzy, you've always done the right thing."

She sighed. "Even when it's gotten me in trouble. But, listen, I owe you, roomy. When I get back, I'm going to treat you to the best meal The Old Mill can offer."

"It's a date," Sarah said. The massive old house itself seemed like one big mystery, and she was going to love poking through its memories.

Besides, she owed Suzy. Her outgoing roommate had taken Sarah under her wing that first year away from home, introducing her to people, badgering her to join clubs and the yearbook staff. Gerry used to call her Suzy Chatterbox because she never stopped talking.

Sarah put the phone back and noted the blinking red light on the answering machine. There were two messages. One from Maggie, Sarah's daughter-in-law, remarking that the twins had mentioned something about a jam party with their Gram. Was Sarah planning to rock out with the twins?

She spoke with amusement in her voice. And when did she want them?

Sarah chuckled. Her jam party consisted of teaching Audrey and Amy how to make strawberry jam and can it in pint-size jars. The party portion of the event would be homemade ice cream to pour hot jam over.

Sarah glanced at the clock. It was after eleven. She would give Maggie a ring in the morning.

The second short message was from Irene Stuart.

"Sarah. This is Irene Stuart. I was thinking that if you ... I mean ... I have a favor to ask if you have some time. It's not urgent ... well, it's important of course. To me. Please give me a call when you have a chance. I'd appreciate it."

Normally, Sarah went to Irene with questions. Irene, the historian at the Maple Hill Historical Society, was very smart and efficient. They had often spent time together hunting down historical facts, but they had never been close friends. Sarah really didn't know much about her personal life other than that Irene had moved to Maple Hill ten years ago with her husband Chris who loved archeology.

She wondered what Irene could possibly want. Maybe it had something do with the Strawberry Festival. A lot of people in town were involved. She jotted down a note to remind herself to call Irene in the morning too.

Returning to her living room couch, she added a couple more stitches to the quilt while humming the hymn "Showers of Blessings," which had been the opening song for church last Sunday at Bridge Street Church. Sarah certainly felt blessed these days with her family being in Maple Hill. She loved her restoration work with the quilts, and now she even had a small mystery to solve. She just hoped Carroll was in a more hospitable mood tomorrow.

She said a prayer for Suzy's daughter and her baby and then gathered up her thread, scissors, and the quilt, and returned them to her sewing room off of the kitchen. She carefully folded and wrapped the quilt in tissue paper, feeling a rush of warm satisfaction. She would call Mrs. Grayson tomorrow and let her know the quilt was finished.

On the way through the kitchen, she paused by the stack of newspapers she planned to put in the recycle bin. She sifted through the daily and weekend editions until she found what she wanted. Tucking them under her arm she headed upstairs to her room.

She reached the second-floor landing where she had made a sitting area for her boarders. She paused to straighten the Flying Geese quilt on the back of the love seat and restack the magazines on the end table. Her current renter, Andi McCormack, must have already retired for the night since no light shone under her door.

Sarah continued on to her room and changed into her nightgown. She pulled back the light floral quilt she'd put on the bed in honor of spring and settled on the sleigh bed. Opening the newspaper, she read the account of Dawn Shepherd's accident. A car in the southbound lane had crossed the median, so Dawn swerved to avoid hitting a school van in front of her and accidentally hit a pole. Her quick act may have saved the lives of the preschool children in the van. Dawn Shepherd was a paralegal and worked at the courthouse.

Sarah flipped the pages and found Dawn's scant obituary, her gaze dropping to the last paragraph.

She is survived by her father, Carroll Shepherd, World War II veteran and co-owner of Shepherd & Stanford car dealership in Pittsfield, and two cousins.

Sarah set the newspapers aside, her eyes misty. Poor Mr. Shepherd. He really was alone now. Losing a spouse— she could relate to that—but how devastating it must be to lose your child. Sympathy for Carroll swelled. She fell asleep praying for Carroll and thanking God she still had her children.

"Mrs. Hart, I was heading out to work and found this on the front porch," Andi said, breezing into the kitchen with a light step and bright smile. Sarah looked up from the kitchen table where she was sipping her morning coffee and reading the newspaper.

Where Andi got her boundless energy, Sarah didn't know. During the previous month, Andi had balanced her work at the Miss Maple diner and her classes at the nearby community college while still maintaining a healthy social life. Sarah got tired just thinking about it.

Andi handed a large manila envelope to Sarah. "I'm late for the diner. I'll catch you later. Have a great day."

Sarah wished her the same and studied the envelope. Sarah's name was slashed across the front in bold letters. She pulled out several sheets of paper. The top one read:

Sarah,

I was able to get an earlier flight home. Enclosed is a list of Carroll's medications, his appointments, and a key to the house. There are also photos he had me take of books in the attic in case he wanted to pick out something different to read. I should be back by the end of the week.

Good luck with the inventorying!

Sarah turned the note over. Suzy hadn't even left a phone number. Carroll must have it. She leafed through the photos of books that had been printed on plain paper. The novels were stacked in shallow crates with their spines upward. Behind the crates she could see other boxes piled almost to the ceiling. What had she gotten herself into?

Oh well, she'd give it her best shot. After all, Suzy said she'd be back by the end of the week. Meanwhile Sarah would concentrate on finding Carroll's tools, and see if Carroll could tell if any other valuables were missing from the house.

She slid the papers and the key back into the envelope, tidied up the kitchen, and called Mrs. Grayson to tell her the quilt was ready. Then she put a call in to Maggie at the store.

"Magpie's Antiques," Maggie's cheerful voice chirped over the phone.

"Hi, Maggie, it's Sarah. I'm returning your call. Are Audrey and Amy ready to jam?" Sarah asked.

Maggie laughed. "Took me several moments to figure out what they were talking about. I had a flashback to college when Jason and I went to a music jam session. Finally, Audrey mentioned strawberries and it all clicked. I think making jam sounds like a great idea. Yummy too. When would you like to have the girls?"

"I was thinking Friday or Sunday afternoon, whichever is more convenient. I still need to get strawberries."

"Sunday would work best."

"That sounds good." It gave Sarah the rest of the week to buy a flat of strawberries. The berry farms in the county had released announcements that because of the early warm weather this year, the luscious berries were ready to be picked.

Sarah gave Maggie a quick overview of the previous evening and mentioned where she would be spending the next few mornings.

"Carroll Shepherd. Why does that name sound familiar?" Maggie asked. In the background the door bell jangled, heralding the arrival or departure of customers.

"His daughter Dawn died in a car accident recently. Maybe you read about it in the paper?"

"Ah yes, that was it. So sad. Did you know she was a paralegal and worked at the courthouse? Jason said he saw her there, but they never actually met. Her poor father. Makes you realize how precious and fleeting life can be."

Sarah agreed, again realizing how fortunate she was to have Jason's family nearby. Sarah enjoyed her chats with Maggie. Jenna, Sarah's daughter, had moved to Texas, and although they talked frequently on the phone, Sarah missed watching her grandchildren grow and being there for Jenna during the ups and downs of her life.

She turned the conversation back to the subject of strawberries, and they chatted about the upcoming festival. Maggie had rented one of the tents to be set up in the park, as an advertisement for the store. She was trying to decide which of her antiques to display. The discussion continued until Maggie needed to assist a customer.

After they said good-bye, Sarah called the number Irene had left and got her voice mail. She left a message to call her back on her cell phone, wondering again what Irene wanted.

Feeling satisfied she'd gotten some things checked off her to-do list, she slipped her reading glasses into her purse and dug out her car keys. Time to do battle with Suzy's Uncle Carroll.

CHAPTER THREE

W hat do you want?" Carroll asked, a growl in his voice.

"Good morning, Mr. Shepherd," Sarah said cheerfully. "I'm here to fix your lunch and to help you start sorting through all this...er...through your belongings. Suzy explained why I'm here, right?"

"I don't need anyone meddling in my life. I'm fine."

Sarah eyed the bear of a man still in the brown armchair, wearing the same slacks and dress shirt from the previous day. Deep creases suggested he'd slept in them. Sarah wondered if he was able to change his clothes without assistance.

"I don't want to meddle, just help. But I can leave if you insist or I can make lunch first. Did you eat breakfast?"

He ignored her question but eyed the brown sack in her arms. "What's in the bag?"

"Chicken, potatoes, and lettuce and cucumbers, plus a homemade apple-rhubarb pie I had in my freezer. I thought

I'd make mock fried chicken, baked potatoes, and a fresh green salad."

He licked his lips. "Well, if Suzy wanted you to make me lunch, we wouldn't want to worry her, now would we?"

Sarah kept her expression serious. "No, we wouldn't. I'll take these to the kitchen." She walked down the hall and unloaded the groceries on the counter. She scrubbed the potatoes and popped them in the oven, and then gathered the ingredients for the baked chicken dish. Dawn had kept Carroll's kitchen well stocked with staples. She found flour and bread crumbs in the cupboard, mixed them together and added salt, pepper, and dried herbs for extra flavor. After dipping the chicken in broth, she dredged the pieces in the flour mixture.

Thumping in the hall heralded Mr. Shepherd's arrival. He made his way into the kitchen and settled heavily on a chair. He watched Sarah put the baking sheet in the oven. "You're not going to fry the chicken?" he asked.

"This is *mock* fried chicken. I like it fried in oil too, but baked is healthier. You can try my recipe and if you don't like it, I'll do it the traditional way next time." *If* there was a next time.

"Healthy my eye. Everyone these day talks about being healthy. I've eaten fried chicken every week my entire life. But what do I know? I'm only eighty-nine years old."

Sarah decided to ignore the sarcasm and proceeded to chop up the cucumbers for the salad, aware Carroll watched every move. Finally she said, "So tell me about your tools. What's so special about them?"

"Ah my tools," he said in a reverent tone. "I've been collecting them for years. The right tool can change your life, you know?"

Sarah turned her head. "I never thought of it quite that way, but yes, I agree. They have changed the world. Like with quilting. Sewing machines revolutionized how efficiently and quickly quilts can be made, although I still prefer to hand-stitch some projects."

"Why?"

"Sewing is an art, and I get satisfaction from doing the stitches myself, although machine quilting takes skill too."

"Humph."

"Okay, why don't we see if we can figure out where your remaining tools are? You mentioned Dawn sold some of them, but maybe the rest are here somewhere."

"That's right." His face flushed. "Dawn had no right to sell my tools. Just because I can't get around like I used to, doesn't mean—"

"She never asked you if she could sell them? Weren't you here when she did?"

"Well, maybe she did. I wasn't paying much attention."

"Who did she sell them to?" Sarah asked.

"Some handyman. She got a bee in her bonnet; wanted to fix up the house before she moved in. There were guys all over the place."

"So your daughter was planning to move in here?"

He shrugged. "Not right away but someday."

Sarah dumped the cucumbers in the salad bowl and found some tomatoes in Carroll's refrigerator. "How valuable would you say these tools were that disappeared?"

"You can't put a price on those tools. They were invaluable. Knowing Dawn's lack of bargaining skills, she probably sold them for far less than they were worth. If I were selling the lot she did, I'd say twelve hundred dollars."

Sarah must've looked surprised because he added, "Quality tools are an investment. They last a lifetime."

"Oh I realize the expense. My husband Gerry was into woodworking." Sarah thought of Gerry's work area in the cellar. She still hadn't had the heart to clean it out. "Do you have a record of the sale or receipt of some kind?"

"Dawn might've gotten one. I don't know."

Sarah suppressed a sigh. "Well, do you remember any of the workers' names?" She finished the tomatoes, rinsed the romaine lettuce in the sink, and tore it into bite-size pieces.

"There was one guy named Joe. Don't know the last name. Never was introduced to the others. Most of them stayed outside or only came into the kitchen when Dawn was here."

"Well, we have forty-five minutes until the chicken is done. Let's take another look for those tools while we wait. Where did you keep them?"

He sighed. "I kept them in my basement workshop until I had my stroke. Then the toolbox was either in the hall closet or here in the kitchen. Over there."

Sarah followed his pointing to the wall under the window. If someone came to the backdoor and found it open, they could've easily reached in and grabbed the toolbox. "How long since you last saw the toolbox?"

"I don't know. A week or so. I just assumed she put it back in the closet."

"Let's walk around the first floor. You can tell me if anything appears to be missing, and maybe we'll run across a clue to finding your tools."

Carroll looked like he might refuse but then he stood, leaning on his walker, and thumped out the door. Sarah grabbed a notebook from her purse and followed.

From Sarah's quick tour the night before, she knew that the downstairs consisted of two large rooms—the living room and the family room—a smaller dining room which had been converted into a bedroom for Carroll, plus the kitchen, a bathroom, and a hall closet.

They searched the hall closet first. No tools, but they found a box of roofing nails. Carroll gestured toward a closed double door. "Dawn was using the family room for storage."

Sarah and Suzy had quickly perused the room the previous evening, and the sunlight that now flooded the room through the tall windows didn't lessen the overwhelming claustrophobic feeling that swamped her again. Newspaper skyscrapers teetered along one wall. Ladies' clothing draped over the two chairs and sofa. Boxes were stacked as high as the mantel in front of the stone fireplace, and more lined up across the floor. Several were labeled Salvation Army. The scent of dust hung heavily in the air and tickled Sarah's nose.

"Looks like Dawn was sorting things," Sarah said to Carroll. "Can you tell if anything is missing?"

"No." He turned and left.

She swept through the room looking behind the boxes and furniture. No tools to be seen. She jotted down a list of things to be done in her notepad. Since they were on the ground floor, maybe Carroll could sort what was in here, or if he refused, at least he could supervise.

The last room was Carroll's bedroom. The bed wasn't made. She looked under it and found a pair of loafers and a sock. This room wouldn't take as much time to clear since Carroll had only been living in it for the last couple of years.

An old metal desk was crammed in the corner with stacks of paper on it. She found a folder with bills and another with bank statements. Under the folders lay a green sheet of paper for a roofing company with an estimate on roof repair, and she took that with her to living room.

"Do you know if these were the people who worked on your roof?"

He glanced at it and shook his head.

"I'm going to take it and give them a call later if we don't find the tools. Maybe they saw them."

"Knock yourself out," Carroll said.

Sarah sighed. Stacks of magazines were piled behind the large sofa. *Popular Mechanics, Sports Illustrated, Newsweek,* and yellowed copies of *Good Housekeeping* and *Knitting Today* dated eight years ago.

Behind one of the two green wing chairs by the fireplace, she discovered a box of new stoneware dishes that Carroll didn't offer any explanation for. A small table by the bay window supported a large chess game board with ferocious gothic-looking game pieces.

"Looks like a game is in progress," Sarah commented.

"The neighbor boy sometimes stops in and tries to beat me. Eddie used to play too. We'd set up a chess set at the dealership and have tournaments," Carroll said. Then he barked out, "That's not right."

"What?" Sarah turned. Carroll was staring at the glass-fronted cabinet that contained a collection of intricately designed small boxes.

"Someone's been messing with Betty's music boxes. They aren't in the right order."

Sarah peered into the cabinet, wondering how he could tell. Dozens of wooden and metal boxes ranging from the size of a breadbox to smaller than her palm covered four shelves.

"Someone dusted recently," Sarah said, "Maybe Dawn—"

Carroll yanked open one door. "Dawn would put them back exactly where they belonged. It was important to both of us that we left them exactly as Betty wanted."

His large hand trembled as he switched two around.

"They're pretty. Do you keep anything in them?" Sarah asked, hoping that talking would ease the telltale flush of high blood pressure creeping up his neck.

"Trinkets and souvenirs we collected in our travels." He selected a redwood box decorated with carved roses and lifted the lid. A tinny version of Sleeping Beauty's waltz played. Carroll let out a sound of disgust. "These aren't supposed to be in here."

Sarah stared at the oblong gold objects, the size of coat buttons, in his palm. "What are they?"

"Old Egyptian coins I picked up in Cairo."

"Fascinating." Sarah took a closer look. "When were you in Cairo?"

"After the war. My platoon had some R & R, and since we were passing through North Africa, we zipped on down to Cairo. Wanted to see the pyramids." He counted the coins. "They're all here." Carroll reached for another box: maple inlaid with yellow flat stones. He was about to drop the coins in when he said, "This is wrong too."

"Is something missing?"

"No, but these postcards aren't supposed to be here." He pulled out the cards. "They go in that chest from Italy. See? These are *Italian* postcards."

"I see," Sarah said. "Carroll, when was the last time you checked these boxes?"

He blinked at her. "I don't know. It's been awhile."

"Weeks, months, or years?"

"Valentine's Day," he said decisively and snatched up a gilded box with red heart-shaped stones on it. He examined the interior and apparently found everything in order because he placed it back on the shelf.

Sarah watched him check and rearrange the other music boxes. Why would anyone bother moving things around and not just steal the boxes or the contents? February was three months ago. If Dawn was starting to go through Carroll's belongings, she could've easily mixed things up.

A ping sounded in the kitchen. "Lunch is ready. Do you need help washing up?" Sarah asked.

He waved her away.

By the time she'd set the table, Carroll appeared in fresh clothes, and he'd combed his hair. Apparently he was capable of some self-care, Sarah noted with relief. His brown slacks were wrinkled but looked clean. Laundry hadn't been on Suzy's list, but Sarah would see if he needed some done.

She prepared a plateful of food, set it in front of Carroll, and then fixed one for herself. When she returned to the table, he still hadn't picked up a fork. "Is something wrong?"

"I was waiting for grace."

Sarah smiled and bowed her head.

"For what we are about to receive, we thank you." Carroll cut into the chicken, the crunchy outside giving way to the tender meat. He took a second bite, so Sarah figured it had met his standards.

"Suzy said that you used to own a car dealership."

"Still do," he said, digging into his baked potato. "I'm a silent partner now. Shepherd and Stanford used to be one of the most successful dealerships in the state. Now, it's barely staying afloat."

"I'm sorry to hear that."

He shrugged. "Car sales aren't what they used to be. Everyone wants green cars, and I don't mean the color. Tiny cars with barely any get up and go. When I started out, no one would've believed we'd be reduced to this state. What we sold was luxury. Still do."

"What kind of cars did you sell?"

"Cadillacs. I started working for Lindberg Cadillac in St. Louis. Worked my way up the chain and branched out on my own," he said. "Before that I used to sell Studebakers and Edsels."

"My great-aunt owned an Edsel," Sarah said.

"The last Edsel rolled off the assembly line in 1959. Eddie had joined the dealership the year before. He almost quit, but luckily he was smitten with our secretary Clarice, so he stuck around." He grinned. "She wore her hair up in one of those beehive hairdos. Could stick a dozen pencils in it and it wouldn't move."

Sarah smiled at the image as Carroll continued. "Also had a young mechanic named Stanley. Bright boy. Wanted to get an engineering degree and work for NASA. I wonder whatever happened to him. Anyway ... where was I? Oh yes, the Edsel. Did you ever ride in one?"

"Once. My aunt lived out of town, but when she came to visit she took all of us for a ride. She loved that car."

He launched into detailed descriptions of engines and horsepower until Sarah thought her eyes would cross. Not that Carroll would notice as he rattled on. She was anxious to get to work. Suzy would be back in a few days, and Sarah wanted to at least track down Carroll's tools. She probably should start with the yellow pages and see how many handymen were listed. Also, there should be some invoices stashed somewhere. Maybe Carroll's desk. And she'd like to speak to the neighbor boy. Suzy hadn't said anything in her notes about him coming around to help.

Suddenly she realized Carroll had stopped talking and was looking at her expectantly. What had she missed?

"Ready for pie?" Sarah asked, pushing back her chair and retrieving the pie from the refrigerator. Luckily, she'd brought whipped cream for a topping since she'd discovered ice crystals had formed on top of the ice cream in the freezer. Sarah needed to start a grocery list.

She placed two slices of pie on small plates and put a generous amount of whipped cream on top. The rhubarb gave the pie a tang which was nicely offset by the sweetness of apple.

"My mother used to make this pie," Carroll said. "Her crust would melt in your mouth. I suggested she should go into the pie business after my father died, but she didn't listen to me."

"Where did your mother live? Here, in Maple Hill?"

He swiped a napkin across his lips. "Virginia."

"Do you still have family there?"

He shifted in his seat and gobbled another bite of the pie. "Never could understand how people can like them frozen store-bought pies. It's good to see that people still make things from scratch. Most people don't make the time these days."

"That's true. It can be hard to find the time, but luckily my granddaughters like to bake. I'm going to teach them how to make strawberry jam next Sunday."

Carroll stared at his fork with a bleak expression. "Betty taught Dawn to bake cookies and I'd take them into the dealership. They'd be gone before the second pot of coffee had finished brewing. There was this one mechanic—we called him Shorty—who'd take extra and hide them in the pocket of his overalls. Never really noticed until one day I went down in the pit to borrow one of his tools and there were cookie crumbs everywhere. We had to bring a cat into the garage because of all the mice Shorty's snacking attracted. Can't remember the cat's name though, not that it matters."

He yawned and Sarah took the opportunity to stand and clear the dishes to the sink. She filled the sink full of sudsy water. She didn't want to be rude or hurt the elderly man's feelings, but time was ticking by. Sarah turned off the water and looked over her shoulder to ask if Carroll would like another cup of coffee. His chair was empty. She'd been so lost in her own thoughts, she hadn't heard him leave.

She wrapped up the leftovers and fixed a plate for Carroll's evening meal before going down the hallway to the living room. Carroll sprawled in his easy chair, his walker parked beside him. His head was tilted back on the cushion and a soft whistle rose from his nose.

Finally. Quiet. Now she could go exploring.

Armed with her notebook, Sarah descended the steep stairs to the cellar. The cool air that bathed her face and seeped into her clothes was especially refreshing after being in the overly warm kitchen with her arms plunged deep in hot sudsy water.

The cellar appeared to be the neatest area in the house. One end of the vast room held plastic storage tubs, neatly stacked along the walls, each labeled with contents such as Christmas lights, extension cords, and motor oil.

Workbenches, with metal cabinets mounted above them on the concrete block walls, occupied the other side of the basement. Except for several small plastic containers of bolts and screws, cans of nails, and coils of fine copper wire, the area had been cleaned out. Sarah rubbed dust off her fingers. It appeared it'd been quite some time since anyone had used the workbench. Carroll couldn't negotiate the stairs with his walker.

Other than a hoe, rake, and shovel leaning on the wall by the bulkhead, there were no other tools. Most likely

Dawn had taken the smaller, important items upstairs after Carroll's stroke.

Sarah turned off the light and returned to the first floor to check on Carroll. His eyelids fluttered slightly at her approach, but he still snored on. She went up the steps to the second story and did a quick scan in the bedrooms. Everything looked the same as last night.

Since Suzy had said the attic would take the longest, Sarah would start the inventory there when Carroll didn't need her and work her way down. She opened the door to the attic stairs and ascended into a wave of stale heat. Maybe waiting until the afternoon hadn't been a good idea. She reached the top of the stairs and gasped. No wonder Suzy had seemed somewhat shell-shocked when she'd returned from the attic last night.

The first half of the attic wasn't so bad. Someone had started organizing the boxes, judging from the inventory sheets taped to the tops of them. The rest of the attic took her breath away.

She maneuvered her way to the middle of the room and turned slowly. From floor to ceiling the room was crammed with old furniture, crates of books, lamps, and trunks. Typewritten sheets of paper and forms were stacked on the floor and scattered about in random places.

She peered around a pile of wooden dining chairs. Edsel, Studebaker, and Cadillac knickknacks and promotional literature made a colorful heap in the corner. A flash of bright blue fabric caught her eye. She stepped over a dilapidated rocking horse and lifted a small quilt off a pile of linens.

She moved closer to the hanging light bulb to examine the quilt. Judging from the creases in the folds, it had been stored for a long time. It was a traditional Nine Patch quilt, pieced from blue fabrics in a variety of patterns. Intricate hand-quilting outlining the shapes of toys adorned the top. Someone had put a lot of time and love into this sweet baby quilt. What a shame it was hidden away in an attic. She wondered who it belonged to. The quilt was definitely too recent to have been Carroll's, although the blue fabrics indicated that it had probably been made for a boy.

She folded it carefully and sorted through the rest of the linens. She picked up four long yellow curtain panels and a flowery bed sheet set and discovered a cardboard box underneath.

She shoved the lid aside, expecting to find more material, but the box contained files. She pulled out a thick folder stuffed with business documents with the letterhead Shepherd & Stanford. She shoved the file back in, replaced the lid, and set the quilt on top. She'd take both down to Carroll later.

Sarah reviewed her scribbled notes. It would take weeks to properly catalog fifty years of accumulated stuff. Suzy was going to need to bring in more people if she wanted to put this house on the market soon. With all the chaos, it was hard to decide where to start first, and the best course of action would be to get organized first. Make a plan. She decided she should draw a map of the attic and jot a brief note of the contents of each box and trunk. When Suzy got back, she'd have something to work from and plot her strategy more quickly.

Sarah started making a crude sketch. Too bad Audrey wasn't here. Her granddaughter loved to draw and could probably do a much better job than Sarah. She worked her way around the perimeter, drawing squares for the boxes and trunks. She wrote numbers on sheets of paper and placed one on each container.

Her cell phone vibrated in her back pocket. She pulled it out and smiled at the name on screen. Martha Maplethorpe, Sarah's best friend.

"Martha, hi!" Sarah said, plunking down on a trunk to rest. "You'll never guess where I am."

"With all your adventures, I'm almost afraid to guess," Martha teased.

"Standing in the attic of an old Victorian on Elm Street."

"Okay...that wasn't one I would've guessed." Martha laughed. "What on earth are you up to?"

Sarah explained about Suzy, Carroll, and the inventorying.

"Oh, I haven't thought about Suzy in years. I don't think I've seen her since your graduation. She was always so bubbly and energetic," Martha said. "How is she?"

"We really didn't get to talk much about her family, but she seems busy and happy," Sarah said. Martha had met

Suzy a few times when Suzy had come home with Sarah for school breaks. Martha had stayed in Maple Hill after high school to finish business classes and help her future husband Ernie set up his furniture store.

"I'm sorry for their loss and I wish I could help you. It must be like one giant garage sale," Martha said. "But I'm on grandma duty this week. I've got Pru and Josiah during the day to give Mandy some alone time with the baby while Colin works. And Ruth and Tim needed to go out of town for a few days so Trina is here too. And of course she and Lexie are joined at the hip," Martha said, referring to the two girl cousins who were Audrey and Amy's age.

"How are the rest of the kids?" Sarah resumed sketching as she listened to Martha's update on her other two children, their spouses, and all of her nine grandchildren. Martha in turn asked about Jason's and Jenna's families. The two woman talked frequently, but it been a couple of days since their last conversation, and they had been accustomed to being enmeshed in each other's lives since grade school.

"Anyway, the reason I called was to ask if you'd like to go strawberry picking sometime soon. I'm—" A crash sounded on the other end of the phone. "Josiah, are you okay?" Martha asked. "Sorry, Sarah, I gotta go. Josiah knocked my basil plant off the windowsill and there's potting soil all over the counter and sink, and on my new kitchen rug."

"Okay. Call me later about the strawberry picking. I'm interested," Sarah said. "Good luck with the kids."

"Thanks. I'll need it." Martha clicked off and Sarah refocused on her map. An hour passed quickly and Sarah wiped her sweaty forehead. Her throat felt as dry as the pile of sandpaper she'd just found. It had to be over ninety degrees at the top of the house. She wondered if Carroll was awake and would like a beverage. A nice cold glass of lemonade would taste so good.

As she turned to the door, she almost bumped into a large spider dangling on its silky thread inches from her nose. She squealed and jumped back, tripping and landing on a pile of rugs, or what she thought was a pile of rugs. Her behind begged to differ. Underneath the braided rag rug were some hard, lumpy objects.

She slowly got to her feet while rubbing her sore spots and scanning the air for the spider. It had gone. She just hoped the creature stayed far away.

She leaned over and lifted the rug.

Tools!

Lots of tools. There had to be at least twenty of them. Most she recognized from Gerry's old garage toolbox—wrenches and screwdrivers. Some were strangely shaped, and several were simply long, thick stainless steel rods. Could these be the tools Carroll said were missing?

She grabbed one of the wrenches and limped downstairs.

 CHAPTER FOUR

T hat's not a wrench. It's a ratchet for a car," Carroll
said. "Very specialized, although now it's basically
useless."

"Useless?"

"Outdated. This one was designed to work on specific engines." He ran his finger along the metal. "Oh, I suppose it
might work on a few current models, and some people still
own the older cars. How'd they get in the attic? They used to
be downstairs in the workshop."

"Are you sure they aren't the tools we're looking for?" She
described some of the others, including the fat steel rods.

Carroll shook his head. "Those are just collectibles now.
The missing ones were bought within the last fifteen years."

Sarah sighed. "Do you want me to bring the tools in the
attic down here?"

"Maybe later. They're probably safer up there. *I don't*
want to get rid of them. You understand?"

That probably went for ninety-nine percent of the rest of the stuff in the attic too, Sarah thought as her cell phone buzzed. She left Carroll cradling the tool in his big hands.

"Sarah? This is Irene. I'm sorry I didn't get back to you sooner. It's been a rather hectic day."

"Is there something I can help you with?"

"Oh yes. I mean, it's not vital, but I was wondering if we could meet this afternoon."

Sarah had already decided to take a break and return in the morning to tackle the attic when it was cooler. Carroll had turned the television on and seemed content watching a ball game.

"Well, I'm across town right now, and I've been working in the heat. I was hoping to get home for a shower. What about later this evening?"

"I have a historical society board meeting in about an hour, and we're working through dinner. I know, how about I treat you to a cold drink at The Spotted Dog?"

Sarah hadn't been in the café for a week and consequently hadn't bumped into Liam, the proprietor and—well, Liam was a special friend. They had been out together a couple of times, but neither was rushing to turn their friendship into anything more. Sarah shouldn't feel nervous seeing him after so long.

Besides, Irene had been extremely helpful when Sarah needed odd facts and historical details. If Sarah could return the favor, she would. "A cold drink sounds great. I'll meet you there in about twenty minutes."

Sarah grabbed her purse and hurried into the down-stairs bathroom. She wiped the dust off her face and arms and spotted a smudge on her blouse. Looking closer, she realized it was grease, probably from carrying that big wrench, or rather, ratchet. She rubbed soap on it and it faded.

She ran a brush through her hair and put on some mascara. She was presentable again but wished she had Martha's rosy cheeks.

She paused by the living room entryway. "Carroll, I'm go-ing now. There are leftovers in the refrigerator for when you want to eat dinner."

He waved a dismissive hand at her as if shooing her away.

"Remember you can call Nancy or Jared next door if you need help. I also left my number by the phone in the kitchen."

"Yeah, yeah, yeah. Go on then."

Sarah shook her head as she walked down the hall and out the front door. He could be so rude. She'd be glad when Suzy got back.

She locked the front door and checked to make sure the door was latched securely. The sound of metal scraping against metal drew her attention and she crossed the square of lawn and peeked around the corner of the house.

A teenage boy was clipping the hedge that ran between Carroll's house and the one next door. Lanky legs poked out from green and black basketball shorts. His green T-shirt boasted the name of the Boston Celtics and he wore nice-looking basketball shoes. From shopping with the twins, Sarah knew those shoes cost close to a hundred dollars. Carroll must pay him really well.

"Jared?"

He didn't answer but continued to methodically work his way down the hedge. Sarah stepped closer and noticed the purple ear buds plugged in his ears. She sidestepped into his line of vision. His brown eyes snapped up, and he nearly dropped the clippers.

"I didn't mean to startle you," Sarah said as the boy tugged a fancy looking MP3 player out of his pocket and fiddled with the buttons. "I'm Mrs. Hart. I'm helping Mr. Shepherd out this week. I met your mom yesterday, and she said you might be able to answer some questions about Mr. Shepherd's house."

"I already talked to the other lady."

"You must mean Suzy Carmichael. She's a friend of mine."

"She came to take him away. I think that really bites."

Sarah sighed. "Oh, Jared, it's more complicated than just that."

"I know. My mom explained. Now that Dawn can't move in with him anymore, he has to leave." He swallowed hard, his Adam's apple bobbing in his skinny neck.

"Did you talk to Dawn often?"

"She was grumpy sometimes, but then Mr. Shepherd can make anyone grumpy if you give him enough time." At least he tried to hide his grin.

Sarah smiled back. "Even you?"

"Sometimes, but then we have fun too. He taught me to play chess and sometimes...," he glanced to the house and lowered his voice, "we even bet."

Sarah raised her eyebrows. "Gamble?"

"Yeah, for M and Ms."

Sarah laughed. The mischievous light in his eye reminded her of Jason at his age.

"Have you noticed anything unusual going on over here?"

He shrugged. "Not me. But Mr. Shepherd once complained he heard footsteps upstairs and called the cops. They didn't find anyone."

"Was anything missing?"

"He claims those silver candlesticks on the mantel were taken, but later Dawn found them under his bed."

"When was this?"

"A couple of weeks ago. Dawn had to take off from work and everything. She wasn't happy."

"Was anything else missing?"

"More like moved around. I told the lady yesterday it wasn't much. His chair was facing the wrong way. Pictures on the wall were crooked."

"Mr. Shepherd mentioned some tools disappeared."

"He grilled me about that too. I used them *once* to fix the shed door. I hit it putting the lawn mower away. The door came right off the hinges, but I put it back."

"Where did you get the tools from?"

"The toolbox in the kitchen. I didn't keep any. Mr. Shepherd believes me. Just ask him."

"I didn't think you took them," Sarah said. "Mr. Shepherd mentioned Dawn had sold some of them, and we're just trying to track down the rest."

"There were some people working on the roof." He looked away, shifting his feet. "I have to go to practice."

"I appreciate your talking to me. I'm going to be around for a few days. If you think of anything else, please let me know."

"Sure. Whatever." He tossed the hedge clippers on the porch and jogged to his backdoor.

Sarah walked to her car and slid onto the hot seat. As she cranked up the air conditioner to high, she noticed a brown van parked across the street one house down. Two people sat in the front. She waited, but they didn't move either. No lettering on the van indicated they were a service of any kind.

Her mind ran over the possibilities. Were they burglars watching Carroll's house? But then what if she called the police, and it turned out they lived there? It wasn't a crime to sit in one's car.

She pulled out her cell phone and called Carroll's number. The phone rang five times. Where was he? There'd been a phone on the stand next to his chair. She hung up and dialed again.

"Yeah?"

"Carroll. This is Sarah Hart."

"Weren't you just here?"

"I was. I am. I'm in my car out front. There's a brown van parked in your neighbor's driveway with two men in it. I was just wondering if it belongs there."

"How would I know? Do you think I spy on my neighbors all day?"

"Of course not," Sarah said with exasperation. "But Jared mentioned you thought someone might've broken into your house a couple of weeks ago. These guys are just sitting here. I think it's odd. Maybe they're canvassing the neighborhood looking for places to break into."

"What year is the van? Model?"

"I don't know. It's brown. Looks like the type to haul cargo or equipment."

"I'll take a look," he said as the van slowly rolled down the driveway and turned east on Elm.

"They're moving now." Maybe she should get the license plate just in case. Sarah had just shifted into drive when a loud crash vibrated over the receiver.

She slammed on the brakes. "Carroll? Are you okay?"

"Yeah. Yeah. I just knocked over the table by the window."

"I'll be right in."

"No. Go on. I'm fine."

"But—"

"I said I'm fine! Just leave me alone!" The phone clicked off.

Sarah took several deep breaths.

Dear Lord, grant me patience.

Sarah stood in the door of The Spotted Dog Café, scanning the crowd for Irene. The air felt unusually warm, and floor fans had been placed about the dining area and in the bookstore.

Karen Bancroft, one of the part-time waitresses, bustled through the sea of tables, holding a large round tray loaded with milk shakes. "Welcome," she called.

She deposited the shakes on a table in front of a couple with three small chattering children, and then sidled over to Sarah. "The AC's out and a tourist bus stopped by about ten minutes ago." She nodded to the packed tables. "There's a stool over at the counter, or maybe you can find a spot on one of the couches in the bookstore."

"Thanks. I'm not in any rush. I'm waiting for Irene. What is that delicious-looking drink over there?" She nodded to a tall icy glass.

"Strawberry lemonade slushy."

"I'll take one of those."

"Good choice," Karen said, swiping back the damp bangs of her stylishly cut hair, and hurried away.

Something cold and wet bumped Sarah's ankle. Murphy, Liam's corgi and the inspiration for the café's name, licked her ankle and grinned up at her, his tail wagging madly.

She bent to pat him on the head. "Murphy, glad to see you. Have you been a good boy?"

"Now you don't think he'd confess to chewing m'favorite pair of slippers, do you?"

Sarah's stomach fluttered at the rich deep Irish brogue. "Now Murphy, I have a hard time believing you'd do such a thing."

"Aye," Liam said. "I believe he did it because I left him home last weekend while I went to Boston."

The rhythm of Murphy's tail slowed as he sat, his chocolate brown eyes gazing up at Sarah.

"He looks sorry to me."

"He does that when a pretty lady is present, but so far I have yet to see any repentance," Liam said with a wink.

"Oh look, Henry, what a cute dog!" a middle-aged woman said to her husband. "I've always wanted a pretty little dog like that."

The round, chubby-cheeked husband pushed his glasses up on the bridge of his nose as they made their way to the door. "Looks like a toy to me. If we get a dog, it'll be a real dog like a German shepherd or a Labrador retriever." The door shut behind them with a jangle of the bell.

Liam gave his head a little shake. "Well, Murphy, after a blatant insult like that, I think we all deserve a cookie."

At the word cookie, Murphy jumped up and danced in a circle. Liam reached in a jar labeled Dog Treats and tossed a dog biscuit in Murphy's dish under the counter. The little dog snatched it up and lay down with the treat between his paws.

"Would you like a cookie as well?" Liam asked. "You don't have to have these. We have a batch of fresh macaroons warming in the oven." He glanced over at the crowd. "At least I hope we have some left."

"I'd love one, but if they're gone, that's fine. I'm waiting on strawberry lemonade. Business is booming today."

"Yes it is. Oh, before I forget, I brought you something from Boston. It's in the office."

A customer tapped Liam on the arm and peered at him through rectangular spectacles. "Sir, do you have any more books on antiques?" He juggled several tomes under his arm.

"Did you check the Local Interest section?" Liam asked, and the man shook his head no. "Well, I'll be happy to show you what we have." Liam leaned toward Sarah and asked, "Are you going to be around a little while longer?"

Sarah nodded. "I'm meeting Irene."

"Good." He gave her another wink and led the customer over to a display of books on local interest.

The door bell jangled again and Irene pushed her way into the crowd by the café. The sunny yellow blouse tucked under her sky blue linen blazer complemented her tanned complexion and dark brown eyes. She smoothed a brunette wisp back into her French twist and her smile widened when she caught sight of Sarah. At the same time, Karen waved at Sarah. She stood by a small round table for two that had just been vacated. Sarah pointed Irene in that direction.

Karen whisked the dirty dishes off the table into a tub and gave the checkered tablecloth a quick wipe. She'd already set Sarah's drink on the table. "Thought I'd grab this table for you before the next wave of customers." She turned to Irene. "What can I get you?"

"I'll have what Sarah's having, thank you." Irene untucked her large white purse from under her arm and sat down.

"Be right back." Karen darted away, pausing at several empty tables to scoop dirty dishes into the tub. Liam motioned to Karen and said something when she got near. Karen smiled and headed for the kitchen.

"Wish I had that kind of energy again," Irene said with a small laugh.

"Oh me too. It's amazing how she juggles school and work. I think she's going to be a terrific architect if she shows as much enthusiasm for projects as she does here," Sarah said as Karen came out of the kitchen with Irene's drink and a plate.

"Macaroons. Fresh from the oven this morning," Karen said. "The boss said you might like some."

"Thank you," Sarah said, feeling a blush tinge her cheeks.

"Sounds like someone's sweet on you."

"He's a good friend," Sarah said. One and a half dates didn't make Liam her boyfriend. She took a gulp of the lemonade slushy. The tartness with a hint of strawberry made her eyes water, but it was pleasant and the iciness cooled her as it slid down her throat. Irene remained silent, but Sarah didn't want to talk about Liam. She wasn't even sure how she felt about their slowly growing affection. She'd never loved anyone but Gerry.

Irene set her drink on the table, the charms on her bracelet clinking on the glass. "How's the family? I haven't had a chance to stop by Maggie's store in ages."

"They're doing great, thank you. The store's been busy with the early tourists, and Jason's had several court cases lately. The twins signed up for some community classes at the old high school. They're offering a great after-school program for the kids."

Irene nodded. "The classes are going to continue all summer. I'm scheduled to teach a short workshop on genealogy in June. I'm going to have the kids trace their family histories, and we're going to make a big family tree of Maple Hill."

"That sounds like fun," Sarah said, wondering if Amy or Audrey had signed up for Irene's class.

"How's Jenna?"

"She called on the weekend to tell me how blistering it is in Texas already. Jonathan and Thomas started swimming lessons this week and they love the pool. Jonathan already swims like a fish, but Thomas is only four and still cautious."

"Understandable. Has Jonathan started school yet?"

"He goes into first grade this fall," Sarah said. Jenna and David's babies were growing up so quickly, and Sarah didn't see them nearly enough. Feeling suddenly blue, she changed the subject to Irene's husband. "How's Chris doing?"

"Work has slowed some since the economy is down. Not as much being imported at the moment. Hopefully it will pick up soon."

Sarah nodded. She wasn't quite sure what Irene's husband did for a living, but it had something to do with importing and exporting goods for several companies and stores. He was able to work online from home and the absence of commuting allowed him time to indulge in his favorite hobby of archeology. He and Irene had been out on several local digs.

"Chris seems a little under the weather. It's almost that time of year for summer colds. I try to get him to take extra vitamin C and drink lots of fluids, but you know how stubborn men can be when they're sick," Irene said and then covered her mouth with her fingers. "I'm sorry. I didn't mean—"

"Oh, I know. Gerry could be such a bear when he had a cold. Stubborn. Hated to take even Tylenol even though he was miserable," Sarah said. She wished people didn't feel uncomfortable discussing Gerry with her. So much of her sadness had faded over the years, and she loved to remember the wonderful life they had shared.

"Chris just accuses me of nagging. How did you handle the grouchiness?"

"Well, if he barked at me too much, I'd set out all the cold medicine, make him a pot of chicken noodle soup, hand him a box of tissues, and go off and quilt or do something with

the children. Eventually he'd mellow and want to be babied."
Sarah smiled at the memory.

"I'll have to try that."

Sarah selected a macaroon and shoved the plate closer to
Irene. "Cookie?"

"They smell great." Irene nibbled on her macaroon,
glanced at Sarah and then away. It was obvious something
weighed on Irene's mind. Sarah sipped her rapidly melting
slushy and waited.

Finally Irene set the cookie down. "Actually, Sarah, as I
mentioned on the phone, I wanted to ask a favor, although
I hate to impose on your time."

Sarah leaned forward. "Well, I certainly would be glad to
help if there's something I can do."

Irene took a deep breath and let it out. "I want to get
published."

"Published?" Sarah had expected Irene to ask her to volunteer on a project for the historical society or even to
ask for quilting lessons, although Irene had never shown
any interest in the sewing arts other than from a historical
perspective.

She nodded. "I've been reading your articles in *Country
Cottage*, and you have so much to share. I want to write articles too."

"Were you thinking you wanted to write for *Country
Cottage?*"

"Not necessarily. I was thinking I'd like to write more
about history, but I've been told my writing is dry as a

textbook, and I tend to ramble. I know this is a lot to ask, but I was hoping you might take a look at one of my attempts and give me some advice, or even show me your process of putting together your column."

"I'm not sure how much help I can be," Sarah said. "I'm just an amateur, but you've been kind enough to help me with my research, and I'd be happy to return the favor."

Irene's face creased into a big smile. "Thank you so much. Maybe we can get together tomorrow morning?"

"I'll be tied up in the morning at the Shepherd house, but we could meet after lunch."

"The Shepherd house? How wonderful!" Irene clasped her hands together. "That's the old Lunderberg place. Mr. Lunderberg is quite a mover and shaker. His ideas on modernizing the town by replacing electric lamps along Main Street with more reliable and brighter 'Star Burners' and campaigning for the first pay telephones are quite ahead of his time."

"Really? I didn't realize," Sarah said with a small smile at Irene's use of present tense. From her faint recollection, Mr. Lunderberg had been a town council member in the late 1800s.

Irene nodded. "Carroll Shepherd's father bought the place from the great-grandson's wife, Mildred Lunderberg. I tried contacting Mr. Shepherd a couple of months ago to ask some questions about the place, but he hung up on me."

Sarah had known Carroll for only a day, but she wasn't surprised.

"Can I get you ladies anything else?" Karen asked. "More lemonade? Cookies?"

Sarah answered she was fine, and Irene looked at her watch. "I'm going to have to run. Board meeting tonight and I have to make copies of last month's minutes. Thanks for meeting me."

"This was fun. I'll give you a call tomorrow when I'm free."

Irene insisted on paying the check on her way out. Sarah drained her glass and glanced around the café. The crowd had thinned drastically, which meant the tour bus had departed, or the tourists had all dispersed to shops around the square.

She turned her gaze to the bookstore, searching out Liam, but he was nowhere to be seen. She moved closer to the café counter so she could see into the kitchen. Liam's legs stuck out from under one of two large stainless steel sinks in the back. At least she assumed it was Liam since Murphy sat next to him, watching intently. A loud banging erupted from underneath and Murphy hightailed it to the other side of the room, barking.

Karen tapped her on the shoulder. "Do you want me to get Liam for you?"

Although she was curious to find out what Liam had brought her from Boston, she shook her head. "That's okay. Looks like he's busy."

Karen nodded. "Poor guy. When it rains it pours around here. First the AC goes out, then one of the ovens refused to heat over two hundred degrees, and now the sink is plugged solid."

Sarah winced as more banging and barking erupted followed by muttering.

"Can you tell Liam thanks for the cookies, and I'll call him later?"

"Sure thing," Karen said, pulling a pencil from behind her ear and heading for a table.

Sarah glanced back in the kitchen. Murphy had ventured closer to his master but stood poised to run just in case. Sarah knew just how he felt.

CHAPTER FIVE

By the time Sarah finished an early supper of soup and sourdough bread, she felt recharged and ready to tackle the job of tracking down the tools Dawn had sold. Andi was out for the evening, so she had the house to herself.

Sarah dug out the invoice she had found on Carroll's desk. Hardies Roof Repair. It was a work order dated April fifteenth. Carroll had said the tools had disappeared recently, but maybe they would know something.

It was five-thirty but she called the number anyway, hoping someone would still be in the office. A man's voice answered on the third ring. Sarah asked him if they'd worked on Carroll's house.

"Shepherd? On Elm Street?" he asked. "Yeah, I remember him. Put up quite a fuss that we had to replace a couple of eaves. Dry rot. Like it was our fault. His daughter's the one who hired us, and I told him he'd have to deal with her. That got me off my back." There was the sound of a file drawer being opened. "I have a copy of the work order here. In fact, it looks like Mr. Shepherd still owes us three hundred and thirty-two dollars."

"I'll mention it," Sarah said. She made a note in her notebook on the page labeled "Things to Tell Suzy." "The reason I called is that some of Mr. Shepherd's tools are missing. His daughter apparently sold some of them, but he doesn't know who she sold them to."

"I bet the old guy thinks we took something."

"No, no, I'm just trying to find the person she sold the tools to. This could just be a mix-up," she added, thinking about what Jared had said about the candlesticks.

"Sorry, can't help you. It wasn't us. Joe and I were the only ones working on his roof. I can double-check with Joe, but we use our own equipment."

"When did you finish the job?"

"Let me see. It's in the paperwork. April twenty-seventh. I put a coat of paint on the new eave."

"Did you see anyone else working around there?"

"Nope. Although the daughter mentioned getting some windows and the porch worked on. I referred her to Sal Martinez."

Sarah wrote the name on her pad. "Do you have a number for him?"

"Yep. Hold on." He came back on a few seconds later and rattled off a local number. "Please pass on our condolences to Mr. Shepherd about his daughter. She was a nice lady."

"I will and thanks. I appreciate your help. I'll let Mr. Shepherd know he has an outstanding bill."

"This is a difficult time so the delay is understandable, but I'd like to get his account zeroed out. And if you know of anyone who needs roofing done, please keep us in mind."

Sarah hung up and dialed the Martinez number, which went directly to voice mail. She left a message and her number.

Tapping her pencil on the table, she reviewed what she'd learned so far, which wasn't much. There was Jared, who seemed to have a lot of nice things for a kid who had to earn his own money and was saving for college. Just how much was Carroll paying him? She thought Carroll's finances were really tight. She hated to think the kid might be stealing from the house, but he did have the opportunity. Other than Dawn, it sounded like he'd spent more time with Mr. Shepherd than anyone else.

Then there were the various workmen who'd been around the house the last few weeks. Any one of them could have pilfered the tools. But even if Carroll insisted on how valuable these tools were, what carpenter or roofer would jeopardize his reputation by stealing?

Sarah wondered how many tools Dawn had sold. Maybe Carroll would let her look at his bank statements. She might be able to detect a deposit that didn't line up with his standard transactions.

The music boxes and their contents were puzzling too. Carroll insisted Dawn wouldn't have moved them. So who did? If someone was searching those boxes to steal something, then why put the gold coins in a different box? Why not just take them?

The problem was that the house was so disorganized and so packed with stuff, it was difficult even for Carroll to tell if anything else was missing. For all they knew, someone could have been steadily pilfering things for weeks.

Her head began to ache. She drew doodles on her paper, but no new inspiration hit her. She glanced at the kitchen clock. The café would be closed by now. She should call Liam. She dialed the number of the café. No one answered, so she tried Liam's home phone. His answering machine picked up.

"Liam, this is Sarah. I wanted to thank you for the cookies this afternoon. And please tell Murphy again that I think he's the perfect specimen of a 'real' dog. I'm sorry I missed you after meeting Irene. You looked like you had your hands full with the plumbing. Hope everything got fixed." Sarah hung up. She wondered again what Liam could possibly have brought her from Boston, but she didn't want to seem too forward by asking.

Gerry used to mail her little gifts when she was in college. Suzy teased her that he was bribing her for her affection as insurance she didn't fall for someone else. But Sarah knew better. The things Gerry sent weren't expensive but little mementos. It was just Gerry's way of saying he was thinking about her when they couldn't be together.

Smiling, she went upstairs to the bedroom and opened the closet door. Carroll wasn't the only one who stored things in boxes. She retrieved one of her mother's old round hat cases from the top shelf.

She hadn't thought about the box in years. In it she'd saved a few things from college. She lifted out a couple of snapshots. One was of Suzy and Sarah, arms around each other's shoulders, smiling in front of a fountain. She set it aside to show Suzy. The other dozen were of various college friends and a couple of her and Gerry.

At the bottom were some of Gerry's "bribes." A pretty pebble he'd picked up when they had driven to their favorite lake in the Berkshires. A napkin from a little diner they found on Cape Cod when a group of their friends rented a cottage for a weekend. And one of her favorites, a thumb-size glass dog they'd picked up at a little shop in Rockport.

Now that she saw it again, the little glass dog resembled Murphy. She smiled and set it on her nightstand along with the photo of her and Suzy. Who knew when something from the past would come sliding into the future and change the course of your life? Carroll with secrets in his old house, Suzy suddenly popping up, and Irene seeking her out to write about history. And here was a little glass Murphy look-alike to remind her of his master, an old friend who went to the trouble of buying her a gift in Boston. A friend who was slowly becoming important in her life. She lay back on the bed with a smile, wondering what lay in store for her tomorrow.

Sarah woke Thursday morning to a rumble of thunder. She threw on her bathrobe and looked out her bedroom window. Gray clouds blanketed the early morning sun, and a fine mist floated over the backyard. Fat water drops dripped off her garden plants, turning the rows between her vegetable plants into a dark mud. There'd be no gardening this morning, but the thought that the cooler temperatures would make it a great day to work in Carroll's attic cheered her.

She chose worn jeans and an old pink floral blouse to wear for the dirty job ahead. She grabbed a bandana to wear on her head, the memory of the spider still fresh.

The smell of coffee filled the kitchen. Andi had obviously been there and gone. Sarah poured a cup and sipped the vanilla-flavored coffee as she opened the cupboard and retrieved a canister of Maggie's homemade granola. She poured some into a bowl and added slices of banana and strawberries. She was just settling in at the kitchen table when the phone rang. It was the handyman she'd called last night, Sal Martinez.

She explained how she'd gotten his number and asked if he had done any work for the Shepherds.

"The house on Elm?" Sal asked. "I never did any work over there. I stopped by and gave the lady an estimate, but she must've gone with someone else. She seemed the stingy type. I do quality work, but you know if people want to cut corners and save a couple bucks, it's their loss when things fall apart."

"Do you have any idea of who else she might have called?"

He hesitated and then simply said. "Nope. Why? Do you need a job done?"

Sarah suspected he didn't want to point her in the direction of his competition. "Well, actually this has to do with some tools. Mr. Shepherd thinks his daughter might have sold some, but others are missing as well."

"Hey lady, I was only there once. I never saw any tools. I didn't even go in the house. I gave her an estimate on what it would take to fix the fence. It was falling over and some of the posts needed replacing. I recommended cementing them in this time and using treated wood."

The roof. Now the fence. Dawn had certainly been busy with repairs over the last couple of months. And where was she getting the money? A historic house that large must cost a fortune to maintain. Perhaps Dawn had been selling things off from the house to help pay for the repairs and hadn't told Carroll.

Sarah sighed. If Carroll or she couldn't find some indication of the other workers at the house, she'd have to start calling the rest of the names in the yellow pages.

She grabbed her notebook, purse, and an umbrella, and hurried though the light rain to the car. She drove across town and as she turned her car down Elm Street, she scanned the street for the brown van. Maybe she was being paranoid. If it did belong to a neighbor, the owners might have driven it to work.

She parked in front of the Shepherd house. The rain was coming down harder now. She unfurled her umbrella and dashed to the dry covered porch. An earthy scent rose from the hedges bordering the house, mixed with the faint scent of paint. She glanced up at the eaves. The paint matched well, but the ones that had been worked on were free of cobwebs and mud dauber nests.

Sarah set her umbrella down and rang the doorbell. When Carroll didn't answer, she stuck her key in the lock. The door creaked open and the stale scent of a house that had been closed up too long wafted out. She pulled the screen door shut behind her and latched the hook to lock it. The place needed fresh air. She would open the backdoor too.

"Carroll?" she called, wiping her shoes on the rug. She went down the hallway, glancing in the living room. On the television, a group of women gathered around a table were chatting cheerfully on a morning show, but Carroll's armchair was vacant. From where she stood she could see into his bedroom. The rumpled bed was empty too.

She called for him again and then continued down the hall to the kitchen. Carroll stood in front of the sink staring out the window. His shoulders drooped over his walker like the soggy, bowed branches outside the kitchen window.

"Good morning, Carroll. I know I'm a little early, but I thought while its cooler, I could get a good start in the attic."

Carroll continued to stare out the window.

"Would you like to me to fix you some eggs?" Sarah asked, moving closer. "Carroll?"

She tapped him on the shoulder. Carroll jerked upward, his walker banging into the counter. He swung his arm back, and Sarah ducked out of the way. He caught his balance and yelled, "What are you doing?"

"I was saying—"

"Speak up, woman!"

Sarah took a deep breath. "I was just asking if you'd like me to make you some breakfast. Didn't you hear me?"

A flush crept up his neck and seeped into his cheeks. His fingers fiddled with his ear and he pulled out a tiny flesh-colored gadget and then another from his other ear, clicking a minute switch on each.

Hearing aids. And Carroll appeared embarrassed by them. Sarah turned away as he replaced them, pretending not to notice. She picked up a carton of milk from the table and put it back in the refrigerator. "I thought with the rainy weather, it would be a good day to work inside and look for your tools. Were you able to find anything in your bank statements that might give us a clue as to who bought them?" She glanced over her shoulder.

"If Dawn paid for work with a check, it hasn't been cashed yet," he said, pulling his walker around. "She probably paid him in cash. A lot of these fellas prefer that."

Sarah nodded, thinking the same thing. "Has Suzy called? I'm wondering if she knows when she's coming back."

"No."

Sarah was worried that Suzy hadn't been in touch. Could it be her daughter and the baby weren't doing well? But then, if Carroll's hearing aids were turned down, he might not have heard the phone. She would give Suzy another day before trying to call her. She didn't want to cause her any more stress right now. She had a big enough job to handle when she got back.

"Do you mind if I go on upstairs?" Sarah asked Carroll as he maneuvered out the door. "I can get in a couple hours of organizing, and then fix you lunch."

He shrugged and shuffled down the hall. She followed and waited until he flopped down in his chair and then set her business card on the small table beside him. "My cell number is on this. Rather than you having to shout up the stairs if you need something, you can call."

He glanced at the card and then at the TV. Sarah watched him for a few moments. She almost preferred his rude feistiness to the silent treatment.

No matter, she'd told Suzy she'd help her out and that's what she intended to do. She climbed the stairs to the attic and flipped on the light. The air felt warmer up here, but not as unbearable as it had been yesterday. The sound of the rain pattering softly on the roof gave the room a sense of coziness despite the jumbled chaos.

Sarah turned to her attic map in her notebook and finished drawing in the boxes and crates near the door, assigning each a number. Now came the fun part of seeing what was stored in each container. She started a fresh page and labeled it number one to correspond with the large black trunk nearest the door. Travel stickers advertising London, Paris, Bali, and other faraway destinations covered the peeling painted surface. Places where Carroll and Betty had probably traveled and where they had collected the items down in the living room cabinet. She wished Gerry and she could have had the chance to travel more, although she had no regrets about the good solid life that they'd had together. Life's tragedies made you pause and wonder what could've been. Carroll was probably struggling with that right now.

She kneeled in front of the trunk and pushed open the lid. The hinges creaked as the smell of moth balls rose from the depths. Coughing, she sat back on her heels, letting the air clear. The trunk appeared to be full of clothes. She lifted out an old houndstooth jacket and suit pants. These probably belonged to Carroll. A navy coat with brass buttons was next and then a layer of tissue paper. Underneath lay a pile of ivory material.

She lifted out a wedding dress with a short-sleeved bodice, an ivory taffeta band around the middle, and a neckline with hundreds of tiny cream-colored faux pearls. The back closed with at least thirty fabric-covered buttons, and the flowery lace overlaying the silk organdy made the dress appear to float. Although the finish on a few of the tiny pearls had left faint tea-colored marks on the fabric, the garment was in excellent condition.

Was this Betty's wedding dress? She tried to picture a younger Carroll standing by the church altar waiting for his bride and smiled. She wondered what he'd been like when his wife was alive. How had they met? And where had they gotten married? If this was indeed Betty's dress, then chances were it had been a fancy wedding.

A gust of wind hit the roof causing the beams to groan. Sarah looked up and realized that if it was taking her this long to go through just one of the containers, it would take her a month to finish the entire attic.

She leaned over the trunk. A hatbox lay at the bottom of the trunk alongside a pair of satin-covered pumps. She opened the box and saw a headdress and veil covered with the same ivory lace and pearls as the wedding dress.

Several sheets of paper lined the bottom of the trunk. Two were army discharge papers dated after World War II for Carroll Shepherd. Another was a diploma. Carroll had graduated from Columbia University in New York, with a degree in mechanical engineering.

She carefully repacked everything and wrote "wedding dress and suit" in her notebook for trunk number one. She set the papers aside to file later.

She moved on to the box beside the trunk, listed as number two. Linens filled it. Unlike the wedding dress, these didn't look expensive and probably could be sold at a yard sale if Suzy chose to do one.

The next box contained paper, pencils, paper clips, envelopes, and assorted papers as if someone had emptied a desk. It also contained Betty's death certificate, various car registrations, invoices for the television and computer, utility bills, and mortgage and bank statements. Nothing was dated recently or was related to the work on the house or Carroll's tools. No copy of Dawn's will either.

Sarah straightened and rubbed her lower back. She glanced at her growing stack of paper. Seeing how important papers were scattered all over the attic, it would probably be best to consolidate them in a safe place.

There had been a file box containing business records. The one under the little blue baby quilt. She could put the papers in there and take it all down to Carroll and have him decide what to do with them.

She spied the quilt in the corner and picked it up. The box under the blanket wasn't the same one she'd seen yesterday. This one contained books.

Where was the box with the business files?

She consulted her crude drawing of the attic and counted the boxes in the corner. The total number was the same, and the box of books even had the paper sheet with the number twelve on it. Something strange was going on. Someone had been in the attic.

But who?

CHAPTER SIX

Carroll wasn't in his chair, and the smell of frying onions wafted from the kitchen. Sarah turned down the hall and heard the sound of a female voice. Had Suzy returned already?

She rounded the corner into the kitchen. Carroll sat at the table and shot Sarah a look from under his bushy eyebrows. A woman dressed in black slacks and a burgundy knit top stood at the stove. Steam rose from a stockpot and onions sizzled in a frying pan.

"My mother used to make this when I was a little girl," she was saying. "It's especially good for cold winter evenings."

"Irene?" Sarah asked.

The woman turned, clutching a long wooden spoon. "Sarah, hi! I was running an errand on this side of town, and thought I'd pop in and see if you needed any help. I hope you don't mind. Mr. Shepherd and I have been enjoying a lovely visit. I also dusted the living room and straightened things a bit."

"That's very nice. Thank you," Sarah said, wondering how long Irene had been there.

"Mr. Shepherd said he hadn't had any lunch so I thought I'd fix beef goulash since he had all the ingredients."

"It smells wonderful," Sarah said and turned to Carroll. "Something strange is going on in the attic. Was anyone up there last night?"

"What do you mean strange?"

"I can't find a box that was up there yesterday. It had your business papers in it. There was a blue baby quilt on top of it. The quilt is still there but—"

"Suzy called," Carroll said.

"She did? While I was upstairs?" Sarah asked. She wished he'd called her down so she could talk to Suzy.

"She said she left you some photos of the books I have stored in the attic. You never gave them to me."

"Well, you can certainly have them anytime you want," Sarah said. "They've been on the counter since yesterday." She crossed the kitchen and retrieved the manila envelope. She yanked the photo sheets out and set them on the table in front of him.

He snatched up the sheets. "I want some of my books."

"Of course. I can get whatever you want. Now about the file box—"

"When?"

Sarah blinked. "When what?"

"*When* are you going to get them?"

Sarah bit back an exasperated sigh. "I can get them now if you want."

"Maybe she can help you." He glanced at Irene, who was adding salt and pepper to the goulash.

Sarah opened her mouth to say it wasn't a two-person job but then noted the strained expression on Carroll's face. He continued to stare at her.

"Oh I'd love to see the upstairs." Irene turned from the stove. "I was telling Mr. Shepherd how much I've always wanted a peek inside of this fine old house." Her cheeks were flushed from the heat of the stove. Brown wisps escaped her bun and floated around her face. "The goulash needs to simmer for about an hour to bring the flavors out."

Sarah wrote down the titles Carroll wanted retrieved and led the way down the hall and up the stairs. "Look at this banister," Irene said. "It's made from an exquisite piece of cherry wood. See? There aren't any breaks in the grain from top to bottom."

Sarah hadn't noticed the detail before and agreed it was beautiful. When they reached the second floor, Irene swept through the rooms exclaiming over the crown molding in the master bedroom, the original glass in the windows and the fine hardwood floors. "I'd love to own a historical house like this, but Chris thinks it would involve too much upkeep. He says we can barely maintain our eighties bungalow and it's a third the size of this place. What do you think? How much maintenance time does your Queen Anne take?"

"I've been fortunate. The house was well built. Gerry and I did a lot of work in the beginning, but then we didn't have many issues at all. When I remodeled for the boarders I had a few repairs done. Now if I keep on top of the small problems they hopefully won't grow into huge ones."

"Would you mind if I brought Chris over to see your place sometime? Maybe I can get him to change his mind. You'd think that two historians such as Chris and I should live in a historical home." Irene stepped back to study the crafted iron chandelier hanging in the upstairs landing. "*This* house should be in the historical register."

"I would've thought it already was."

Irene shook her head. "I've sent several letters over the years to Mr. Shepherd, but he's never replied. I even stopped by once and his daughter answered the door. She said she'd discuss it with him, but I never heard anything back from her."

Irene turned into the second bedroom. "This must've been Dawn's childhood room," she said coming to the same conclusion Sarah had from the pink flowery wallpaper and mementos on the shelves. "It's so sad, how quickly some people go. No warning. No time to say good-bye. One day they're here and the next gone," she said with a catch in her voice.

Sarah nodded, a lump rising in her throat. She'd had a chance to say good-bye to Gerry and her mother, and although their passing left a painful hole in her heart, she was glad she'd been there at the end. She'd had a chance to tell them how much she loved them. Carroll hadn't had the opportunity with Dawn.

Irene gave her head a little shake and walked out of Dawn's room and peeked into the room that had been turned into an office. "There's a lot of stuff that needs to be packed," she finally said.

Sarah stepped toward the staircase. "Wait until you see the attic."

Irene followed Sarah up to the attic, then turned in a slow circle as she surveyed the room. "Wow. The history just in this room must be incredible." She darted about the cramped space like a kid in a toy store.

"Look at that chair. Looks like a Chippendale. I wonder if Mr. Shepherd would sell it to me."

"He might." Sarah looked at the dilapidated dust-covered furniture with new eyes. Perhaps she should get Maggie up here to distinguish what might be valuable antiques.

"I better find those books he wanted." Sarah moved toward the section of attic where she had seen the books.

"Yes, he did seem persistent about it." Irene scooted in between the chairs to a large cabinet in the middle of the room. "This armoire would probably sell for over a thousand dollars if it was restored."

She pulled on the china knob and opened the door. "Oh how pretty."

Sarah paused in lifting one crate of books off another as Irene pulled out a white gown covered in clear plastic.

"I think it's a wedding dress." Irene held it up in the light. "Oh I love the bows at the waist and on the sleeves."

Another one? Sarah stepped over a chair to get a closer look. This gown was a simpler design than the dress she'd found in the trunk. Long white satin panels flowed from the empire waist.

"I would've loved to have had a dress like this for my wedding. Chris and I ended up eloping, so no fancy dress. Just a suit that I could wear to church later," Irene said as she smoothed the wrinkles on the skirt.

"Eloping sounds romantic, though," Sarah said. "How did you and Chris meet?"

"He visited the John F. Kennedy Library and Museum when I was working there. I noticed him in the crowd because he had grass stains on his jeans and a spot of dirt on his cheek. His blonde hair was sticking up as if he'd been in a wind storm. Later I found out he'd been doing gravestone rubbings for a class.

"Anyway, he didn't say one word to me, but then he came back the next day, and then the next. I thought he was interested in my co-worker Wendy, who was gorgeous. Finally, he asked me a question about Brookline, where JFK was born, and whether I had any old maps of the area from around 1917." Irene's eyes sparkled.

Sarah smiled. Irene loved maps. Her most prized item in the historical society was a beautiful set of Maple Hill maps that showed how land ownership had changed over the decades.

"It was just an excuse, of course, to talk to me. Chris's real passion for history focuses on events that occurred before the turn of the century or on anything else ancient that can be dug up." Irene let out a little laugh. "Anyway, we hit it off and it's been fifteen years now. How did you and Gerry meet?"

"Nothing quite as intriguing as meeting in a national museum. We went to Maple Hill High together. He was a grade ahead so he didn't pay too much attention to me in the beginning. We ended up working together on the yearbook during my sophomore year. He was one of the photographers and my job was to collect interesting tidbits for the captions. We became friends and starting hanging around the same people."

"Did he ask you to the prom?"

"His senior year." She smiled at the tingle running up her spine as she recalled how Gerry had leaned against her locker and asked if she already had a date. Seeing how it was five months before the prom, she, of course, didn't.

"I didn't go to my prom," Irene said. "Didn't have time for many social activities. I got a job at a diner when I turned sixteen and worked the evening shift, saving for college. Put myself through school. Never had any regrets."

Except maybe not having a wedding, Sarah thought as Irene continued to stroke the silky fabric of the dress.

"Such a fabulous dress. I wonder who you belong to." Irene said to the garment as she tucked it back in the armoire. She closed the doors and stepped back. "Was Dawn ever married?"

"Not that I know of," Sarah said. Although it was possible Dawn had been divorced and had gone back to her maiden name.

"Seems a shame to hide it up here," Irene said. "Maybe someone else in the family will have a use for it someday."

Sarah went back to the books and compared them to the photos in her hand. "That's strange. These aren't in the right order."

"What do you mean?" Irene came up behind her and stared at the four crates of books.

Sarah held up a sheet of paper with the snapshot of one of the crates. "Suzy took these for Carroll so he could see what was up here in case he wanted to read. But compare this line of books with the photo. There are at least three that have been moved, and I can't find the Clancy book he wants. It should be right here."

Irene took the photograph and bent over the crate, running her fingers along the books' spines. "When did she take these photos?"

"Day before yesterday, I think," Sarah said. "I think someone's been up here. There's a file box missing too."

"Are there any other relatives nearby who might've wanted to look over Dawn's things?" Irene asked.

"He didn't mention anyone, and apparently he sometimes turns off his hearing aids at night." She told Irene about the missing tools.

Irene pressed a finger to her lips as she surveyed the attic. "How very odd. Too bad we don't have a video camera we could run up here."

Sarah's cell phone vibrated. She flipped it open and Carroll's voice boomed over it before she even got it to her ear.

"What is taking you so long? I think the stew is burning," Carroll thundered.

"Can you turn the flame down?" she asked Carroll.

"Oh my!" Irene dashed out of the attic. Sarah took one last look around, wondering if anything else would be missing tomorrow.

"Nonsense. You must be imagining things. All I wanted was a couple of books, and you're trying to turn this into a big mystery," Carroll said, thumping about the kitchen with his walker.

"I'm just trying to tell you that I think someone may be sneaking into your attic," Sarah said.

"Yeah, you!"

Sarah took a deep breath. "Maybe you should call the police again."

"To report what? That you think that a box is missing and you can't find a couple of books? They'll think I'm an idiot."

"There are your missing tools too."

"The tools are different. That happened down here. Why would anyone go all the way into the attic to steal junk?"

Good question. She'd been wondering that herself.

Irene stirred the goulash on the stove, which had bubbled over some.

Carroll's chest heaved. A sheen of sweat coated his red face as he continued to pace with his walker.

"Carroll, why don't you sit down?" Sarah asked. He'd been in a state when they'd arrived back downstairs.

"Don't tell me what to do!" He swayed slightly.

"It's time for lunch!" Irene said.

Sarah slid a firm hand under Carroll's arm and guided him to a chair. She'd seen an automatic blood pressure cuff in one of the cupboards. It took her a couple of minutes to find it. Irene placed a bowl of the rich stew in front of Carroll.

Sarah wrapped the cuff around Carroll's arm before he could protest and took his blood pressure.

"That's high," Irene commented as she watched the needle bounce on the dial. Sarah didn't bother to ask Carroll if he needed his meds. She got the pills off the windowsill and plunked them down in front of him.

"I'm going to pester you until you take the recommended dose," she said as he opened his mouth to protest. He clamped his lips shut and then after several sighs, he swallowed his medication.

Sarah waited until Carroll had eaten his lunch and settled back in his armchair before gathering up her purse, the notebook, and her umbrella. She wasn't hungry, but she took a bite of the goulash and thought it was the best she'd ever had.

Irene waited for her on the front porch. The rain had stopped, and Sarah breathed deeply of the freshly washed air.

"I hope he'll be okay." Irene fiddled with the charms on her bracelet.

"He should be. The blood pressure medication makes him sleepy." Carroll hadn't even told her good-bye, let alone thanked her or Irene.

One more day, Sarah told herself. It'd be a relief not to have to come back here again.

Irene patted her bag. "I brought my several pathetic attempts at articles I wanted you to see. Should we go to The Spotted Dog again? It's my favorite."

Sarah's too, and she'd like to see Liam. He hadn't called her back last night. She agreed and they drove across town.

The square appeared quieter than the day before, with few people on the sidewalk. She could see a couple of people in Maggie's store and she wondered what the twins were up to today. She was looking forward to seeing them on Sunday.

"Hello, ladies," Karen said. "You have your choice of tables today. No tour buses so far."

Sarah let Irene pick a table by the window as she glanced around the café and bookstore. Liam was nowhere to be seen.

"These are the articles I started," Irene said after they had settled at the table and Karen took their order. "I don't know what I should focus on. I know quite a bit about architecture, and of course I get out with Chris on his archeology expeditions."

Sarah skimmed Irene's article on the history of an old bench in the park. It had been placed there in 1928 and stirred a controversy on whether it should face the fountain or the playground. Eventually the disagreement was put to rest by getting another bench. Irene had done a good job reporting the facts, but she was right when she'd said her writing was dry. The style was fine for an academic magazine, but not very entertaining for the average reader.

"This is a good topic. You describe the facts and history clearly."

"But?"

"I think you might try adding a human interest angle. Like interviewing people who actually sat on the bench. Have them share what the bench means to them."

Irene nodded.

Karen set their drinks down and patted her forehead with a bandana she pulled out of her pocket.

"Is Liam here?" Sarah asked her.

"He's off running errands. He's been trying to fix things around here."

"Did he get the sink fixed?"

"Depends on how you define 'fixed.' He got it unstopped, but now it's leaking. Duct tape will only hold for so long. The plumber is due anytime. So is the air conditioning guy."

"If you get a chance, can you tell Liam that I said hello?"

"Sure thing, Mrs. Hart."

Sarah turned her attention back to Irene. "Where were we?"

"Human interest angle. I'm going to try that. How would you open the article though?"

Sarah started to answer when her cell phone rang, and Maggie's work number popped up on the screen.

"Sorry. Do you mind if I take this?" Sarah asked.

Irene shook her head. "Not at all."

Sarah moved to a quiet corner of the bookstore. "Hi Maggie, what's up?"

"Strawberries. That's what," Maggie said. "Ever since you mentioned strawberry jam, I can't get strawberries off my brain. I decided to make strawberry shortcake for dessert tonight. I wanted to know if you'd like to come over for dinner."

"Love to." Sarah smiled. "What time?"

"Around six."

Sarah glanced at her watch. It was almost four thirty. There was enough time to run home and shower off the attic dust before dinner. Sarah said good-bye to Maggie and returned to the table. Irene was reading a page, her pencil poised over the words.

"I'm afraid I need to get going," Sarah said. "Family time tonight."

"Oh, I understand," Irene said, setting her pencil down.

"Why don't you let me have the articles, and I'll read the rest of them tonight."

Irene smiled. "Oh would you? Thank you so much." She straightened the sheets together and handed them to Sarah.

"I'm so excited to be working on this with you. This is going to be great."

"Grandma, come see what I drew in art class today," Audrey said as Sarah entered the kitchen. Her granddaughter popped up from the table, nearly knocking over her chair.

"Audrey, I'm on the phone." Maggie stood in the corner, holding her hand over the receiver.

"Oh sorry," Audrey said and lowered her voice. "We worked on drawing faces today. We were supposed to draw a child and then an older person." She handed two sheets of sketch paper to Sarah.

Audrey had drawn a good likeness of Sarah's father, William Drayton, and another of a girl around the age of five who looked vaguely familiar.

"These are really good, Audrey. Did you draw them from memory?"

She shook her head. "We took in photos to look at."

"Who's the girl?"

"That's mom when she was little." Audrey smiled.

"She has the same nice smile now," Sarah said, "It's just like yours."

"That's what Dad says too." Audrey took the pictures back and studied them.

"So how do you like the after-school activities so far?" Sarah asked, referring to the new community youth classes being offered at the old high school. Amy had opted to work on her basketball skills while Audrey selected an art class.

"It's fun. It's not like regular school. We don't have to go every day, and we get to choose what we want to do," Audrey said. "Tomorrow the teachers have an in-service, so we have the day off and we're taking a babysitting class. We have to review first aid and everything so we can be recertified. Trina, Pru, and Lexie are taking it too."

"That does sound like fun," Sarah agreed.

Maggie hung up the phone. "Audrey, could you go find Amy and your father? It's time to eat."

After Audrey skipped out, Maggie turned to Sarah.

"Hi, Sarah. I didn't mean to ignore you when you came in."

"No problem. Audrey was telling me about their classes. I'm glad the kids are getting opportunities to try different things."

"I just hope the girls get to go tomorrow. Normally they can catch a bus from the school, but there's a teacher's conference tomorrow so they're off. I'm trying to find them a ride. I just found out there's an estate auction up north. The house has been in one family for four generations and it's loaded with antiques. Jason is in court all day, or he'd take Audrey and Amy over."

"Audrey said Martha's grandkids are going. Maybe they can carpool."

Maggie opened the oven door and lifted out a roasting pan. "I talked to Christine, and she said Martha is taking them, but her minivan is full. I tried a couple of others, but no luck. I guess I could leave early from the sale, although sometimes they leave the best pieces for last."

"I can take the girls if they don't mind going with me to the Shepherd house first. I can drop them off in the afternoon and take them home afterward."

"Oh that'd be wonderful, if you have time. I didn't ask because I figured you had your hands full over there. How's it going, by the way?" Sarah grabbed the salad bowl and followed Maggie to the dining room table. "It's … okay," Sarah said, not sure if she should to try to explain the strange happenings at Carroll's place. "Mr. Shepherd isn't the easiest to work with. He's not happy about having to go into assisted living and tends to bark at people a lot."

"There isn't any way for him to stay in his home? What about hiring help?"

"I think there are some financial issues. Suzy's counting on the sale of the house to help him get into a good place, and apparently with government assistance he'll be able to cover the monthly costs."

"It's sad he can't stay in his home, but then, Grandpa William seems to enjoy the company at Bradford Manor. The last time I visited him, he was the only male at the dining room table and seemed to be having a grand time. The ladies flock around him."

"That's because at their age, good-looking, charming bachelors are in hot demand," Jason said as he entered the kitchen. "Hi Mom. I hear *you've* been hanging out with a charming, eligible bachelor." He bent to kiss her on the cheek.

Sarah chuckled. "Carroll may be eligible, but charming he's not, at least not with me."

"I think it's great you're helping him out." Jason scooted over to give his wife a smooch.

"I would've left by now if it wasn't for Suzy Carmichael." And if she had to admit it, the mystery of the missing tools and the odd things happening in the attic intrigued her.

"Who's Suzy Carmichael?" Amy asked, settling in the chair across from Sarah.

"My college roommate."

"Wow, that's a long, long time to be friends."

"It's been over forty years."

Audrey looked up from cutting her roasted potato in fourths. "Wow, she must be *really* old."

"Audrey—" Maggie said.

"Yes, positively ancient," Jason said, winking at Sarah.

Maggie shot him a look that clearly said he wasn't helping.

Sarah chuckled. "It won't seem so old when you're my age. The time flies by. There are days I feel like it was only yesterday your grandpa Gerry was driving up in his convertible to visit me on campus."

"Let's say the blessing," Jason interrupted and they bowed their heads while they prayed.

As soon as Jason said amen, Audrey asked, "Did you wear a miniskirt, Grandma?"

"Not the real short ones," Sarah said, "but my skirts were shorter than they are now."

Audrey looked disappointed but brightened when Sarah added, "But Suzy did. She was a wild one."

"Wild?" Amy asked. "Like how?"

"Maybe *wild* is exaggerating. She was involved in a lot of campus activities and didn't study a lot."

"Did she smoke pot?"

Maggie dropped her fork and stared at her daughters. "Girls! Where are these questions coming from?"

"We saw a documentary in social studies on the old days," Amy explained while cutting her roast. "Talked about the war and the hippie generation."

Audrey looked at Sarah again. "Were you a hippie, Grandma?"

Jason laughed and nearly choked on the carrot he was chewing. "Sorry. I was just picturing Grandma at a sit-in with love beads around her neck."

Sarah smiled. "Hey, I picketed one time with Suzy. We were protesting the cafeteria food. We wanted more fresh fruit and vegetables instead of the processed stuff."

Amy made a face. "You protested because you *couldn't* have vegetables? Weird."

"People were starting to get interested in organic foods," Sarah said, but clearly the girls weren't impressed.

Amy continued the interrogation. "How come Grandpa Gerry didn't go to war? Grandpa William did."

"He would've, but he'd hurt his knee in high school playing football. He was exempt," Jason explained.

"Exempt?"

"It means he wasn't allowed to go," Maggie told Audrey. "You need to eat before your food gets cold." She turned to Sarah. "What does Suzy's husband do?"

"The last I heard he was a prosecutor in the DA's office, but I don't know if he's retired yet or not. They live in Arizona. Maybe you'll get a chance to meet Suzy. She should be back tomorrow."

"It must be really hot in Arizona this time of year," Jason said. "The temperatures are supposed to climb here the rest of the week. May be in the nineties by the weekend."

All the more reason she needed to go through Carroll's attic quickly.

"It seems way too early for a heat wave," Maggie lamented. "I probably should get some more fans for the store. I hate to think what my utility bills will be, assuming my air conditioning system can even keep up. The unit struggled last year, and it wasn't nearly as hot."

"The air conditioning went out at The Spotted Dog. I stopped in on the way home." Jason reached for more potatoes.

Sarah nodded. "I was there today too. Karen said someone was coming in to look at it."

"Do you know who Liam used?" Maggie asked. "Maybe it would be a good idea to have my unit checked out. The vents might need a good cleaning."

"Karen didn't mention a name, but speaking of repair-men, I was trying to find some names of local handymen."

Jason paused, his fork halfway to his mouth. "Do you need something repaired?"

"No, I was trying to find out who worked on the Shepherd place." She briefly explained about the missing tools.

"I haven't used anyone recently. Jason's been repairing everything at the shop." Maggie gave her husband a fond smile. "But you could ask Dave Diamond, although he's not working as a handyman anymore."

"I thought of him, but I'd heard he'd gotten a job at the lumber store after the baby was born." Sarah had been happy about the news since she remembered Dave's wife Liz telling her once that he didn't work well for others, which was why he had started his own business. Dave spent lots of time actively helping veterans in the area, and ca-reer goals weren't high on his priority list. But having a baby changes the list a bit, and Liz had mentioned that the health and retirement benefits were good at the lumber store.

"He still might know people." Maggie pointed to the veg-etables on Amy's plate with her fork and Amy made a face.

Sarah smiled. "Thanks, Maggie. That's a good idea. I'll check with Dave."

The dinner talk shifted to Jason's work. His clientele was steadily growing; his reputation as being a kind, competent lawyer spread by word of mouth. The twins finished eating and asked to be excused to watch a favorite TV show. Maggie said she'd call them when she dished up the strawberry shortcake.

After the girls took their plates to the kitchen and took off down the hall to the living room, Maggie lowered her voice and said, "While I was dropping off the girls the other afternoon for their classes, Trina Carper asked me if they could throw a surprise birthday party for the twins here at the house."

"That's sweet of them," Sarah said, "but I thought you'd already made plans to go out to dinner."

"I know, but I think it would work out. We could still go out to dinner, and while we're gone Trina and the others can set things up before we bring the girls home."

"Sneaky but fun," Jason said. "I'm not so sure about letting a bunch of teenagers in here to decorate while we're not here. How many are we talking about?"

"Twelve or thirteen. Trina said she was going to ask her mother or grandmother to help, so it's not like they'll be unsupervised. But I'm worried that if I start amassing large amounts of party-type food here, the girls might get suspicious."

"I'd be happy to keep the food and stuff at my place," Sarah said. The girls were going to be so surprised, and more important, it would show them how much their friends cared. The twins had been through a lot of changes over the last year after moving from California.

Maggie turned to her husband. "What do you think, Jason? Their friends really want to do this for them. Should we try it?"

Jason rubbed his chin and then grinned. "Oh why not? As Mom would say back in college, it sounds 'groovy!'"

CHAPTER SEVEN

The porch boards groaned softly as Sarah rocked in her chair. The balmy air held a hint of crispness, and a wet, earthy scent rose from the lawn, drifting in the gentle breeze. A cricket chirped from somewhere close by.

Light glowed from her neighbors' windows as people settled in their living rooms for the remaining hour or so before bed. Sarah wiped her reading glasses with the end of her blouse, feeling content.

She'd had a nice visit with Jason and Maggie, and watched an hour of television with the girls. The strawberry shortcake had been a hit, although the berries were a little tart. They were early strawberries, but tasted of summer and no one complained.

Before she left, she'd asked the girls about going to Carroll Shepherd's house in the morning. Amy seemed enthused after Sarah explained what she was doing. Her granddaughter had inherited a penchant for mysteries, and snooping through an attic appealed to her.

Audrey appeared less enthusiastic, but seemed more agreeable after Sarah suggested she bring her drawing stuff with her. Mr. Shepherd had all sorts of interesting things she might want to sketch.

When Sarah had gotten home, her answering machine was blinking. Liam had called her back, joking that they were playing phone tag and she was "it." She wondered why he hadn't called her cell phone, but then he probably assumed if she wasn't home, she was busy. Since it was already ten thirty, she decided to try to catch him in the morning.

The porch light shone over her shoulder, illuminating the sample articles Irene had given her. Historical details about Patriot Park and the surrounding buildings were crammed onto the three pages. Sarah had no doubt the information was accurate. Irene was an excellent historian and extremely intelligent, but her prose read more like a textbook than an entertaining commentary. She tapped her pen on her knee as she mulled over the different directions Irene could go.

The sound of her telephone ringing propelled her upward. Maybe it was Liam again. The ring stopped before she reached the kitchen. Andi, dressed in a fuzzy yellow bathrobe and slippers, had the receiver pinned between her ear and shoulder as she stirred a tablespoon of cocoa powder into a mug. She smiled when she saw Sarah.

"Oh, here she is. Hold on." Andi handed the phone to Sarah. "It's Suzy Carmichael."

"Sarah! Sorry to call so late. I keep forgetting the time difference."

"That's all right. I'm still up," Sarah said. "I'm glad you called."

Andi clinked her spoon on the mug rim and stuck the utensil in the dishwasher. She gave Sarah a little wave and headed for the stairs.

"How are your daughter and the baby?"

"Jessica is doing fine, although they had to do a cesarean. She'll be here for a couple more days. My grandchild's name is Michelle, after her grandpa. She's still in neonatal intensive care. She went for a time without oxygen, but the doctors say there's no sign of any brain damage," Suzy said, her voice low.

"I'm so glad they're going to be okay," Sarah said, sending up a prayer of thanks.

"How's it going there? Is Uncle Carroll behaving himself?"

"Define behaving," Sarah said. "He's yelled at me and is basically being an old grouch, but he hasn't forbidden me to come back yet."

"Wow. That's cheerful for him. You must be doing something right then," Suzy said, humor creeping back into her tone. "Find out where his tools have gone?"

"Not yet. I've talked to a couple of people but no real leads. There's something strange still going on." She updated Suzy on her progress in the attic and the missing file box, as well as the rearranged books.

"Oh the books!" Suzy said. "I'm afraid that's my fault. I was looking for something to read on the plane and must've moved them around after I took the photos. Sorry to be so ditzy."

"It's okay. I'm glad there's a logical explanation."

"I don't know what to tell you about the file box though. It's such a disaster zone up there. Are you sure it just didn't get swallowed up in that horrendous mess?"

"I don't see how, unless someone else moved it," Sarah said. "In fact, there was a blue baby quilt on top of the file box. That was moved too. The only reason I noticed the box missing today was because I wanted to put some important documents I'd found around the attic in it."

"How odd. Has Carroll had any other visitors?"

"Not that I know of, but he can be a little short in the pertinent information department," Sarah said. She wondered whether she should share her concern about the brown van and decided it was better to share just in case. "Do you know if any of the neighbors own a brown cargo van? There have been two men hanging around the neighborhood in one."

"Not that I've noticed. Any idea who they are?"

"No, but I worry they may be up to no good. They seem to park in people's driveways or in the street and just sit there. If I can get a license plate I'll report them."

"Thanks for keeping on top of it," Suzy said. "Any luck on finding Dawn's will?"

"No, but I haven't gone through everything yet. I found some other interesting things, though. Like two wedding dresses."

"Two? What did they look like?"

"One was quite old-fashioned, and I'm assuming that it may've been your aunt's. The other is newer with lots of pretty bows. Did Dawn ever get married or plan to get married?"

"I never got an invitation if she did."

"What about the baby quilt?" Sarah asked. She described it briefly. "Do you know whose it was?"

"Nope. I'm afraid I don't know much about that side of the family. Listen, I've got to go."

"Well, I was just curious. Maybe Carroll will know. If he hadn't been in such a flustered state, I could've asked him today."

"Thanks again, Sarah. I should be out by next Monday. I appreciate your helping me out, but you know if it gets too unbearable, I can see if I can get meals-on-wheels to deliver food until I get back. Just say the word."

"I'll let you know. Give that baby a kiss from your old roommate."

"Will do."

After Suzy hung up, Sarah stared at the phone. Her friend had given her a way out of going back to the Shepherd house. Was she crazy not to have taken her up on it?

One thing was for certain, her curiosity was aroused. Feeling too keyed up to head to bed yet, she went into her office and fired up her laptop.

She searched Carroll Shepherd's name online, and to her surprise numerous links started to pop up, including the online encyclopedia. Most were for the dealership, but with some digging she found some references to Carroll's receiving company awards for designing various parts and tools for automobiles. His degree in mechanical engineering had been put to good use, she mused.

The search also retrieved some images, one with a short, attractive man standing beside a much younger Carroll. The caption read Shepherd and Stanford Motors. So the short man must be the partner who owned the other half of the failing dealership. According to the article the two men were receiving an award for the most cars sold in northwest Massachusetts. Too bad the article wasn't more recent. Better sales might mean Carroll wouldn't have to move into a retirement home.

A huge yawn brought tears to her eyes. She printed out some articles to read later.

Lastly, before she shut down, she typed in *vintage wedding dresses*. Multiple sites popped up, including some that showed styles by decade. It might not be as hard as she thought to pinpoint the approximate age of each gown. She bookmarked the search and shut the computer down. She headed upstairs with a spring in her step. Tomorrow she was going to find some answers.

Sarah, Amy, and Audrey stood on the sidewalk looking at Carroll's house. The day had dawned with full sun, and already the heat beat heavily on their heads.

"It looks old," Amy said.

"That's because it is."

Amy glared at her sister. "I was going to say that I bet there are lots of cool things in the attic."

Audrey shrugged and tucked her sketchbook and the vinyl bag with her colored pencils under her arm. She had made it clear on the way over; she did not want to go in any dirty attic.

The twins had wisely dressed in shorts. Audrey was wearing a pretty blouse that hung down past her hips, and Amy had on her Sox T-shirt. Sarah had popped over to their house after breakfast and before Maggie left for her drive north.

"Now, Mr. Shepherd can be a little grouchy, but don't let it bother you. He's sad he lost his daughter recently, and he's not happy because he's going to have to move."

"That's terrible," Audrey said. "I bet he doesn't want to leave his friends."

"Could be." Although Sarah wasn't sure what friends, if any, Carroll had. Other than Jared and his mother next door, Sarah hadn't seen anyone visiting. Of course, that didn't mean people didn't drop by in the evening. Carroll had been closemouthed about it if they had.

They trooped up the steps to the porch. Sarah rang the bell and as she inserted the key, Amy asked in a loud whisper, "Grandma, who's that?"

Sarah shifted her gaze in the direction the girls were looking. Jared was in his driveway, dressed in his basketball garb, shooting at the hoop mounted above the garage.

"He's cute," Audrey said. Sarah hadn't gotten used to her darling granddaughters growing up so fast. In her eyes, her granddaughters were still babies even though they'd be thirteen next week. Boys and dating weren't too far off.

"His name is Jared, and he's sixteen." In other words, he was too old for them, but the girls didn't seem to mind. Jared glanced over and spotted the girls, missing an easy layup. Audrey giggled, but Amy just shook her head.

Sarah waved at him. "Good morning, Jared."

Jared sauntered over to the hedge dividing the properties. "Morning, Mrs...."

"Hart. How are you this morning?"

"Okay." He stole a glance at the twins.

"These are my granddaughters, Amy and Audrey," Sarah said.

"You go to Maple Hill High?" Audrey asked.

"Yep," Jared said and subtly squared his shoulders. "Where do you go?"

"Hawthorne Middle." Audrey smiled.

Amy looked him up and down. "Are you on the basket-ball team?"

"I'm trying out. The coach thinks I have a chance if I work hard this summer."

"Cool," Amy said.

"Jared, I have a question for you," Sarah said.

"Shoot."

"I saw a brown van parked across the street the other day. Two men were sitting in it. I was wondering if they lived there."

"Nope. That's the Keller place, and they have Toyotas," Jared said. "Some of the people living on this street drive minivans, but nobody owns a brown one."

"This one was more like a cargo van. If you see it, could you let me know?"

"Sure."

Sarah glanced at Carroll's house. "Everything been okay around here?"

"I guess. I haven't seen Mr. Shepherd yet. Usually he comes out early to get his paper." He nodded to the plastic-wrapped newspaper on the lawn.

Apprehension shot through Sarah as Amy jogged over to get the paper. "I better go check on him."

"See ya later." Jared dribbled the ball and lobbed another shot.

Sarah unlocked the front door. "Mr. Shepherd?" she called as she walked down the hall with the girls on her heels. She turned the corner. Carroll slumped in his arm-chair. His head hung forward and his chin rested on his chest. A glass lay on the floor by his slippers.

"Is he dead?" Audrey asked, horror in her voice.

Amy stepped closer. "No. Can't you hear him snoring?" A soft sound whistled out of the old man's nose.

"He may have fallen asleep here last night," Sarah said, noting he had on the same clothes as the day before. "Good morning, Carroll."

No response. His hearing aids were probably turned off. She stepped around his walker in the middle of the room and shook his shoulder. "Carroll? Are you all right?"

His head rolled to the other side and his snore grew louder.

"He sure is a sound sleeper," Amy said.

"Quit fooling around, Eddie, it's your move!" he barked out and both girls took a step backward.

"Eddie?" Audrey asked. "Who's that?"

Sarah gave him another shake. "Carroll. Wake up."

He jerked upright. "What?" He gazed at them with blurry-looking eyes. "What in tarnation? Where am I?"

"Your living room. Did you sleep here all night?"

He rubbed his hands over his face. "I guess so."

"Was Eddie here last night?"

"Who?" He snorted. "No. Why would he be here?"

"You said his name."

"I did?" He gazed around him, color seeping into his face. He focus narrowed on the twins. "Who are they?"

"These are my granddaughters, Amy and Audrey. I'm taking them to their class later, so they're here to help out this morning. I hope that's okay with you."

"Why ask me? My opinion doesn't count for much anymore. It's rotten getting old, you hear me?" He poked a finger toward the girls. "Just don't break anything. Kids are always breaking things."

Sarah stepped in front of Audrey and Amy. "They're good helpers and will try to be careful as always."

"Humph."

"If this is a problem, we can leave right now," Sarah said lightly with a smile for the girls. "I can bring you lunch later this afternoon."

Carroll scowled. "Don't get all huffy now."

"All right," Sarah said. "Why don't you go change your clothes and freshen up? I'll make you a hot breakfast." She pushed his walker to him, then stopped and looked back to where it had been. It had to be at least six feet from the chair. "Did you leave your walker over here?"

He blinked several times. "I don't remember."

"Are you sure no one was here last night?"

Carroll scowled. "I said no. Quit asking me the same thing like I'm a crazy old coot." He winced and rubbed his temples with his fingers. "I have a terrible headache."

Sarah slipped her hand under his arm and helped him stand. She waited beside him until he took some steps behind his walker. He seemed steady enough.

"Come on, girls, let's go," Sarah said.

"You're right, he *is* a grouch," Audrey said, after entering the kitchen. She set her sketchbook and pencils on the table.

Sarah opened the refrigerator and took out an egg carton and cheddar cheese. She would make Carroll an omelet. "He's going through a hard time. Which is no excuse for bad behavior, but we can try to be extra patient. Amy, can you please try to find me a small mixing bowl?"

Sarah washed her hands as Amy searched the cupboards. Instead of the usual pile of dirty dishes and glasses, the sink was empty and the stainless steel shone. "Doesn't look like he ate dinner last night either," Sarah said.

"Maybe he has trouble with his memory like Grandpa William," Amy suggested, carrying a small ceramic bowl.

"He could, but most of the time he seems sharp," Sarah said. She glanced at the bottles above the sink and wondered if he'd taken enough of his medication last night. Suzy had mentioned that his high blood pressure could cause blackouts, and when Irene and Sarah had left him yesterday afternoon, he'd been agitated.

She sighed. If Carroll was trying to prove he was capable of taking care of himself, today wasn't a good example.

"Can I crack the eggs?" Amy asked.

"Sure, sweetie, but I think we'll make this mostly an egg white omelet. We'll want one whole egg and four whites. Do you know how to separate eggs?"

"I've seen Mom do it," Audrey said, scooting back her chair and coming over.

"So have I!" Amy said, sidling in front of her sister. "I want to do it. I asked first."

"How about you each separate two?" Sarah said as Audrey jostled Amy with her hip to get closer to the bowl.

Sarah gave them a quick demonstration of how to rock the yolk back and forth so the white dripped into the bowl.

Amy, who was the more coordinated of the two, handled the separating like a pro.

Audrey did her first one perfectly but dropped the second yolk in the mixture. "Oops. Amy bumped me."

"I did not. *You* bumped into me."

Sarah reached for the bowl. "Girls, you both did a great job." Sarah left the extra yolk in the bowl and beat the eggs with a fork.

Amy found some frozen hash browns in the freezer and Sarah threw those into another skillet. By the time the omelet had cooked and the coffee brewed, the thump of the walker sounded in the hall.

Carroll came around the corner in fresh brown slacks and a short-sleeved plaid shirt. His hair was wet and combed, and he had shaved the white whiskers off his chin.

"You look nice," Sarah said, turning the fire off under the skillets.

"Breakfast ready?"

"Almost. Have a seat." Sarah got down a plate.

Carroll shuffled over to the table where Audrey was sketching. "What are you drawing?"

"I'm trying to figure out how to draw cars." She pointed at a salt and pepper shaker set shaped like Model T Fords that Amy had found in a cupboard and used to replace the plain ones that had been on the table.

"My wife picked those up in St. Louis. She wanted Edsels, but they were sold out. I have some models that were made for advertising, but they're in the attic. We didn't have any use for them after they stopped making the cars. Designed them myself. Want me to draw them?"

"Sure."

"I'll need some paper."

Audrey flipped a page and handed him the sketchbook and a pencil.

"You see, the trick is to get the line right," he said, stroking lines across the paper. "Every car model has its own distinct line. When you see the silhouette, most of the time you can figure out what car it is."

"Cool." Audrey watched him draw, and Amy went over to watch too.

"This is a Studebaker. Those were fine old days when people wanted good, heavy cars, not these tin cans you see today."

Sarah set the plate down by Carroll. His face was animated and a hint of a smile played around his lips. Sarah was just relieved he'd stopped barking at the girls.

"You draw very well," Audrey said.

"Thank you, young lady. I've had lots of practice."

"Did you draw when you were a kid like me?"

"I did, but then I got an engineering degree and went into the car business. I decided I didn't like working for the big companies and opened a business of my own. The sales side of it kept me so busy, I only had time to draw for things at work."

"Do engineers draw?"

"Yep. I used to draw designs for my inventions. I designed—"

"Sorry to interrupt," Sarah said, anticipating Carroll was going to launch into one of his long stories again. "I'm going to head back upstairs to the attic to finish inventorying things."

"Well, get on with it then," Carroll said.

"You should tell Grandma thank you for breakfast," Audrey whispered. "It's polite."

A flush crept up his wrinkled neck. He glanced at Audrey and then back at Sarah. "And thank you for breakfast."

"You're welcome," Sarah said with a small smile. "If you need anything, call my cell phone."

Amy scooted around the table. "I'm coming with you, Grandma."

"I'll stay here with Mr. Shepherd." Audrey flipped the pages of the sketchbook. "I want to show him some of my drawings. Maybe he can help me."

"As long as it's fine with Mr. Shepherd. His breakfast is getting cold though."

"I'll make sure he eats," Audrey said, pulling the plate in front of Carroll.

Carroll glanced at Audrey's big smile and looked up at Sarah. "We'll be fine."

Sarah smiled as she followed Amy down the hall. It was nice to see Carroll enjoying himself. Audrey was no threat to him, and she probably reminded him of Dawn when she was young. It was a shame he had no grandchildren. Sarah sure loved hers. They made life much more meaningful.

Amy bounded up the staircase. "The attic stairs are next to the front bedroom," Sarah called after her. By the time she reached the attic, Amy stood in the middle of the crowded room.

"Cool, Grandma. Look at all this stuff." Amy spun in a circle. "It's like finding pirate's treasure."

Sarah grinned. What were some people's treasures were junk to others.

"Are we looking for anything special?"

"If we see any papers, especially ones that have to do with Dawn Shepherd, we need to take them to Mr. Shepherd." Sarah tapped the pencil on the clipboard. "Which would you prefer? To dig into the boxes or write?"

"Dig of course."

"That's what I thought." She smiled. "Let's start with this one." She pointed to a medium-size box. It turned out to be another one filled with miscellaneous household items, but the process went much faster with Amy calling out the things she found, as Sarah jotted notes.

Their system worked so well, an hour and a half went by before she knew it. They'd reached the corner where the

Cadillac and Edsel items were stored. Amy pulled out a box that had gotten shoved deep against the wall where the roof met the floor. "This one is full of paper, Gram."

Sarah looked up from her clipboard and maneuvered to Amy's side, ducking so she wouldn't bump her head. It looked like the same box that Sarah had said was missing yesterday. "Help me pull it out." Amy grabbed the other side, and they dragged it out under the light.

Amy flipped the lid off revealing the familiar manila files labeled for various business dealings, invoices, and catalogues. "What's wrong, Grandma?" Amy asked, brushing the dust off her shorts.

"This file box wasn't here yesterday."

"Are you sure?

She nodded. Even if it had gotten shoved back under the eaves, she would have seen it. Besides, it still meant someone had moved the box. She told Amy about the box disappearing and how the blue quilt had been moved.

"What blue quilt?" Amy asked looking around.

Sarah gazed at the box where she had left the quilt yesterday.

"It's gone."

CHAPTER EIGHT

I found something blue," Amy called from the other side of the attic. They'd split up and done a hasty search of the vast room. "It's stuck."

Sarah hurried over to the wall beside the stairway. A blue scrap of fabric hung on a protruding nail.

Amy yanked it off. "It looks like it's part of a quilt." She handed the scrap to Sarah. With a sinking feeling, Sarah recognized the quilting pattern.

"This is it, or what's left of the quilt. Good eyes, Amy." She rubbed her thumb over a dark spot on the fabric. Was that grease?

"Do you think someone was taking it to the stairs and it got caught?"

"Certainly appears that way." Sarah's heart thumped. "I need to speak to Mr. Shepherd." She set her clipboard and the scrap on the file box and hefted it into her arms. She staggered toward the stairs.

"That's too heavy. Let me help, Grandma." Amy grabbed one end. Between the two of them, they managed to get the load down the two flights of stairs.

Audrey and Carroll had moved to the living room and were playing a game of chess. Carroll didn't look up when Sarah and Amy entered the room. "We're not finished yet," he said.

"I don't mean to interrupt your game, but I need to talk to you. You weren't imagining things. Someone has definitely been in the attic. Here's the box that I told you had disappeared yesterday. Amy found it. And now a baby quilt is gone too."

Carroll dropped the rook in his hand and it clattered onto the chess board, knocking over two of Audrey's pawns.

"This is all that's left of the quilt." She handed the scrap to Carroll. "Amy found it near the stairs. It looks like someone may have been in a hurry to leave and it caught on a nail. I think we should call the police."

Carroll shook his head.

"Mr. Shepherd, you may be in danger. You really should make a police report and change the locks."

"Over what? A file box you say moved? A scrap of fabric? They're going to think I'm crazy." His voice rose. "This is still my house, and no one has the right to tell me what to do."

The girls looked wide-eyed at Sarah. She gave them a gentle smile. "Girls, can you go in the kitchen and start making salad for lunch? There's lettuce, cucumbers, and tomatoes in the refrigerator. I'll be there in a few minutes."

Audrey got up from the table and followed Amy out of the room. Sarah waited until their footsteps faded before turning back.

"Carroll, contrary to what you may believe, I'm trying to help you. I think you may be in danger being here all alone."

"I've lived here for fifty years. You can't make me afraid to be in my own house."

"Even though someone is apparently breaking in while you're asleep? You turn your hearing aids down at night, so you wouldn't be able to hear anyone. And this morning I had a tough time waking you up. What about your missing tools? What if they weren't sold? Suppose someone took them? Did you ever think someone could be in here right now?"

"*Someone* is in my house right now!" Carroll's eyes narrowed as he looked around. Sarah just waited until he took a few shallow breaths. "Okay. So? You may have a point."

"I'm just wondering how they got in. The doors were locked when I got here this morning."

"I usually check before going to bed."

"Maybe there's an open window somewhere."

Carroll rose, his legs slightly shaking. "I'll check the downstairs."

"Okay, I'll go to the basement and upstairs," she said, but decided to pop into the kitchen first to check on the girls. Amy stood at the sink. Audrey was on her phone, exclaiming, "You've got to be kidding. That's so cool."

"Be right back," Sarah called cheerfully and ducked down the cellar steps. She flipped on the light. The basement appeared as neat as it had the last time she was down there. She walked over to the two narrow windows set high up on the wall. Both latches were closed.

She turned to go back up the stairs when something caught her eye. The metal doors to the cabinets above the work benches were cracked open several inches. Surely she'd closed them, hadn't she? Or had someone else been looking for something?

She pushed one door shut. The door bounced back. She pushed it more firmly, and the magnet caught, holding it shut. Maybe she'd been in such a rush, she hadn't made sure they were closed. She checked the bulkhead doors. Locked. She hurried back upstairs to where the girls were.

Amy was still at the sink rinsing lettuce leaves in a colander. "What's going on, Grandma?

"I'm checking the windows to make sure they're locked." She spied a glass on the counter and held it up. The glass was spotless. "Was this Mr. Shepherd's glass from the living room?"

"Yes, Audrey brought it in. I washed it before I put the lettuce in the sink. Why?" Amy said, a worried wrinkle forming between her eyebrows.

"Oh, nothing. You're doing a great job," Sarah said.

She moved to the refrigerator. The pitcher wasn't on the shelf where she'd left it. Carroll either drank all the lemonade or someone poured it out. She opened the cupboard and found the empty pitcher, washed and clean.

Maybe she was being overly paranoid. There could be a logical explanation. Maybe Nancy had popped over to check on Carroll and cleaned up after him. Or maybe Carroll's blood pressure had spiked, and he had a memory lapse.

"There are some turkey slices. Can we make sandwiches?" Audrey asked.

Sarah picked up the package. It was still sealed from the grocery store. "Sounds good." She pulled out some individually wrapped cheese slices and a tomato.

Sarah glanced at the clock. They had about an hour before she needed to get the twins over to their class. She darted upstairs to check the windows. They were all locked too.

She returned to Carroll in the living room. "All the windows in the basement and on the second floor are secure."

"Same with the first floor."

Sarah paced the room in front his chair. "What do you remember from last night? What did you do?"

"I watched the news and must've fallen asleep."

"So you didn't eat dinner?" Sarah asked.

"I had some of that stew that woman left."

"But there were no dishes in the sink and the lemonade pitcher was empty and in the cupboard. Did you wash them?"

He ran his hand over his face. "I don't remember. Everything seems fuzzy. I must've been tired. I could've washed them."

Having to deal with Dawn's death and funeral must have taken a toll on Carroll, but it seemed too coincidental considering she was positive someone had been in the attic. "Did you take any more of your medication last night?"

"No. I told you I don't like taking it. Makes me too sleepy."

"Anything else to eat or drink?"

"Just the lemonade you made."

"Did it taste funny?"

"No, it tasted like lemonade," Carroll said. "What's with all the questions?"

"I'm just trying to figure out what happened," Sarah said, rubbing the back of her neck. "Do you know who that baby quilt in the attic belonged to?"

He shrugged and shifted in his chair restlessly. "Dawn went to a lot of garage sales."

"Why would someone take it?"

"Who would want an old quilt?"

Sarah for one, but he was correct in that the quilt probably wasn't worth more than a hundred dollars and only if he sold it to a collector. "What about your files? Is there anything important in them worth stealing?" She shoved the heavy box over by his feet and flipped off the lid. He looked at the contents.

"There are some files labeled by year with spreadsheets in them," she said, digging into the packed box, using her fingers to separate the files so she could read the labels. "What are these?" She pulled out some charts.

"Market projections of car models that my partner was always working on. He tried to predict the future. Never very good at it though, considering the place may go bankrupt." He leaned closer as Sarah pulled out some pink sheets.

"Invoices for special deliveries," Carroll said. "I liked to keep a copy for custom jobs."

"What are XT-9-52 and TR-16-20?"

"Just old designs of mine that didn't go far. There's probably more in there." He shook his head. "I can't imagine anyone would be interested in anything in there but me. It's stuff from my office at the dealership. After my stroke, Dawn went over there one day and threw it all in a box. There's nothing valuable in there."

Sarah pulled out a file labeled Personal. "Did you know your house title is in here? And here's one for a car."

"Those were in the safe in my office. I'd planned to move them to a safe-deposit box, but forgot."

Sarah pulled out two passports. She glanced inside. The book had expired, but it was loaded with stamps. Betty and Carroll had traveled a lot. Two folded multisheet documents slipped out and fell to the floor.

"That should be my will and life insurance papers," Carroll said as Sarah shoved everything back into the file and set it on the table beside the chessboard. She'd find a safe place to keep it until Suzy got back. "Is Dawn's will in there too? Suzy mentioned it was missing."

He shook his head. "It wouldn't be here. It was never in my safe."

"But someone might've thought it was." Sarah knew she was grasping at straws, and judging from Carroll's expression, he thought so too.

"Just figuratively speaking, who do you think would gain from her will?"

He rubbed his chin. "Me, I guess. Betty left half the house to Dawn, and we were supposed to have stipulations in our wills that our share of the house would revert to the other if..."

"I realize this is difficult, Carroll, but I'm trying to find a motive for someone breaking into your house. Maybe it's someone you know. Someone who's looking for something specific."

He sat back. "The house and any savings left would've been hers. Same with my share in the dealership, which is practically worthless at the moment. Dawn could've changed her will for all I know. She could be fickle at times, and we bickered a bit over the last year. None of this should've mattered. I was supposed to go first anyway."

Sarah couldn't imagine the pain of losing a child, and even though Carroll tried to act tough, it had to be devastating. "Was there anyone else in the family she was close to?" she asked softly.

"A couple of cousins, but everyone left Maple Hill. I suppose she could've still been in contact with them."

"Did any come to the funeral?"

"A nephew on Betty's side whom I didn't expect to see."

"Why not?"

Carroll waved his hand in a dismissive manner. "Ancient history. I don't want to talk about it."

"But—"

"I said I don't want to talk about it." His gaze shifted back to the marketing charts on the floor. "Did you know that Cadillac was the first American manufacturer to win the coveted Dewar Trophy for standardization of automobile parts?"

"Um, no," Sarah said.

"That was the area that I was interested in. Streamlining the manufacturing process even more and making repairs easier. I came up with several innovative ideas, but most of the time management was too shortsighted."

"I saw an article online about you. You won an award for something to do with electronic fuel injection."

He raised his eyebrows. "Checking up on me?"

"I was curious. It was dated in the seventies."

"I designed a part for the fuel injection system, but several months later someone in their research department came up with what they thought was a better version. Cheaper."

"Why didn't you work full-time in research if you liked it so much? Obviously you had a gift for it." She turned her attention back to the file box. Could the answer to what was going on be in there?

"Oh they offered me positions, but let's just say I did better working independently. I made a good living in sales and if I ever happened to invent something, there'd be higher compensation selling the patent than there would be if I had been on their research payroll."

Sarah finished emptying the file box as Carroll rambled on about the various virtues and assembly problems of the Cadillac versus the Lexus versus the Mercedes. "The reason they don't want standardization across models, of course, is because then any part would do."

Sarah stifled a yawn.

"Lunch is ready," Audrey called. Sarah waited for Carroll to get to his feet and then followed him to the kitchen. He seemed more stable than he had that morning.

The girls had set the table. A sandwich, cut on the diagonal, adorned each plate. The green salad was in the center of the table with a vase of pink roses.

"Girls, the table looks so nice," Sarah said, nearly bursting with pride.

"Where'd you get the roses?" Carroll said sharply.

"From the backyard. There are lots of them. I hope that was okay," Amy said.

He glanced at her and then sat with a "humph."

Through the window, Sarah spied Jared wheeling his bike down his driveway. "I'll be right back."

She went out the backdoor and crossed the lawn as Jared swung a leg over the bike.

"Jared!"

He screeched to a stop, hopping on one foot to keep the bike upright. He looked over his shoulder. "Mrs. Hart?"

"I'm sorry, but I was wondering if you saw anyone visiting Mr. Shepherd last night."

He shook his head. "I didn't notice. I was in all evening watching a game."

Sarah thanked him, and he flew down the street. A brown van was parked several houses down behind a silver sedan. Sarah looked more closely. Sunlight reflected off the windshield, making it difficult to see in. Was that someone sitting in the front seat?

Sarah rounded the corner of the house and cut across the front lawn to the neighbor on the opposite side of Carroll's house. Someone must know if the van belonged to anyone in the neighborhood. The split-level ranch had probably been built in the sixties but looked very modern next to Carroll's nineteenth-century home. Toys littered the small front lawn and a swing set occupied the side yard.

She knocked on the front door, and after a few moments, a woman answered. She cradled an infant in one arm and a toddler clung to the hem of her shirt. A gray tabby darted between her legs and dashed across the porch.

"Robin!" she yelled. "Get back here."

The cat's green eyes peered over his shoulder before he slipped under the railing and into the bushes."

"I'm sorry," Sarah said. "Do you want me to try to catch him?"

"No, he'll come back in when he's hungry. I just didn't want him sneaking in and bothering my neighbor right now."

The curly-headed boy pointed a finger at the yard. "Robcat."

Sarah smiled. "Robin is an unusual name for a kitty."

"It's after the Winnie-the-Pooh series. Betty Shepherd's cat had kittens. There was a Christopher and an Eeyore and a Tigger. Robin is the only one left of the litter. The others were given to people not in the neighborhood." She adjusted the baby in her arms. "I've seen you over there. How's Mr. Shepherd doing? Poor guy has had it rough."

"He's ... managing for now. I'm helping his niece out."

"It's sad about his daughter."

"Did you know Dawn well?"

"Not really. I knew her mother better. She was so friendly after we bought the house and would visit every week. She would've loved to have known my kids too. She wanted grandchildren so badly. This is Matthew." She placed a hand on his head. "And the baby is Olivia. She just turned five months old."

"They're so precious. I have four grandchildren myself. I'm Sarah Hart."

The woman smiled "Theresa Nottingham, and my husband is Shane. I'm sorry, where are my manners? Would you like to come in? The house is a wreck though."

"Oh I don't want to be a bother. I just popped on over to ask you about that van parked down the street. Do you know if it belongs to anyone around here?"

"What van?" She stepped out farther on the porch, tugging Matthew along. "That one in front of the Parkers? I've seen it around a couple of times, but I don't know who owns it. Why?"

"The last time it was parked in the driveway across the street. I saw two men in the front, just sitting there. I'm worried they might be casing the neighborhood."

"You mean like burglars?" Theresa frowned, backing to her doorway. "There haven't been any reports of break-ins that I know of. And I never saw anyone get out of the van. I just assumed they were working around here. Dawn had people working on Mr. Shepherd's house. Did something happen?"

Sarah explained about Carroll's missing tools and the possibility that someone had been in the house the previous evening. "Did you notice if Carroll had any visitors last night?"

"Only you."

Sarah's heart skipped a beat. "I wasn't here last night."

"Oh?" Her gaze darted toward the Shepherd house. "I just assumed since I'd seen you earlier in the day. It was dark. I thought I saw a woman going around the side of the house to the back."

"What time?"

"Just before nine. Robin got out again and I was chasing him down. I wasn't paying much attention. Maybe it was Nancy, Carroll's neighbor on the other side. We've all tried to keep an eye on him from time to time for Dawn, even though he doesn't want any help. He just seemed so lonely after Betty passed away, and then of course, he had his stroke which made him even more homebound.

"You could ask Jared. He was outside shooting hoops last night. I could hear his basketball."

"He plays outside that late?" Sarah asked. Hadn't Jared just said he was in all night watching a game?

"Sometimes," she said. "Poor kid. Took it real hard when his dad left and got in a bunch of trouble last year. Fell in with a bad crowd for a while."

"I'm sorry to hear that. He seems to be a nice, responsible boy. At least Carroll relies on him."

"Yeah. I don't know all the details, but Jared did some community service, and his mom says he's fine now. Playing basketball has kept him focused." Theresa shifted Olivia in her arms. "Would you like me to call you if I see that woman again? Assuming it's not Nancy."

"I'd appreciate it. I'll drop by my business card when I take my granddaughters to their class."

"I'll tell my husband about the van too, and if I see anything suspicious I'll call the police. I feel pretty stupid for not being more aware. I used to be so organized and active in the community. My brain has been in a fog since Olivia was born." Her dark eyes glistened.

"Oh please don't feel that way. You're raising young ones, and that's the most important job in the world. From the looks of these two, you're doing wonderfully."

"Thank you," Theresa said with a small smile.

"I better get back over to Mr. Shepherd's. I'll drop my phone number by when I leave."

The van still sat under the oak behind the sedan. Something moved in the window, and now she could make out two people. So they were just sitting there again.

A car had parked behind them. If she could get a little closer she would be able to make out the letters on the license plate.

She set out down the sidewalk at a leisurely pace, trying to look relaxed and just out for a stroll. As she got closer, she could hear the engine idling.

Almost there. From the new angle, she could make out that the man in the passenger seat wore a Lakers basketball hat and held a cell phone to his ear. A few more steps and she would be able to see beyond the sedan's trunk to the van's front plate.

The man with the cap lifted his gaze and spotted Sarah. He gave her a little wave and the van backed up with a spin of its tires. It made a U-turn and roared down the street, a cloud spewing out of the exhaust pipes. Sarah could make out only the first two letters T and S and the last number 7.

Hands on hips, Sarah watched the van turn the corner and roar away. "Well, so much for my skills at stealth surveillance," she muttered and turned back to Carroll's. She went in the front door to discover that Audrey and Mr. Shepherd had moved to the living room. Audrey sat cross-legged on the carpet by the large cabinet. The bottom doors were open and photo albums were piled around her.

"What took so long, Grandma?" Audrey asked, looking up from a yellowed page with black and white photos. "You didn't finish lunch. We left your sandwich on the table for you."

"Thanks, sweetie, I didn't mean to be gone so long. I got to talking to Mr. Shepherd's neighbor." She turned to Carroll. "Theresa says she saw a woman heading to the backyard last night."

He kept his gaze on the lively talk show host. "I already told you I didn't have any visitors."

"Well, someone was out there after dark."

"Maybe Suzy's back."

"I talked to her on the phone last night. She said she wouldn't be back until next week. What about Nancy Ferguson? Does she have a key?"

He shrugged.

"Who else might have a key to your house?" When he didn't answer, she asked, "Carroll?"

He looked at her. "I don't know. Me, Betty, Dawn. Betty may have given the key to someone so they could feed our pets when we were gone. And there was a time Betty used to hide one outside in case she forgot her key ring. We've been here forty years, and I've never changed the locks."

"Mr. Shepherd, as I said before, I really think we should file a report with the police. And we should get your locks changed just in case."

"I'll think about it."

"At least let me mention the break-in to Officer Hopkins."

"I *said* I'd think about it."

The man was impossible. "Audrey, we better get going."

"Okay." She carefully set the photo albums back in the cabinet.

Sarah regarded Carroll, intent on his show. Since they had had sandwiches for lunch there weren't leftovers for tonight. "I'll be back later this evening to make sure you have something for dinner."

He didn't answer.

Audrey followed Sarah to the kitchen. Amy's arms were plunged into the soap suds in the sink.

"Amy, that's so nice of you. I would've cleaned up."

Her granddaughter shrugged. "I like helping Mr. Shepherd. He's grumpy, but he doesn't have anyone right now."

"No, he doesn't. I appreciate all your work today. I think we should get an ice cream after your class if you don't think it'll spoil your dinner."

"Not a chance," Amy grinned, wiping her hands on a towel.

"Can we go to The Spotted Dog?" Audrey asked. "They've got a new, three-berry chocolate sundae. Trina said it was amazing."

"Sounds like it, and we can go there if you like. Okay with you, Amy?" Sarah picked up her purse and locked the backdoor.

Amy shrugged. "It's ice cream, so I'm happy."

They trooped to the front door, calling a good-bye to Carroll who grunted in return.

As Sarah turned and locked the door, a sense of foreboding swamped her. What would she find the next time she returned?

arah shifted on the metal chair, trying to get comfortable in the back of the classroom where the baby-sitting first aid class was being taught. Amy and Audrey sat on the floor near the front of the room watching the instructor set up the baby mannequin to teach infant CPR.

Martha Maplethorpe slid into the chair next to her. "Doesn't this bring back memories? I had French for two years in this room."

Sarah grinned. "We just need sweater sets and pleated skirts, and no one would even know we left high school."

Martha laughed. "Wish it were that easy." She set a large tote bag decorated with palm trees at her feet and lifted out her current crochet project, which appeared to be a vest. "I'm sorry I couldn't pick up the twins. My minivan was full with my grandkids and a couple of their friends."

"That's fine. I enjoy the time with the girls. They helped me this morning at the Shepherd house."

"How's that going? I've been dying for an update," Martha asked, her fingers flying as her crochet hook flashed around the yarn strands creating another sunny row.

"Well, there's still a lot to do. Suzy will have to finish it up. The attic is a huge job by itself, but strange things have been happening." She told Martha about the missing items and moved objects.

"A mystery!" Martha exclaimed, setting her crocheting in her lap. "Do you have any leads?"

They exchanged a smile. Martha enjoyed helping Sarah sleuth. "Right now I'm trying to contact handymen around town to see if they worked at the Shepherds'. Someone has to know something. As far as who has access to the house, there are a number of people who may have been inside. There's Jared, the neighbor boy who Carroll hires to do yard work. He comes in to play chess with Carroll sometimes. His mother Nancy is another, although she says she hasn't been in there for a long time.

"There's also the unknown handyman. Dawn said she sold him some of Carroll's tools, but what if he saw some other things worth stealing? One of them may have somehow gotten hold of a key. Carroll mentioned a nephew and hinted about bad blood on that side of the family."

She looked down at the fingers she'd used to tick off the possible suspects and wondered how many more she hadn't thought of yet. "If I can figure out why someone would want these things, I might be able to narrow it down."

"What about Mr. Shepherd? Does he have any friends? Or enemies, for that matter."

"Not sure. Carroll has mentioned someone named Eddie a couple of times. Once, I think, in relation to the dealership. Only I don't know who Eddie is. I've asked Carroll, but he always changes the subject. He's vague about family matters too."

Martha paused as she counted her loops. "Doesn't sound like he's very cooperative."

"Not at all. I think he's in denial about all the changes coming, and he's still hurting over his daughter's death. I just hope he's not in danger. There's this brown van that's been hanging around the neighborhood. I tried to get the license plate, but they drove off."

"You think they may be sneaking in?"

Sarah shrugged. "Could be. I had a talk with one of Carroll's neighbors, and she's going to keep an eye out for it."

Martha set her crochet hook down again. "So somebody or somebodies stole his tools, a baby quilt, a file box, and possibly some novels."

"Well, the file box and books are still there, but they'd been moved. I know the whole thing sounds far-fetched, but it's scary if someone is entering Carroll's house without his knowledge. What if they try to harm him?" Sarah recounted the trouble they had waking him up that morning and her suspicions about the lemonade.

"You think maybe somebody might've put something in that drink to help him sleep?" Martha asked.

"Anything's possible at this point," Sarah said, picturing the living room in her mind. "He hadn't changed out of his clothes from the day before and—"

"What?"

She looked at Martha. "When I went into the room, his walker was in the middle of the floor. Why would he have left it there?"

"Can he walk without it?"

"Yes, but not very well. And he was unsteady on his feet this morning."

"So someone else may have moved it." They both fell silent for a few moments. The big question was why?

"I can almost hear the gears spinning in your brain," Martha said.

"It helps to be able to talk to you about this."

"I just wish I had time to help more," Martha said with a glance toward her grandchildren. "So what kind of quilt was taken?"

"A sweet little baby quilt. Actually, I have a piece of it with me." She reached into her purse and extracted a plastic bag with the quilt scrap inside. "It's such a shame. It was a pretty quilt. Someone put a lot of time and love into it."

Martha took the bag. "Oh I like the pattern."

"It's a Nine Patch and all the quilting was done by hand."

"You could fix it if you had the rest of the quilt," Martha said in a confident tone. "What did Mr. Shepherd say about it?"

"I asked him if it was Dawn's, and he said she'd gone to a lot of garage sales. He wasn't sure though."

"Maybe someone heard the house was going to be sold and came back to get it."

"That's possible. But why not just ask Carroll for the quilt instead of sneaking in?" Sarah asked. "Unless, of course, they were looking for something else too. There's other evidence around the house that someone is searching for something," Sarah added, thinking about the music boxes and open cabinet doors in the basement.

"But what?" she continued. "The house is jammed with stuff. There's no way of knowing if they took anything else. Only Carroll can tell if something valuable is gone. Instead, he grumbles and watches TV. I've been trying to be patient because I figured his bad mood had to do with the loss of his daughter, but I'm starting to think that maybe he's always been this way. Miserable."

"So what's your plan?"

"I'm going to try to track down everyone who may have had access to the house and—" Sarah's cell phone rang and she fumbled for the Quiet button as the instructor looked at her. "It's the historical society number. It must be Irene. I meant to call her earlier today."

"Go ahead and take the call. I'm going to get a drink of water, assuming the drinking fountain still works." Martha and Sarah both darted through the door into the hallway.

"Sarah, I've been sitting here trying to work on a new article, and I'm stuck," Irene said. "I was wondering if you had a chance to read my work."

"I have actually, and they're very good. They seem...," Sarah tried to find the right words to protect Irene's feelings, "... very thorough. But I would suggest breaking the articles down into smaller bites or topics. Pick out one or two interesting aspects and expand on them. Like, take the town square. Instead of trying to write about the history of all the buildings, try doing just one or two and give the reader a chance to experience the past personally."

Silence stretched. Had she offended her? "Are you there?" Sarah asked. "This is just an opinion. It doesn't mean you should take it."

"On no. You're right," Irene said. "I'd like to talk about this more in-depth. Maybe you can give me some more examples, and I can write the beginning with you. I know I'm imposing again, but are you busy today?"

"You're not imposing," Sarah said as Martha strolled down the hall toward her. "I'm happy to help if I can, but I'm afraid it can't be today. I'm with my granddaughters right now at their class, and I still need to get back to the Shepherd place this evening."

"How's the attic inventory going?"

"Slowly."

"If you need help, I can always drop in again. I enjoyed finally meeting Mr. Shepherd, although he wasn't very talkative. The house is fabulous, really well preserved, even if you can't see the details with all the stuff lying around. Imagine how that place must've looked at the turn of the century. Heavenly. The floors alone are treasures. That type of hardwood isn't easy to find these days. I wish I could—"

"Irene," Sarah interrupted, "there *is* actually something you can do to help."

"Just name it."

"If it's not too much trouble, I'd like information on Dawn Shepherd's relatives, especially those who might still live nearby. Baby and wedding announcements would be helpful too."

"I can get most of that through county records and archived newspapers. This will be fun."

"Thanks Irene, I—"

"How soon do you need this?"

"As soon as it's convenient."

"Okay, I'll get right on it. Talk to you soon."

Martha had slipped back inside the classroom. The instructor glanced at Sarah as she returned to her chair. Sarah put her phone on vibrate before dropping it back in her purse.

Martha continued to crochet and didn't ask any questions but waited for Sarah to share.

"Irene's going to do some research on the Shepherd house and family," Sarah said. "That may give me more to work with since most likely there are things in that attic that belonged to other family members. If I can figure out

who might want those particular items that were taken—
like who the quilt belongs to—I might be able to figure out
who's been breaking into the house." She paused, taking a
deep breath. "Am I making any sense?"

"You are to me, but I've known you for over forty years."

Sarah smiled. Now to see if her plan would work.

The class ran overtime, and it was nearly three by the time
each girl completed the CPR recertification process. Audrey
chatted with her friends while Amy cruised over to where
Sarah sat. "I only missed three on the test."

"Good job!" Sarah took the CPR card Amy proffered and
admired it.

Martha stuck her crocheting into her tote bag and stood
with her hand on her lower back, stretching the kinks
out.

"Sarah, I'm taking my girls strawberry picking at the
Brewsters' farm for about an hour. Would you and the twins
like to come? It looks like it's going to be a gorgeous afternoon."

Sarah waved Audrey over. "Decision time. Would you
rather go strawberry picking with Trina, Pru, and Lexie or
go for ice cream?"

"Ice cream," Amy said at the same time Audrey pro-
claimed, "Strawberries."

Of course. "Well, how about a compromise? We could go
pick strawberries and then you can put them over ice cream

tonight at home. And I'll take you to The Spotted Dog for an extra special treat next week."

"Well..." Amy glanced over at the crowd that was leaving. Trina and Lexie waved at her. "Okay."

"Let me ring your mom and clear it with her. She may be home by now." The twins ran ahead to be with their friends as the crowd of parents and students flowed out the door. When Sarah reached the parking lot, she called her daughter-in-law.

"I'm heading back as soon as I make arrangements for delivery," Maggie said. An auctioneer's voice bellowed in the background. "The sale is terrific. I snagged a pristine nineteenth-century dining room set and the chandelier, plus a gorgeous maple sleigh bed. Right now they're selling off some of the jewelry. I found some lovely cameo pins too. How's it going there?"

"The girls passed their babysitting recertification and were a huge help this morning. Audrey kept Mr. Shepherd entertained while Amy helped me go through the boxes in the attic. The inventorying went so much faster with Amy helping. Then they offered to make lunch."

"Wow. I'm impressed. Now if we could only get them to take that kind of initiative at home." Maggie chuckled. "I know, I know. It's much more fun helping other people than picking up your own room. I'm glad they did so well."

"They did, and I thought they deserved a treat. I was going to take them for ice cream at The Spotted Dog if you were okay with that, but Martha is here with her granddaughters, and they're going strawberry picking at a farm just outside of town. The girls are willing to go, and I suggested they could put strawberries over ice cream after supper tonight."

"That sounds yummy. I used up all our strawberries on the shortcake. If the berries look good, I'll take a bucket. I'd like to freeze some to save for this winter."

"Okay, we'll see what they have. We should be out there for about an hour or so."

"That'll work out great. I'll give Jason a call to let him know what's going on. Can you stay for supper again?"

"I'd love to, but I need to drop back by Mr. Shepherd's place and fix him some dinner. We had sandwiches for lunch and I'd like him to have something hot and hearty." Plus she wanted to stick around until Carroll went to bed. It seemed that the strange occurrences in the attic were happening at night.

"Well, I better go. A lot number is coming up that I want to bid on. Thanks again for taking the girls."

Sarah started to disconnect when Maggie exclaimed, "Oh wait, before I forget, I wanted to tell you something. Remember how we were talking about Dave Diamond last night? Well, I ran into Clarisse Green who is friends with his wife Liz. She's here bidding on some china for her niece's wedding. Guess what? Liz is expecting again. She's fifteen weeks."

"That's terrific," Sarah said. She and Maggie had been with Liz when she went into labor with her son.

"I'm getting sidetracked. What I'm trying to tell you is that Liz and Dave are on vacation with relatives on the Cape, so they won't be home until this weekend if you're were trying to call Dave."

"Thanks for letting me know."

The auctioneer's voice grew louder and boomed across the cell phone connection. "This collection of antique jewelry's estimated to be from the time period of 1900 to 1945 and—"

"Sorry. Gotta run," Maggie said and the connection clicked off.

"What did Mom say?" Audrey asked as she snapped her seat belt into place in the front seat.

"She should be back in a couple of hours and thinks the strawberry idea is yummy." Sarah waited for Amy to get settled in the back and then pulled behind Martha's van packed full of kids.

When Sarah was a girl, the Brewsters' farm had seemed way out in the country, but over the years Maple Hill had expanded, gradually creeping out into the farming valley surrounded by rolling hills.

They turned onto a dirt road and parked with several other vehicles by a sprawling farmhouse with a porch that circled the entire house. Behind the house stood a large barn. The wide doors were open, and people meandered in and out.

Martha and Sarah set the girls up with buckets. Mrs. Brewster's daughter instructed them to be careful not to step on the rows and suggested the berries on the west end of the field were riper than those closest to the barn. Trina and Audrey led the merry band across the field, Sarah and Martha following.

"This should get me enough to can some jam," Martha said.

"I was going to have the girls over on Sunday to do the same."

Martha placed her hand on Sarah's arm and slowed her steps to let the girls get farther ahead. "Trina told me all about the surprise party for the girls. If you and Maggie want, I can supervise them while the rest of you go out to dinner."

"Maggie thinks the surprise is a great idea, but I think she'll be relieved if you're there to help."

"The girls are so excited, but I also know how rambunctious they can get. On the way over, they were singing some songs and bouncing in their seats to the beat. For a moment I thought we were having an earthquake." Martha laughed. "I'll call Maggie then, and she can get me a key before the big event. I'll make sure the house stays in one piece. They want to hang streamers and balloons and I heard something about Silly String, but I'll nix the string if it sounds too messy."

"That'll be appreciated." They closed the distance to the girls.

Since the Brewsters allowed customers to sample the strawberries while they were harvesting, Sarah plucked a bright red strawberry, dusted it off on her jeans, and popped it into her mouth. "That one was really sweet."

Martha tasted a berry and gave her a thumbs-up. They moved to the end of the row opposite the girls and started picking. Sarah's bucket was half-full when her phone rang.

"Hi Sarah, sorry to bother you again," Irene said, "but I'm just starting to run names through the newspaper archives and wondered how far back you want me to go."

"Probably just the last hundred years, if that's possible. Mr. Shepherd is eighty-nine. See if there's any mention of relatives on his side of the family and Betty's too."

"In addition to birth, wedding, and funeral announcements, I'm running an obituary search," Irene said above the sound of the clicking keyboard. "I had another idea too. Since I'm doing all this research on the Shepherds, do you think there might be a good story in it for a magazine?"

"Probably, but you'd want to clear it with Mr. Shepherd first. He seems to value his privacy."

"Oh, of course. I'll ask him first," she said. "Are you busy right now? Maybe we can do some brainstorming."

"Actually, I'm standing in a strawberry field with Martha Maplethorpe, our grandchildren, and some of their friends." Sarah propped the phone between her ear and shoulder as she gathered more berries.

"That sounds like fun. I grew up in the middle of the city and I've never had a chance to go berry picking."

"This was a spur of the moment decision on my part. If you're interested, I'll let you know if we go again."

"I'd like that."

"Grandma, we're done." Amy ran over, her bucket wobbling. Several berries fell out, and she bent to pick them up.

"I'll let you go," Irene said. "I'll call later when I have some results, okay?"

"Thanks, Irene. Whenever you have time, really." Sarah clicked the phone shut and rejoined Martha, who'd filled her bucket until strawberries mounded in a hill over the top. She poured the excess into Sarah's bucket so they were both full.

Sarah smiled her thanks. "Sorry I fell behind. That was Irene again." She explained to Martha about the articles. "I'm just not sure why she picked me. I don't have that much writing experience compared to some other folks in town."

"You're such a sweetie, you can never say no to anyone, that's why." Martha said. "First Suzy Carmichael, then Carroll Shepherd, and now Irene."

Martha had a good point. Maybe Sarah said yes too often. In Carroll's case, he'd certainly not asked for Sarah's help, but he was going to get it anyway.

CHAPTER TEN

I don't want broccoli. I don't like broccoli, and I'm not going to eat it!" Carroll declared from his easy chair.

"That's fine. You don't have to," Sarah said, praying for patience. Carroll was worse than usual tonight—if that was possible. "I just asked because there's a bag in the freezer. What else would you like?"

"Corn."

"I didn't see any corn, but there are peas. Those will go with Swiss steak and mashed potatoes."

"No peas."

Sarah sucked in a deep breath and let it out slowly. "Okay. I'm going to make a salad. You don't have to eat it if you don't want to."

Sarah spun and walked to the kitchen, fragrant with her bubbling entree. She yanked open the refrigerator door and grabbed the leftover salad from lunch and the rest of the lettuce Amy had washed earlier.

The minute she'd come in the door after dropping off the girls at home, she'd sensed Carroll was in a foul mood. He sat sprawled in front of the TV, a scowl on his face. She asked him how his day had gone, and he snapped back.

She'd been tempted to leave then. After all, she was giving up dinner with her family. She had brought the strawberries along to see if Carroll wanted some, but he'd been so cranky she hadn't even asked him about dessert.

She gazed out the window at the Ferguson house. No car in the driveway. Nancy might be pulling a double shift again. She wondered if Nancy had been the woman Theresa had seen last night. The hedge between the houses would have made Nancy come up through the front yard and around the side to reach the backdoor.

Sarah checked the index card taped to the wall by the phone and found the Fergusons' number. Their phone rang several times until finally a young male voice said, "Yeah?"

"Jared? This is Mrs. Hart next door with Mr. Shepherd. Is your mother home?"

"She's working late."

"Do you know if she visited Mr. Shepherd last night?"

"I don't know. Like I told you earlier, I was watching the game."

"Okay, thanks," Sarah said and then asked, "Have you had dinner? I made Swiss steak for Mr. Shepherd. There's plenty if you want to come over."

"I'm fine. Mom leaves stuff in the Crock-Pot, but thanks."

Sarah hung up the phone, pulled the casserole out of the oven, and set it on the counter. After she stirred the mashed potatoes on the stove, she fixed a plate for Carroll, poured a glass of grape juice, and carried the items to the living room.

"Since you're watching the news, I brought dinner in here if that's okay." She grabbed a TV tray from the corner and set up his dinner. "I'll be back in a minute." She returned to the kitchen and assembled a plate of food for herself.

On her way back to the living room she checked to make sure the back and front doors were locked.

"I think I'll join you in here." She sat on the couch and noted Carroll hadn't touched his food yet.

"I'm ready to say grace if you are," she said.

He bowed his head. "For the bounty we are about to receive, thank you." He hesitated and continued, "And bless the hands that prepared it."

"Thank you, Carroll."

He grunted and dug into the mashed potatoes. The meteorologist predicted wind and possibly a stray shower tonight but still projected temperatures to climb for the next couple of days. Sarah decided she needed to get in the attic as early in the morning as possible if she wanted to finish before Suzy came back.

Tomorrow afternoon she'd try to cajole Carroll into joining her in the family room where Dawn had begun sorting.

If that didn't work, she'd start bringing the boxes in here to sort them with him.

She finished eating before Carroll did. The news had given way to a game show she wasn't interested in. She glanced at the lower section of the cabinet where Audrey had returned Carroll's photo albums. Maybe there was some clue in those about the wedding dresses and baby quilt. "Mr. Shepherd, would you mind if I looked at your photo albums?"

"Suit yourself."

She pulled out a black leather-bound book and settled back on the couch. She flipped through the pages and came across wedding photos. "You look so handsome in your uniform. Did you get married before you went off to war?"

"After." He glanced at her. "I stayed in the army for several years until I finished college."

"That's such a beautiful dress Betty wore for your wedding. I saw it in the attic. There was another one up there too, stored in an armoire. I was wondering whose it was."

"I've never seen it."

"I thought maybe it was Dawn's but—"

"Dawn never married." He turned up the volume on the TV.

Sarah scanned through more pages until she came to a photo of another wedding. This time Carroll was dressed in a tux and stood beside the groom. Brown ringlets framed the bride's pixie face. Pretty lace adorned her dress, but it wasn't the one in the attic.

"Who's this?" she asked, sliding off the cushion and carrying the book over to Carroll. She set it on the arm of his easy chair.

He sighed. "My baby sister Shirley. That's her first husband. Named Danvers. Didn't last long. He was killed in the Korean War."

"How sad. Did she ever remarry?"

"Yeah. She was young when Danvers died, but she waited for about fifteen years before marrying the other one. Bach was his last name."

"Did they have children?"

"Two sons, but one died in a plane crash. The other came for Betty's and Dawn's funerals. Probably won't show up again until mine and the will reading. The joke is on him though. His formerly well-to-do uncle will be lucky to have two nickels to rub together by the time he goes."

"I wish you wouldn't talk like that."

"Just stating the truth. What?" He furrowed his brow. "You can't handle the truth?"

"That's a good Jack Nicholson," Sarah said, pleased that Carroll had made a joke and that she actually recognized the phrase from the movie Jason liked.

"Betty liked my John Wayne better. I haven't lost my temper in forty years but, Pilgrim, you caused a lot of trouble this morning," he drawled.

Sarah laughed. Who would have known that under that gruff exterior lurked a sense of theatrics? She glanced back down at the album. "Do you keep in touch with your sister?"

"That was Betty's department. But my sister passed away. So did my brother. I was the oldest, fought in the war, raced cars, smoked most of my life, drank like a fish in the army, ate lousy food, and had a stroke, but I'm still here. Some folks might not think that's fair, but that's the way life is."

Sarah had no answer for that other than God had deemed to bless Carroll with a longer life. "Did your brother live around here? What was his name?"

"Ronald. He was a judge and the apple of my mother's eye," Carroll said. "Why all the questions?"

"Sorry, I was just curious because I wondered if any of your family might be interested in the things in the house." She put the photo album back and gathered up his and her plates.

Since Carroll didn't respond, Sarah offered dessert. "I brought fresh strawberries. I can slice them and put them over ice cream. You have a carton of vanilla in the freezer."

"I like them with just plain cream poured over them."

"Okay, I'll see what I can do. I'll be right back."

The kitchen clock hands had crept around to the seven o'clock position. She set the dishes in the sink to soak and got out the bowl she had sliced the berries into. Carroll had half-and-half in the refrigerator. Not as thick as cream, but it would have to do. She was fixing them each a bowl when she thought she heard a noise. A creaking that raised the hair on the back of her neck. She froze, listening. Could it be the wind causing the house to shift?

She peered out the window and noted the branches of the neighbor's maple trees swaying. She finished pouring half-and-half over the fruit and hurried down the hall.

Another soft creak caused her to pause by the stairs. The second story was pitch-black. She reached for the switch, and yellow light flooded the stairwell.

Maybe her nerves were just stretched too thin. How could anyone get upstairs without coming through the first floor? All the second story windows were too far off the ground unless someone had a ladder. She had made sure the doors were locked when she had left earlier in the day. Of course, she hadn't been here all afternoon and Carroll could have gone outside.

She waited a few more seconds and turned off the light. She stepped toward the living room, feeling a little foolish, when someone pounded on the front door.

Sarah jumped and one of the bowls of strawberries slipped out of her fingers and clattered to the floor.

"What's going on?" Carroll thundered.

"It's okay. I just dropped a bowl," Sarah called, surveying the white puddle dotted with red disks. "And someone's at the door."

"Well are ya gonna answer it?"

Sarah held her tongue. She set the remaining bowl on the staircase and shook half-and-half off her shoe. She turned on the porch light and looked through the peephole. Irene stood on the porch with a file tucked under her arm.

"Well? Who is it?" Carroll called.

"Irene. The woman who made you goulash."

"She's annoying. Chatters constantly. Tell her to go away."

"I'll do no such thing. Behave yourself. I'm opening the door."

Sarah unlocked the dead bolt and swung open the door, thankful it was a solid thick piece of oak. Irene stood there smiling, apparently not having heard Carroll's opinion of her.

"Sarah, I was so excited about what I found, I couldn't wait until tomorrow to show you. I took a chance you were still here."

Sarah stepped back to let Irene in. "I could use some good news right now."

Irene caught sight of the puddle on the floor. "Oh my! What happened?"

"Just me being clumsy." And overly jumpy. "Why don't we go on back to the kitchen, I feel like a cup of coffee. Would you like one?"

"That sounds good."

Sarah fetched the bowl on the staircase and took it into Carroll. "We'll be in the kitchen if you need anything."

By the time Sarah reached the kitchen, Irene had already commandeered the coffeepot and was filling it with water.

"Be right back." Sarah grabbed a roll of paper towels, wet a few, and returned to the mess in the hall. The floor really needed a good mopping, but she'd do that later.

"Carroll's almost out of coffee, so this may be a little weak," Irene said when Sarah put the wad of paper towels in the trash.

"Thanks. I'll make a note of it. I'll probably get him some groceries before Suzy gets back. Would you like some strawberries?"

"I'd love some, but I better not. I don't like eating after dinner. My metabolism just isn't what it used to be."

Sarah observed Irene's petite, trim figure. "I don't think you need to worry. You've always looked great."

"Thank you. You're so sweet. I appreciate hearing that, but both my parents were overweight and I want to make sure I don't follow the same unhealthy path." Irene forced a smile that didn't quite reach her eyes. "Chris is still a skinny beanpole, no matter what he eats."

Irene flipped open the file she had placed on the table and extracted copies of newspaper pages. "I found two wedding announcements and several obituaries. I'm not sure they're all related to Carroll. Most of the Shepherds moved away from Maple Hill in the eighties. I also brought the research I collected on the house."

Sarah sat, eager to see what Irene had uncovered. The first announcement, dated 1943, was for a Garfield Shepherd and his bride Mable Orman. She would have to ask Carroll about that one. She picked up the other and scanned it.

Gus and Mary Shepherd are pleased to announce the wedding of Shirley Shepherd Danvers and Irving Bach, June 12,

1967. The ceremony was conducted in Pittsfield where the couple will reside.

"This is Carroll's sister," she told Irene. "We were just talking about her. She passed away."

"I found obituaries for both her and her husband." Irene dug through the sheets inside the file. "Here's Shirley's. She died after Irving. It says she left behind a son Lucas. It says he was from Pittsfield."

"That's good." Sarah said. Pittsfield wasn't too far away, and she should be able to track him down if he still lived there.

"Betty's maiden name was Morgan and she was born in New York State." Irene pulled out Betty's obituary. "Apparently Betty and Carroll were married away from Maple Hill."

"Carroll mentioned he was on leave from the army, and they married in New York."

"Well, that would explain why there wasn't anything in the Maple Hill paper. The Shepherds, Carroll's parents, didn't purchase this home until 1953. I'd assumed they came from around here, but they might've moved in from out of town."

Irene squinted at the tiny print. "Betty's obit just says she was survived by Carroll, Dawn, and a niece and nephew." She looked up. "Can't you just ask Mr. Shepherd about this?"

Sarah wrinkled her nose. "I've tried. I've managed to get a few details from him, but he's reticent about discussing family. He'd much rather discuss cars and work."

"Sounds like a typical male." Irene grinned. "Chris will talk your ear off about an archaeological dig, describing every minute detail of every object found, where on the timeline they located it, and the possible implications of the find. But ask him his nephews' middle names or their ages, and he gets them mixed up. He can remember the date of every battle of the Revolutionary War, but he forgets my birthday and our anniversary and has to scramble at the last minute. He's a dear, sweet man, but I've lowered my expectations a little when it comes to family-oriented stuff. Was Gerry a workaholic too?"

"Sometimes," Sarah said. "Especially during tax season. He brought his work home from the office in the evenings, so he still had dinner with us every night. Even now in the spring I miss the sound of his fingers clicking on the adding machine and the *ca'ching* when he'd hit total."

"Did he get along with your parents? I mean, did they like each other?"

"Well enough, I suppose," Sarah said, wondering where the conversation was going. "Dad and Gerry would have their political differences sometimes and debate for hours. My mother called it bickering, but I think they really enjoyed it."

"What about your mother?"

"In the beginning she worried some about Gerry since we met when we were young. She wanted us to finish school, which we did, and that's how I met Suzy Carmichael."

"And ended up here tonight." Irene's grin broadened. "Funny where life can lead."

"What about Chris and your parents?"

She shrugged. "There weren't any issues between Chris and my folks." She popped up from her chair. "Coffee's done." She brought two mugs and the pot to the table.

Sarah poured herself a cup. The brew was a bit weak but still pleasant.

"When will Suzy be back? I'd like to meet her," Irene said.

"Monday. I thought I'd try to get some inventorying done for her tonight. Was there something you needed me to help you with on your article first?"

"Oh yes, I wanted to show you how I shortened my new beginning." Irene reached into her tote bag and then pulled it onto her lap. "They're not here. I must have grabbed the research for you and left the articles at the office. I had highlighted the sections I had questions about. Well, no matter. I can help you with the inventorying, if you'd like."

"I'd appreciate any help, but won't your husband miss you at home?" Sarah asked.

Irene waved her hand in a dismissive gesture that jangled the charms on her bracelet. "Chris drove over to Concord for a lecture tonight at the library, so I'm free as a bird."

"Okay, I was going to sort through some of the stuff in the family room, but I figure with the hot weather coming, it'd be best to try to finish up in the attic while it's cooler." Sarah glanced at Irene's smart tan and black pantsuit. "It's dusty up there though. We can stay down here if—"

"Oh I think the attic's a good idea. I don't mind dust."

"There are a couple of things you need to be aware of." Sarah explained about items being moved and disappearing. She thought it only fair to inform Irene about the strange occurrences in case she wanted to back out.

"Certainly strange, but I love a good mystery." Irene bounded to her feet. "This will be fun."

On the way to the stairs, Sarah stopped in the living room and told Carroll about their plans. He said he had a headache and was going to bed soon.

"All right, I'll make sure everything is locked up when I leave."

He gave her a nod, and she said good night. No thanks for dinner, but at least he wasn't grumbling now. She followed Irene upstairs. The second floor seemed foreboding at night. Street lamps outside the windows cast long waving shadows across the office and master bedroom. They hurried to the attic stairwell where Sarah flipped on the light switch.

She could feel herself involuntarily holding her breath as she climbed the last few stairs and turned the corner in the attic. Had anything been moved since her last visit? Sarah took a quick look around and let out her breath slowly. Everything appeared the same as when she left the room this morning.

"I can see why the inventory is taking so long," Irene said and then sneezed. "Excuse me." She rubbed her nose. "Strange, the dust didn't bother me when we were up here before."

She sneezed again and wiped her watery eyes. "What are the numbers for?"

"That's just my system of keeping track of the contents of each container without having to move any of them."

"Good thinking." Irene smiled, clasping her hands together as she surveyed the room. "Where'd you leave off?"

"Number forty-one over by the wall. By my initial count that leaves twenty-three more to go."

Sarah handed the clipboard to Irene. "Do you mind writing the contents down while I dig?" Sarah asked. "Writing is less messy." And dusty. Irene's eyes continued to water. Sarah wondered how Irene managed out on dig sites with Chris. But then those activities were outside instead of in a stale attic. The circular air vents under both ends of the peaked roof looked like they'd been painted over, blocking some of the circulation. No wonder it got so stuffy in here.

Sarah opened box forty-one to reveal newspaper-wrapped lumps. She lifted a small one out, carefully pulling back the paper. "Oh it's china." She held up an ivory teacup rimmed with a gold leaf pattern. "The price tag's still on it."

Irene moved closer. "That's really nice-looking china. Expensive. It really shouldn't be wrapped like that. The newspaper's dated September 13, 1970. I wonder why they packed it up without even using it."

"Good question," Sarah said. It was probably futile to ask Carroll. She glanced down at the box. "I don't think I'm going to risk breaking any by unpacking the rest of it. Let's just write down 'china' for box forty-one."

"Done," Irene said with a flourish of her pencil. "Next?"

They moved on to box forty-two, which contained toys from different decades, including a pink suitcase holding several Barbie dolls and their extensive wardrobes.

"Oh wow, I had a Barbie, but not this many clothes." Irene set the clipboard on a trunk and sorted through a pile of miniature clothes to fit every possible social occasion: mini skirts and blouses, boots, shoes, dresses, and even a faux fur coat. She held up a long, glittery blue gown and tiara.

"Whoever these belonged to must have had such fun," Irene said with a wistful sigh. "My parents were frugal and my mother made doll clothes, so nothing was ever as elaborate as this." She fluffed out a miniature boa scarf. "I hated not having the store-bought clothes like other girls had, but now ... I wish I had the ones my mother made. I came across them the last time I was home. Stuffed in a shoebox in my old room."

"Maybe you still can get them. If your parents are anything like the Shepherd family, they don't throw anything away," she said, meaning it to be a joke, but Irene continued to stare at the toys. "I'm sorry. Did I say something wrong?

"What?" Irene lifted her chin. "Oh no, I'm just being silly." She set the clothes back in the box and sneezed. "These are still in good condition, and there's an excellent chance they're collectibles that could fetch good money."

Sarah repacked the box while Irene made notes. She had started on a couple of hatboxes when a faint creak sounded near the door.

"Did you hear that?" Sarah asked, standing. Was someone on the stairs? "I thought I heard something similar earlier."

Irene paused in her writing. "I didn't hear anything."

Sarah put her finger over her lips to signal quiet. The stairs creaked again.

Irene took a sharp breath in as they both froze, waiting. Sarah felt her pocket for her phone and realized she'd left it downstairs. She leaned close to ask Irene if she had hers when a small box on top of the stack blocking the view of the door fell over with a thud.

Irene screeched and grabbed Sarah's arm.

"Who is it? Who's there?" Sarah demanded. Irene tightened her grip on Sarah's arm as the silence stretched.

"Do you think someone's still behind there?" Irene whispered. "Maybe we scared him off."

"Do you have your cell phone?"

Irene shook her head.

"Anyone there?" Sarah stepped toward the stairwell, Irene on her heels. She reached the box that had fallen and then peered around the stack, holding her breath. The stairs were empty.

Irene let out a little giggle. "Guess it was nothing."

Sarah nodded. "Maybe the vibration from us moving around caused the box to fall."

"Meow!"

Irene jerked back, nearly colliding with Sarah. "Oh my!" She gasped as the gray tabby cat leapt up on top of a trunk.

Sarah put a hand over her pounding heart. "It's Robin. The neighbor's cat."

"Well that explains why my nose is itching so much," Irene said, sneezing. "I'm allergic to cats."

"Here kitty, kitty. Come on, Robin," Sarah wheedled. "Let's take you downstairs."

Robin hunched down and stared at her with huge green eyes. Sarah slowly reached her hand out and stroked his ear. "Don't you want to go home?"

The cat remained still as a statue until Sarah stepped closer. Then he sprang past her and darted down the stairs.

"I should go make sure he gets back outside." Sarah looked at her watch. "I can finish up here tomorrow. It's after nine thirty."

"Really? I didn't realize it was so late." Irene said. "Chris should be home by now."

Sarah switched off the light and they headed downstairs. They checked the second floor rooms for the cat, but Robin was nowhere to be seen. He wasn't in the kitchen or the living room either. The family room and basement doors were closed.

Sarah paused by Carroll's bedroom. A snore reverberated from the bed, but she couldn't see Robin. The cat could be under the bed, but she wasn't going to risk disturbing Carroll.

"I wonder how he got in the house." Irene had stopped sneezing, which meant the cat had put some distance between them.

"He might've snuck past Carroll if he went outside." She explained how Robin had been born in this house.

Irene tucked her tote bag under her arm. "I'll leave you the file on the Shepherd family, but I'm still going to see if I can uncover anything else. Are you leaving now too?"

"As soon as I check to make sure the doors and windows are locked. But it won't do any good if the person who's been in the attic has a key."

"No it won't," Irene agreed. "But you know what? I have an idea about how you can at least know if someone goes up there tonight."

CHAPTER ELEVEN

By the time Sarah crawled into bed the clock on the nightstand indicated it was after eleven. Exhaustion weighted her limbs, yet she felt restless. Not a good combination.

The unsettled feeling might be coming from the fact that she had missed Liam's phone call yet again. He had called her cell phone this time, when she had unintentionally left it in her purse in Carroll's kitchen. In the voice message, Liam teased her that either she had been trying to avoid his phone call, or she had accidentally sewn herself into one of her quilts, and he hoped she would escape soon. By the time she heard his message, it was too late to call back.

The restlessness also stemmed from the feeling she wasn't getting anywhere with her investigation into Carroll's missing tools and moving possessions.

She had stayed longer at Carroll's than she had intended. Irene's idea about the attic had been to string a thread loosely across the stairwell so that if anyone went into the attic before Sarah got back, the thread would be moved. Irene had read about this trick in a mystery novel and sounded so enthusiastic Sarah had agreed to give it a try.

Hunting for thread in Carroll's house took some time, especially since he was asleep and couldn't point them in the general direction. They finally found a spool tucked into a drawer in the kitchen. They had managed to hook the thread on slivers of wood in the stairwell and string it across. It was almost invisible.

She and Irene had gone through Carroll's house making sure everything was locked and secure. They hadn't found the cat, and Sarah wondered if Robin had a secret way in and out. She would call Carroll first thing in the morning and let him know the cat had been in the house and still might be there.

Before heading home, she had circled the three blocks near the Shepherd house, scanning the streets for the brown van. If the owners lived in the neighborhood, they didn't leave the van on the street or in the driveways she passed.

Sarah leaned back against her pillow and reached for a devotion book. She had been so busy lately she hadn't taken much time for worship. She read through the lesson on trust and felt comforted. Everything would work out according to God's will. He had a plan, just as a quilter did when she planned a quilt. At first the pieces might look like scraps of mismatched fabric, but the quilter would eventually skillfully fit it all together to make something beautiful and useful.

She reached for the torn piece of the baby quilt on her nightstand and once again admired the tiny stitches and the detail. A lot of time and love had gone into this quilt. Had it been made by a young mother preparing for the birth of her first baby? Or perhaps by a grandmother who wanted to bestow a loving gift on a new grandbaby? Even if Dawn had purchased it from a yard sale, the quilt had a history.

It was sad that this quilt had ended up in the attic without anyone seeming to know anything about it, and even more devastating that it had been damaged.

As she drifted off to sleep, determination surged through her. She felt she owed it to whomever created the sweet quilt to discover its history and what had happened to it.

"Good morning, Dad," Sarah leaned over to kiss William's weathered cheek. "It's a great day to be outdoors, isn't it?"

She had arrived before lunch to find that some of the residents of the Bradford Manor Nursing Home were outside on the back lawn enjoying the sunny weather. Her father had been wheeled to a table shaded by a large floral umbrella.

He nodded with a vague expression and she wondered if she had awakened him.

"You're not too warm, are you?" A lightweight blanket draped across his lap. A half-empty glass of ice water sat next to his elbow, and the sweating pitcher nearby had created a wet ring on the checkered tablecloth.

"I'm fine." His eyes focused on her, and he grinned. "Sarah! How's my girl doing?"

Relieved, Sarah dragged a deck chair closer to him. William's memory had been slipping for years, but lately it had seemed to her that his awareness of his surroundings was growing worse. "Doing well, considering that other than seeing you, the day hasn't gone as planned."

He patted her on the knee. "Anything wrong?"

"No, it's just that I was going to get over to the Shepherd house early, before it got too hot to work in the attic, but I got a call from a potential client this morning. She just bought this lovely antique Amish Wedding Ring quilt and decided to give it to her son, who's getting married in two weeks. The quilt needed some minor repairs. Well, she said she'd be right over, but then got delayed. And what she thought was a minor repair is going to take hours if it's going to be done right.

"Anyway, by the time I got to the Shepherd house, Carroll's physical therapist was there working with him, and it was already beastly hot in the attic so I came here instead."

"What are you doing in the Shepherds' attic?"

Sarah poured herself a glass of water. "A favor for a friend. Do you remember Suzy Carmichael, my college roommate?"

He thought for a moment. "I remember the name."

"She came to visit only a couple of times. Her parents lived over in Pittsfield. Mr. Shepherd's wife Betty was Suzy's mother's sister." She explained about Dawn's death, and how

Carroll needed to be moved into assisted living. "So I've been trying to help out a little."

"Is that right?"

"Suzy's due back Monday." Sarah sipped the ice water. "Did you happen to know the Shepherds? They lived over on Elm not far from the old high school. Carroll owns a car dealership in Pittsfield, but moved into his parents' house when they passed away. His parents were Mary and Gus."

William stroked his chin. "Don't recall having met them. I'm sorry I can't be any help."

"That's okay, Dad. I didn't know them either. Just thought I'd ask. I'm trying to find out some history on them. Mr. Shepherd isn't very forthcoming with information, and there are some problems going on that may be related to the past."

"Mrs. Whitney might know them," William said. "She knows a lot of people. She's sitting over there." He gestured toward the shade under a big oak tree where four ladies surrounded a small square table playing cards.

"Really? Which one is she?"

"The one with the hat. Why don't you go ask her now?"

"I think I will. Thanks, Dad." She stood. "Oh wait, I almost forgot. Guess what I brought you?" She reached in her purse and extracted a small Tupperware container that held freshly washed berries. She pulled off the lid and handed it to him. "Strawberries. I picked them yesterday with the twins and Martha and her bevy of grandchildren."

"Thank you. I was just talking to Martha's mother yesterday about the new fountain they're building for the park. She's collecting donations to put up more benches around the perimeter."

"Dad," Sarah said gently, "Martha's mother passed away several years ago."

"Is that right?" William stroked his chin.

Sarah suppressed a sigh and refrained from also reminding him that the "new" fountain had gurgled merrily by the rose garden for years, a nearby bench displaying a small plaque that read: Donated by the Drayton Family.

"Aren't you going to try the strawberries?" Sarah asked. "They're really sweet."

William patted the container. "I will in a bit."

For as long as she could remember her father had eagerly looked forward to May and the arrival of fresh fruit, especially berries. Usually he dived right in.

"What's wrong? Not feeling well?" Sarah asked.

"Just tired today. I haven't been sleeping well."

"Have you told your doctor?" Sarah asked. The weary note in his voice shoved her worry over into fear.

He shooed away her concern with a small smile. "Don't worry about me. I'm fine."

"Okay," Sarah said. "I'll be back in a few minutes." Sarah strolled across the lawn to the four women. The air temperature under the hundred-year-old trees was pleasantly mild. She recognized two of the ladies from previous visits, Nellie and Alice.

"Hi Sarah. How nice to see you," Nellie said with a quick smile.

"This is William's daughter Sarah," Alice said to the other two ladies. "I know you've met Nellie before," she addressed Sarah, "and these are Laura Miller and Claire Whitney."

"We tried to get your dad to play Rook with us, but he wasn't up to it today." Claire's white hat with the daisies bobbed as she talked.

"I appreciate your asking him. He used to like to play cards with my mother." Sarah smiled at the pleasant memory of her parents sitting by the fireplace, snow drifts outside the frosty windows, enjoying each other's company over a game of Go Fish.

"Oh it's our pleasure. William is such a nice gentleman." Laura tucked a loose red strand of Lucille Ball-colored hair into the bun on her neck.

"Mrs. Whitney, my dad suggested that one of you might've known Betty and Carroll Shepherd on Elm Street. I've been helping Mr. Shepherd with some things for the last few days and—"

"Shepherd? The name does sound familiar," Claire said.

Laura nudged Claire with her shoulder. "You knew Betty Shepherd. She used to walk her cocker spaniel past our houses once in a while. Her daughter played with Tanya's daughter across the street. They lived in Mary and Gus's old house." Laura smiled at Sarah and added, "Claire and I were neighbors for thirty-two years and then ended up here, neighbors again."

"Oh! Betty Shepherd. Yes, I remember now," Claire said. "She was really soft-spoken and so sweet."

"Her husband was very nice. So charming." Laura said with a dreamy look in her eyes. "I used to jog past their house, and sometimes he'd be out doing yard work. Always had pleasant things to say to me."

Carroll, nice? Charming and pleasant?

Alice smiled up at Sarah. "What did you need to know, dear?"

Before Sarah could answer, Claire said, "I remember thinking Betty was older than many of the mothers with similar-aged children. They must've started their family later than most folks did back then."

"I got the impression that maybe he'd been widowed or something," Laura added. "He was such a handsome man."

"Yes, he was," Claire said. "He had wavy thick blond hair. I wonder if he still does."

Laura shook her head. "Such a shame when men lose their hair, but then look at me. Wheelchair-bound. I used to have the nicest legs from all my running."

"Yes, Mr. Shepherd still has thick hair, but it's white now." Before the conversation took another turn, Sarah asked, "So you think Betty was his second wife?"

"I didn't know Betty well enough to ask," Claire said. "I don't like prying into other people's business. I did hear Betty passed away awhile ago. Is Mr. Shepherd still single? Do you think he might ever consider moving in here?"

Alice and Nellie exchanged an amused glance.

"He's single, and I'm not sure what his plans are." She glanced back at her father. His chin had dropped on his chest. Good, she thought, he looked like he needed sleep.

"You said you knew his parents? Mary and Gus?" Sarah asked Laura.

"Briefly, and I didn't really know them well," she said. "My parents moved us into the neighborhood when I was sixteen. Carroll was older than us, and he'd left home already. He returned years after I married Robert, and we bought our place on Cypress."

"Right next to mine." Laura shared another shoulder to shoulder nudge with her buddy.

"Did either of you know Dawn?" Sarah asked.

"Other than in passing, not really. She was much younger than my two," Laura said.

"Same here," Claire said.

Sarah saw a nurse in pink scrubs approaching William. "Well, thank you so much for the information, and it was nice meeting you ladies. I probably should get back to Dad."

The ladies said good-bye and Sarah hurried across the grass. The nurse smiled at Sarah. "I was just about to take William back to his room. Looks like he needs his nap."

"He mentioned he hasn't been sleeping well at night lately. Do you know if he's in any pain? He'd never tell me if he was. Doesn't want to be a bother."

"Hmm. I didn't see anything in his chart, but I'll make a note for the doctor next time he comes in. Like you said, William doesn't like to complain. He's a sweet guy."

Sarah followed the nurse inside and waited by William's door while the nurse and an orderly helped him back into his bed.

She went to kiss him good-bye. "I'm sorry, Sarah," he said wearily. "Don't mean to be a party pooper."

"You're not a party pooper. You just need your rest. I'm going to give these strawberries to the nurse to put in the refrigerator for later. Love you, Dad."

"Love you too, sweetheart." He closed his eyes. Sarah lingered in the doorway until his breathing became deep and steady, just like she had at home when her children were small. Time was passing so quickly and she could feel him gradually slipping away from her. Her heart ached that she couldn't do more than pray for God to keep her father safely in his hands.

The cricket was back under the porch boards, singing happily as Sarah took a break in her rocker after working the rest of the afternoon on the Amish ring quilt. She had spot treated a few dark places on the ivory fabric and then hand washed the quilt in the bathtub. Her back ached from bending over the tub for so long, but her efforts had paid off. The spots had faded to being almost unnoticeable, and the blue, green, and red in the rings popped out with more vibrant color.

Once the Amish quilt dried, she would fix some of the quilting where it had unraveled. Luckily this quilt wasn't old enough to have faded much, or it had been kept in a dark place, so she wouldn't have trouble finding a matching thread or have to stain the white thread with tea. The biggest challenge would be to fix the corner of the quilt where a small chunk of fabric had been torn out. The ragged tear reminded her of the baby quilt that had been in Carroll's attic, only she had been left with the scrap instead of the quilt.

She sighed over her lack of progress with the Shepherd house today. She had learned that there was a possibility Carroll had had an earlier marriage, but she had already dismissed that idea as being of no use to her investigation. Even if Carroll had been married before or had other children, the fabrics in the baby quilt were of a much more recent vintage. The quilt wasn't old enough to relate to an early period in Carroll's life. Nor was the wedding dress in the armoire old enough either, although ... it was one of those simple, timeless styles. Hard to put a date on it without more research. So far, none of this information gave her clues to why someone would be in the house and what they would be looking for.

At least no one had been up there last night. Sarah had checked Carroll's attic stairway on her way back from the nursing home, and the thread still hung between the walls. She left the thread in place.

Carroll had seemed worn out by his physical therapy session, and he had accepted her offer of chili, cheese, and crackers without complaint, but he had declined her offer to drive him to church tomorrow. He said he could manage fine until she got there in the evening. She had a full afternoon planned with the girls.

The sound of a car engine approached. Sarah looked up as Liam's pickup rolled to a stop at the curb.

Her heart skipped a beat. She ran a hand over her hair and smoothed her shirt. To work on the quilt, she had dressed in old bleach-stained jeans and a worn Cape Cod T-shirt she had picked up fifteen years ago when vacationing with Gerry. No time to change, for Liam had already hopped out of the cab and started up the sidewalk with his strong, confident stride.

He was dressed in black jeans and a striped long-sleeved dress shirt. The deep green in the shirt accented the color of his eyes, which twinkled when they caught sight of her. "Since phone calls weren't working, I thought I'd try the person-to-person approach and take a chance you were in."

"I'm glad you stopped by. I'm sorry we kept missing each other."

He walked up the steps, clutching a small paper bag. "I brought your gift. I hope you're not disappointed after all the unintended suspense in waiting. It really isn't much, but when I saw it, I thought of you." He handed her the bag.

"I'm flattered you thought of me. Thank you so much." She pulled out a fat black metal tube about ten inches long with slits cut in the sides and one around the middle. She turned it over, perplexed. "What exactly is it?"

Liam roared with laughter. "That's what I said when I first saw it. Here, let me show you." He clutched the tube on both ends and twisted them in opposite directions. The slits widened, revealing tools.

"It's like a giant Swiss army knife," Sarah exclaimed. Measuring spoons pulled out on detachable hinges at one end. Candy thermometer, pastry brush, scissors, and knife on the other.

Liam chuckled. "I don't know how useful it actually is, but it sure is neat."

"And this reminded you of me?" Sarah asked, amused.

"At the convention it was labeled Mystery Gift, and I know how you like a good mystery."

"Well, thank you very much," Sarah said. "Do you have time for a glass of lemonade?"

"Karen's closing the store tonight so I have time for a couple of glasses on one condition," Liam said, a stern expression on his handsome face.

"What's that?"

"That you update me on your latest adventure."

"I think I can manage that," Sarah said with a big smile.

CHAPTER TWELVE

On Sunday morning Sarah sat in a pew with Maggie, Jason, and the girls. The announcements for the coming week's events were being read, but Sarah was having a hard time concentrating. Instead, her mind kept replaying the conversation she'd had with Liam last night. They'd had a nice friendly chat until Liam had expressed concern over the idea that Carroll had an intruder.

"I don't like the idea that someone might be in there when you go up to work," he had said. "I think you need to report this to the police and get the locks changed. An alarm system would be an excellent idea too."

"I wish I could, but Carroll refuses. Doesn't want the police involved, although they have come out before. Turns out that last time, the items reported stolen turned up later. Really must've been embarrassing for him. It's his house, as he likes to remind everyone."

"But we've taken some precautions," she had said with a smile and told him about Irene's idea about the thread across the stairwell.

Liam had smiled back but then said, "I'm still going to worry."

So was Sarah, but she didn't want to admit it. "Well, the thread hasn't moved."

"Yet."

"True. The only things that we know for sure are missing are the quilt and his tools, and there may be a plausible explanation for the missing tools."

"Okay, tell me what you have so far." He had listened intently as Sarah outlined her progress.

Audrey nudged her, snapping Sarah out of her daydream. She handed Sarah the hymnal. "Grandma, what are you smiling about?"

"Oh, nothing. Sorry," Sarah whispered as the organ started playing. She leafed through the hymnal to find the opening song, and someone tapped her on the shoulder. She looked up to see Irene standing in the aisle.

"Morning. Is anyone sitting here?" Irene asked in a hushed tone. Sarah shook her head and scooted closer to Amy.

"Thanks," Irene whispered, shaking off the jacket of her jade suit, revealing a pale silk blouse. "Chris's cold has wiped him out and he stayed home. I didn't feel like sitting by myself."

"Glad you came," Sarah said. She hadn't even realized Irene attended church here. Was this something new? She shared the hymnal with her as they stood to sing.

The morning sped by. Pastor John's sermon was on how past sins will find you out. Was there something in their lives that needed to be brought back into consciousness to ask God forgiveness for?

As Sarah mulled over her past, her mind tripped over to Carroll. Was there something in Carroll's past, some wrong he had done that was surfacing now? Had he hidden something in the attic that someone wanted back? Chances were, if he was so adamant about the authorities not been brought into it, it was illegal. There had to be something up there, some small detail she had missed that would give a clue to what was really going on.

Nothing Carroll had done or said gave her reason to believe he had done something criminal. She was grasping at straws again, but just in case, she was going to do a little more research on him.

After the sermon concluded and they had surged forward with the exiting crowd to the front steps, Irene turned to her. "Since Chris was sick last night, I went down to work and spent some time on the computer putting together a Shepherd and Morgan family tree. There are still a lot of blank spots, but I came across something interesting. Did you know Dawn Shepherd didn't attend Maple Hill High School all four years?"

"No, I didn't," Sarah said. "How did you find that out?"

"By chance. I got to thinking maybe some of Dawn's friends might be able to fill in some blanks, and frankly I was curious about Dawn. We have the school yearbooks catalogued. She's in the class pictures for all but for what would've been her junior year."

"Interesting," Sarah said. She would like to find Dawn's personal yearbooks. "Maybe she skipped a grade or went to a private school."

"Maybe. Here, I wrote it all down." Irene handed her a folded sheet of paper.

Sarah glanced at Irene's extensive notes on each of the Shepherd and Morgan family members going back three generations. "This is great," she said, although she realized she shouldn't be surprised. Irene was meticulous to a fault when it came to historical details. "Thank you. This will save me lots of time."

"I'm glad," Irene said. "If I find anything new, I'll let you know. I'm enjoying this."

"Grandma, are you coming?" Amy called from the bottom of the steps. "I'm hungry." Maggie gave her a playful whack on the shoulder, saying something about being polite.

"Sounds like you're wanted. I better go too," Irene said but didn't move.

Something about Irene's expression prompted Sarah to ask. "Would you like to come for lunch? We always have plenty."

"Thanks, I would, but I probably should get home and baby Chris. I'm going to make him some chicken noodle soup."

Sarah said good-bye and continued down the steps. On the way to the car, Martha waved at her and hurried over. "I see your new buddy is here." She grinned. "I thought she'd transferred over to a church on Pine Avenue."

Sarah shrugged. "Her husband is sick so maybe she wants to see some other people for a change."

"The only one I saw her talking to was you. Are you still helping her with her articles?"

"I was. I guess I still am, since she still wants to show me some of her revisions, but we haven't really talked about it. She brought me some more information about the Shepherd family." Sarah's gaze shifted to the parking lot where Irene was getting into her car.

"I'm glad you've befriended her," Martha said. "Other than her husband, I get the impression she doesn't get out much, happier cooped up at historical society talking about historical figures as if they were right in the room with her. Maybe she needs a real friend right now."

"Could be," Sarah agreed watching Irene drive away.

"Before I go, I just wanted to tell you I talked to Maggie and the party's all set. Trina and the rest of the girls have been gathering supplies and giving them to me to keep until Wednesday. They're so excited. I just hope they don't accidentally give the surprise away."

"I hope not too. But even if they do, this is going to mean a lot to Amy and Audrey," she said as Jason's car rolled past. Amy gave her a wave over Audrey's head, but Audrey stared at something in her own lap.

"I better run. I'm having lunch at Jason's, and apparently, Amy is *starving*."

"I understand." Martha grinned. "We wouldn't want her to faint from hunger because we stand around 'gossiping,' as Lexie accuses me of."

"If Amy only knew what we were planning, she wouldn't be so grumpy." Sarah pulled her keys out of her purse. She hurried over to her car, and as she drove to Jason's house, she mulled over what Martha had said about Irene.

Maybe Martha was right. Maybe help with the articles was just an excuse. Maybe Irene needed a friend.

"Gram, why are you looking at wedding dresses?" Amy asked, leaning on her elbows across the kitchen table. Her freckled nose was inches from Sarah's computer screen. After Sunday lunch, Sarah and the girls had taken leftovers from Maggie's over to Carroll and then had gone to Sarah's to make jam.

Audrey turned from the stove where she stirred the hot strawberries and sugar. "Wedding dresses? No way. You're not getting married."

Was it so hard to believe that their grandmother could find another husband? Not that she had spent any time thinking about it. Gerry had been her first true love and one of a kind. She still missed him every day in the six years he had been gone.

"Oh I must've left the computer on this morning," Sarah said. "And no, Audrey, I'm not getting married. I was doing research on a wedding dress we found in the attic."

"In Mr. Shepherd's attic?" Amy asked.

"Yes, there were two dresses. I already know that one of them belonged to Mrs. Shepherd from the photo album Audrey was looking through."

"Mrs. Shepherd was pretty in an old-fashioned kind of way," Audrey said, lifting the spoon from the pot and catching a red drip with her finger. "Ouch, that's hot." Audrey popped her finger in her mouth.

"You okay?" Sarah asked Audrey.

Audrey nodded. "It tastes good."

"Okay, well keep stirring the jam so the pectin gets mixed in. We'll put the jam in jars in five minutes."

"Then ice cream, right?" Amy exclaimed. "I'm going to check on it." She jumped up from the chair and went out the backdoor where Sarah had set up her old electric ice cream maker.

"It's making chugging noises," Amy called.

"Can you keep stirring for a few more minutes, Audrey?"

She sighed. "Okay, but my arm's getting tired."

Sarah grabbed a teaspoon and hurried out to the back porch. After unplugging the machine from the outlet, she opened the metal container surrounded by ice and salt and lifted the paddle. The cream had solidified to a soft state. She scooped up a spoonful and handed it to Amy. "What do you think? Does it taste like ice cream?"

Amy licked the spoon and her eyes grew wide. "Yum. This is the best vanilla I've ever tasted."

"Hey, I want some too," Audrey called.

"Don't worry. We're all going to have a big bowlful as soon as we get the strawberry jam in the jars." Sarah walked back inside with the ice cream container. She wiped off the outside and shoved it in the freezer.

"You can stop stirring now, Audrey. Let's grab the jars and start filling them."

The pint jars had already been washed and were lined up on the counter. Sarah grabbed a measuring cup and pot holder, and they each took turns pouring the steaming jam.

"They look so pretty," Audrey said after they had filled six pint jars and there was about half a cup left in the bottom of the pan.

"I thought we'd have way more jam. The strawberries shrank a lot," Amy commented.

Sarah smiled as she screwed on the lids and dropped the jars into her big black canning pot to seal them. "So what do you think about making jam?"

"I think it's a lot of work when you can just buy a jar in the supermarket," Amy said.

"This tastes way better than store-bought." Audrey held the stirring spoon covered in jam for Amy to taste.

"It's okay," Amy said, but Sarah noted she licked every drop off the spoon.

"Well, let's see what you think about it over ice cream." Sarah scooped up generous servings and drizzled warm strawberry jam over the top.

After Amy finished hers, she let out a contented sounding sigh. "Okay, I take it back. This is better than jam from the store, but I still think it's a lot of work."

After the girls finished helping with the cleanup, they dashed off to the living room to watch a movie. Sarah retrieved her laptop and settled on the couch. She had searched online for wedding dresses early that morning and was amazed at how many vintage gowns were for sale. She perused the gowns sorted by decade and came to the conclusion that the dress in the armoire could have come from the late fifties through the sixties. This ruled out the notion that Carroll had been married to someone else before Betty, at least not someone who wore that dress.

So who in the family would have been married during that time period?

Sarah realized that the time period might not be conclusive. The bride could have chosen a vintage dress to wear or the dress may have been passed down from one generation to the next. It was time she talked to someone in the family other than Carroll to get information.

She brought up the online white pages and typed in Carroll's nephew's name, Lucas Bach, and the city as Pittsfield. The girls were still engrossed in their movie so Sarah carried the laptop back to the kitchen so she could talk in private. She dialed the number. The call connected, but no one spoke.

"Lucas Bach?" Sarah finally asked.

"Yes..." the deep male voice answered. No doubt he probably thought she was a telemarketer.

"My name is Sarah Hart. I'm a friend of your cousin Suzy Carmichael, and I've been helping out with your Uncle Carroll Shepherd." Sarah hesitated, not sure how to continue. "I was wondering if I could ask you a couple of questions."

"About what?"

"I was hoping you could help me with some family matters."

"I don't think—"

"It's about Dawn."

There was a long stretch of silence. "Look, I don't have time right now, but Dawn was a good friend as well as cousin." He sighed. "Tell you what, I'll make you a deal. Dawn used to have a photo of the two of us when we were about ten and on a trip to the Adirondacks. She once told me she still had the framed photo in her room. I'd really like to have a copy. It's my favorite memory of the two of us when we were young.

"I asked Uncle Carroll about the photo at the funeral, but the old grump just brushed me off. If you could get me a copy, I'll tell you anything you want to know, which I warn you probably won't be that much. After Uncle Carroll and my father quarreled, I didn't see much of Dawn."

"I'll see what I can do," Sarah said and he suggested meeting at a Pittsfield coffee shop the next day. Sarah hung up the phone, considering his request. Was he really sincere in wanting a memory of Dawn, or was he up to something else?

She checked the jars in the canning pot. They were sealed tight, so she grabbed her tongs and pulled them out to cool on the counter. Amy was right. Her bucket hadn't produced as much jam as she would have liked. An idea occurred to her and she phoned Martha.

"Oh, I'm glad you called," Martha said. "Lexie was just asking me to find out what Audrey's and Amy's favorite colors are."

"Hold on a minute," Sarah peeked in the living room. Both girls were still on the floor in front of the TV. Audrey had pulled her sketchbook out of her backpack but seemed too intent on the movie to draw.

Sarah returned to the kitchen and walked into her office, shutting the door. "Sorry about that, but the girls are here visiting. We just finished making jam. I didn't want them to overhear. I think Amy's favorite color is blue. It's hard to say with Audrey. She seems to change her mind every other week, but judging by the colors in her room, lime green and orange seem to be popular with her right now."

"Great. I'll tell Lexie," Martha said. "So how did the jam lesson go?"

"Great, although Amy thinks it's a lot of work compared to buying a jar."

Martha laughed. "I agree, but wait until she tastes your jam in the dead of winter. Nothing tastes as good as home-made strawberry jam on hot biscuits on a cold morning."

"Oh I agree, which is why I'm calling. I got only six pints of jam out of that bucket and I'd like to make some more. I'm going to Pittsfield tomorrow and there are some great produce stands along the way. I wondered if you wanted to go. Or I could get some strawberries for you if you need any."

"That sounds like fun. I'm off car pool duty tomorrow and I could use more berries. Some rhubarb too. I'm thinking of making a strawberry rhubarb pie. Why do you need to go to Pittsfield?"

Sarah explained about Dawn and Lucas Bach. "If Carroll won't give me the photo, Lucas might not answer my questions, but I'd like to see him face-to-face. Something happened between his father and Carroll, and the anger I heard in Lucas's voice stemmed from more than being denied a photograph."

"Do you think Lucas might've been the one in Carroll's house?"

"At this point, I can't rule anyone out."

CHAPTER THIRTEEN

As Sarah parked in front of the Shepherd house, the gray cloud cover slid away and morning sun streamed in through the windshield, blinding her. She shaded her eyes and reached for the bag of groceries on the passenger seat. She looked up just in time to see Carroll's front door open. Jared slipped out and jogged across the lawn to his driveway.

She climbed out of the car. "Jared!" she called. His step faltered as if he'd heard her, but he darted up the steps and into his home.

Sarah shook her head, wondering what was going on. She started up the walk and noticed Nancy's car in her driveway. Sarah hadn't been able to talk to her since Theresa had told her about the woman at Carroll's house the other night.

She set the groceries on Carroll's porch steps, walked to the Fergusons' front door, and rang the bell.

Nancy answered, dressed in a bathrobe with mussed hair and dark circles under her eyes. "Mrs. Hart? Is something wrong? Is Carroll all right?"

"I assume so; I just got here and saw Jared come from Carroll's house—"

"I didn't even know Jared was home," she said, and before Sarah could explain, Nancy called, "Jared. Come here please!"

"Actually, I just wanted to ask you something."

"Oh sorry. I'm not really awake yet. I worked doubles over the weekend." She gave a weary smile.

Footsteps sounded in the hallway, and Jared appeared behind his mother. His stopped when he saw Sarah. "I didn't take anything. He gave them to me! It's not my fault he forgets later."

"Gave you what?" Nancy's gaze shifted from Jared to Sarah. "What's going on?"

"I don't know," Sarah said. "I haven't seen Carroll since yesterday."

"Jared, please explain what your outburst is all about."

Jared's face flushed. "Nothing. It's not important."

"Jared." His mother's tone held a warning.

"Mr. Shepherd just gave me these." He reached into his pocket and then held out his hand with four gold coins, the same coins that had been in Mr. Shepherd's cabinet.

"Those are pretty," Nancy said. "Put them somewhere safe. I don't want to find them in the washing machine."

Jared nodded and darted away.

"Does Mr. Shepherd often give things to Jared?" Sarah asked.

"Occasionally. He's been very generous, especially over the last year. Why?"

"I'm just trying to get an idea of where some of his belongings may have gone," Sarah said. "Things have been disappearing."

"You're not implying Jared has anything to do with it, are you? He doesn't steal."

"I'm sorry. I didn't mean to upset you. I actually came over to ask you about something else," Sarah said. "Someone kindly helped out Carroll the other night and tidied the kitchen. I was just wondering if you were over there. A neighbor said she saw a woman heading toward the backyard."

"Wasn't me," Nancy said. "I've had hardly a moment to do anything except work and sleep, and now I'm going back to bed. I have to work this evening."

The door shut with a firm click. Sarah turned back to the Shepherd house. That could have been handled better, but Jared's outburst had caught her off guard. Had he been accused of taking things before? Was that the trouble he'd gotten into last year? His mother was quick to jump to his defense.

Sarah grabbed the sack of groceries. She truly hoped Nancy was right about her son. Unfortunately, Jared had more access to the Shepherd house than anyone else so far, which made him a prime suspect. He also seemed to like expensive things.

Surely, Mr. Shepherd couldn't be paying Jared as much anymore on his dwindling income, which could explain the gifts from the household. But what if Jared had become so accustomed to receiving tokens that he helped himself sometimes? Even so, Sarah doubted a sixteen-year-old boy would take a baby quilt. Not when there were more valuable things lying around like the gold coins.

Carroll's front door was unlocked, and as she stepped into the foyer, she could hear his voice booming from the back of the house and the sound of drawers slamming.

"Carroll, what's wrong?" She rounded the corner into the kitchen. Carroll stood by the counter, yanking one drawer open after the next and then slamming them shut.

"I want my tools. I need a hammer! Now!" he shouted. Sweat dripped down his glistening red face and his shirt clung to his back.

"All right. All right. Just calm down. You're going to burst a blood vessel if you keep going like that." Or have another stroke. Sarah pulled out a chair. "Come over here and sit. I'll look for one."

His arms trembled as he maneuvered his walker, but he didn't argue. He collapsed onto the chair. Sarah got him a glass of water and handed his pills to him. He held the pills in his hand for a moment, then gulped them all down with the water.

She waited until his color faded and his breathing normalized. "Now, why is it so urgent you have hammer?"

"I knocked a picture off the wall."

Sarah refrained from giving him a lecture. A picture was not worth risking a stroke over. "Would there be any hammers in the basement?"

"No, Dawn cleaned my workshop out. There were two hammers in my toolbox. There should be at least another one, if not down here in the kitchen, then maybe in the attic."

"But you said that those tools up there were for automobiles and I don't remember seeing a hammer. Are you sure there isn't one in your shed? What about—"

"Just stop talking and check the attic!" he bellowed.

Sarah left the room before she gave the rude, ungrateful man a good talking-to. She stopped in the hall to take a deep breath. Again she wondered about the man the ladies at the nursing home had described. They'd thought he was charming. Apparently old age and losing Betty and Dawn had taken their toll.

"Hurry up!"

Sarah almost marched out the front door, but instead she climbed the stairs and kept repeating to herself. "Suzy is coming back today. Suzy is coming back today." And then Sarah would be done.

If Suzy wanted her to continue to track down the tools and the quilt, she would continue to investigate, but Suzy would have to deal with Carroll. Sarah was at the end of her patience. She'd feed the man lunch for the last time, and then leave for Pittsfield.

She stormed up to the second floor and yanked open the attic door. She'd stomped halfway up the stairs before she remembered the thread she and Irene had strung across the stairwell.

She stopped in her tracks. She must have walked right through it. She examined her slacks and shoes, running her hand down the fabric. No thread. She backed down and searched each step and along the walls. If the thread wasn't on her or anywhere in the stairway that meant someone else had gone into the attic.

She backed down the stairs, shut off the light, and opened the attic door. She paused a few seconds, the time it would have taken to walk through the doorway, and then shut the door. She stood in the semidarkness listening intently. No sound from above. She waited for her eyes to adjust to the dimness and then crept up the stairs until she could peer around the corner into the attic. Sunlight poured in through the two vents, casting shadows over the room. Nothing stirred.

She stepped higher, staying behind the stack of boxes by the door, and inched her way until she got a good view of the room. The attic appeared lifeless, just the same old piles of stuff. She flipped the wall switch and the attic flooded with light.

Nothing appeared to have been moved. Her clipboard still rested on the trunk where Irene had left it on Friday.

She leaned against the wall, letting her pulse slow.

Hammer. She had come up here for a hammer. She didn't want Carroll going ballistic, especially when she had to inform him that unless he had sent someone up here, someone had broken into his house again.

She circled the big pile in the middle of room until she found the rug that had covered the pile of tools she had landed on last week. She hadn't reached that section of the attic yet on her inventory. She lifted the bulky rug and stared at bare floor.

Not again.

She did a quick search of the area, circling round, checking behind boxes. The tools were gone. She had to tell Carroll. But maybe this time he would call the police.

She took one last look around and then headed downstairs. She sure hoped Suzy's plane arrived early in the day. As Carroll's niece, she would hopefully have more influence on his decision making than Sarah did.

It was quiet when she got downstairs. Too quiet. Not even the television was turned on. Carroll had made it back to his easy chair, but his head was flung back on the cushion and he was clutching a wooden picture frame.

"Carroll?" Sarah asked, walking across the room intending to wake him but stopped when she got closer. His eyes were shut and there was moisture on his cheeks. Were those tears?

Sarah gently tugged the frame from his fingers and turned it over. It was a portrait of Carroll, Betty, and Dawn that appeared to have been painted a couple of decades before. A dent marred one corner. It had to be so frustrating for such a strong-minded man not to be able to do a simple task like hanging a picture on the wall.

She remembered the waves of helplessness, followed by anger at the unfairness of it all, as Gerry battled cancer. She understood loss. The denial. The pain. The anger. But yet, she hadn't raged at people like Carroll did.

Sarah placed the photo on the end table. She wouldn't wake Carroll yet. He obviously needed the sleep. His tools could have been taken anytime since Saturday night. What was another hour?

She would use the time to do some more investigating. What was the connection between a missing quilt, a wedding dress, and two sets of tools? And what about the file box that still sat beside the couch?

First things first. She needed to find out whom that baby quilt belonged to. Since it was the most personal, unique item, it might point to who was searching the house and taking things.

Lucas Bach might be able to shed some light on the family, but she needed to find that photo he had requested. She looked at Carroll. A slight chill hung in the living room and she grabbed a light blanket from his bedroom and draped it over him before heading upstairs.

Dust coated everything in Dawn's old bedroom. A violet bedspread covered the canopied four poster double bed. Boxes had been shoved in here too, but books and other girly trinkets and treasures still lined the shelves. The advantage of being an only child and living in a big house. There probably hadn't been an urgent need to clean out the room, especially if Dawn had planned on moving back in someday.

Sarah picked up a trophy and brushed dust from the inscription. First place Freestyle High Dive.

Dawn? A diver?

There were several smaller diving trophies on the shelf and ribbons had been pinned on the wall. She scanned the novels on the shelves, noting some that had been her own daughter's favorites.

Lucas had said that Dawn kept a photo of them in her old room. There were a dozen or so small frames scattered around the room. No photos of Dawn at a lake.

Several boxes were shoved up against the bed. As she sat on the bed to open a lid, the mattress bumped the nightstand, setting the lamp shade to swaying and knocking over a horse figurine.

Sarah scooted closer to the headboard and reached her hand down between the mattress and the nightstand. Something made a crinkling noise and she pulled out a candy bar wrapper. She tried again, and this time her fingers brushed something cold and solid. She dragged up a frame shaped like a bear. Inside was a photo of a teenage girl and boy standing knee-deep in a sparkling lake. This had to be what Lucas wanted.

She set it on the bed and turned back to the shelves. Now that her main mission for coming in here was accomplished, she could concentrate on learning more about Dawn. She wondered where Dawn's high school yearbooks or her photo albums were. She scanned the shelves again and checked in the closet. Maybe she had taken those items to her apartment, or they could be in one of the cardboard boxes.

Sarah glanced at her watch and headed for the stairs. An hour had passed and she needed to fix lunch for Carroll and find out what he wanted to do about the missing tools.

His face had such a peaceful expression, she hated to wake him. She would let him sleep a little longer while she got some canned chicken soup on the stove and doctored it up with the chopped green beans and carrots she had picked up at the market on the way over and a handful of tiny shell pasta she found in the cupboard. She brought the soup up to a boil and then down to a simmer.

Dreading what she had to do, she went back to the living room and gently tapped Carroll on the shoulder. "Carroll. Time to wake up. Lunch will be ready soon, but I need to talk to you."

He groaned and opened his eyes. "What?"

"I went to the attic—"

"Did you find a hammer?"

"No. In fact, I didn't find your other tools either. They're gone. Someone has been up there. Last Friday Irene had an idea to run a thread across the stairwell and it was gone when I just went up there."

"What's this about thread? You're not making sense."

Sarah sighed and explained what they had done and why. "You need to make a report to the police."

"I'll think about it."

"And you should seriously consider getting an alarm system put in."

"Why? I won't be living here much longer."

He had a point. Sarah sighed. "What's so important about those tools? Why would someone keep searching your house?"

"I don't know."

"What about Jared?"

"What about him?"

"Does he ever wander around the house? Jared said you've given him things, like the Egyptian coins. I hate to suggest this, but maybe Jared thinks your gifts entitle him to poke around the house and help himself to other things."

"No. He wouldn't. He's a good kid."

"Someone said he got in trouble last year. Was it for stealing?"

"Jared told me it was a misunderstanding, and I believe him. And besides, this isn't any of your business!" Carroll's voice rose and he banged his fist on the armrest. "I can give my things to whomever I want! I could leave him this whole house if I wanted to."

He took several deep shaky breaths and his voice softened. "It's not like I'll ever have grandchildren now that Dawn..."

A lump rose in Sarah's throat. She reached for his hand. "I'm sorry."

"You didn't even know her." Carroll's hand stayed lax in her hand. Sarah squeezed tightly for a moment before letting go.

"But I know you," Sarah said. "Come on to the kitchen. The soup's ready." As they walked down the hall, she asked, "Okay, who else might want your tools? What about this Eddie you keep mentioning?"

"Eddie? Touch a tool?" Carroll laughed. "He'd tarnish his image. No grease monkey business for him. Why, I remember one Christmas his car had a flat tire on the way to our corporate party, and his date had to change it so he wouldn't get his tux or hands dirty."

"You're kidding! You were friends with the guy because...?"

"He was great with numbers and a dynamite salesman. He could sell ice cubes to an Eskimo. Did you know Eddie came on the year before the Edsel tanked in 1960? But he negotiated so we got some of the Comets that were being assigned only to Mercury dealerships, and he was able to swing deals that rid us of the last of our Edsel stock. We went back to Studebakers, but he foresaw the demise of that company and switched over to Cadillac. As he said, we weren't brand loyal, but who cared? We stayed afloat when other dealers went under."

As Sarah dished up the soup, he rambled on about the Edsel being the wrong car at the wrong time and about its design flaws. On the fifty-eight model, for example, the taillight lenses were boomerang-shaped so it looked like the arrows on the turn signals were pointing in the opposite direction. Then there was the toilet seat grill and a widely circulated wisecrack at the time that the Edsel looked like an Oldsmobile sucking on a lemon. He chuckled.

"Do you want a peanut butter and jelly sandwich?" Sarah asked.

He nodded. "Did you know that mechanics were wary of the 410-cubic-inch Edsel 'E-475' engine because of its cylinder head design? Very innovative, so that the combustion took place entirely in the cylinder bore. It cost less to manufacture and minimized carbon buildup, but regular mechanics were unfamiliar with it. I tweaked a tool that would've made it easier to work on the cylinders, but they were already talking about shutting the line down and refused to pick it up for the dealerships. Could've made a fortune." He shook his head as he picked up a spoon.

"What happened to Eddie?"

Carroll studied his spoonful of soup, took a sip, and reached for the pepper shaker on the table. He looked at her. "What?"

"I was asking about Eddie. Does he come to visit often?"

"Used to." He banged his spoon on the table. "Loyalty, friendship, common courtesy no longer exists these days, you know?" His voice rose. "You'd think—"

"Suzy is due back today. Have you heard from her?" Sarah interjected. Carroll blinked and his mouth flapped shut as if the sudden change in topic had derailed him, which had been Sarah's purpose.

"When I talked to her last week," Sarah continued, "she said mom and baby had a complicated birth, but were doing well. You have a grandniece, isn't that wonderful? I'm hoping she brings photos."

"I haven't heard from her." He retrieved his spoon which had landed in the middle of the table. He started eating again, and Sarah waited until they had both finished their soup.

"Speaking of relatives, I want to ask you something, but I don't want you getting upset and shooting up your blood pressure. I need to borrow this." She showed him the photo of Dawn and Lucas in the lake. "Lucas wants a copy. It'd mean a lot to him. He says you got angry at him when he asked."

"Lucas hasn't seen me in years, but the first thing he asks me at the funeral home is when we'd read Dawn's will. As if it's any business of his! Of course I was angry with the insensitive clod. All he cares about is himself."

"That brings up another question," Sarah said. "Suppose Dawn didn't leave a will or it's never found. Who'd stand to inherit?"

"There isn't anything to inherit."

"But what if there was. You mentioned originally that you and Dawn had specified that you each would get the other's share of the house. Could she have changed the bequest?"

"She wouldn't do that," he said.

"Does Lucas know that? Were they in contact over the years?"

He shrugged.

"I know I'm getting really personal here, but this could be important. What about your will? If Dawn is gone, who stands to inherit?"

"I guess Suzy and Lucas would have to duke it out, assuming there's anything left to fight over. I really don't care anymore. If I have to move and sell this place, the money will be gone soon enough." He shook his head. "I should've sold off my share of the dealership before the economy took a dive.

"Remember the Fleetwood series in the sixties?" He leaned back in his chair, a dreamy smile on his face. "Now those were luxurious cars. Big and roomy. You felt like a king riding in them. Sales were great. People were optimistic and weren't afraid to indulge themselves with nice things."

Sarah took her dish to the sink as Carroll rambled on about car sales and designs. She should count her blessings that Carroll had discussed family for as long as he did. And now she had more to ask Lucas Bach.

Why was he so concerned about Dawn's will? And had he come looking for it?

CHAPTER FOURTEEN

arah grabbed a sweater, locked the front door to her house, and joined Martha on the porch.

"I'd like to get some herbs to grow on my kitchen windowsill too," Martha said. "I'm hoping one of the stands we stop at will have some."

"Hi Sarah, Martha!" Irene strolled up the walk, a manila file tucked under her arm. She stopped when she saw them leaving the house. "I'm sorry. Are you on your way out?"

Sarah nodded. "We are. We're just on our way out to Pittsfield to visit with someone and then hit the produce stands."

"Really?" Irene looked from Martha to Sarah. "I've always wanted to visit the produce stands near Pittsfield, but it never seemed any fun going alone." She shifted the file to her other arm. "I have the day off, and I wanted to show Sarah the progress I've made with my articles."

"Why don't you come with us?" Martha asked.

"Sure, the more the merrier," Sarah said. "As long as you don't mind waiting while I'm in my meeting."

"I don't mind at all," Irene said with a big smile. "This will be so much fun. A Girls' Day Out! Let me get my purse." Irene spun and hurried down the walk to her car.

Martha bumped shoulders with Sarah as they walked to Sarah's car in the driveway. "Girls day out? Why would she want to spend the day with us? We're at least twenty years older than she is."

"You don't still consider yourself fun, Martha Maplethorpe?" Sarah teased.

"Well I do, but she might not." Martha laughed. "I wonder if she's having some sort of troubles at home. Are she and her husband okay?"

"Chris has a cold, but other than that, she hasn't mentioned anything wrong."

"I'm ready," Irene called and crossed the lawn with a bouncing step. She slid into Sarah's backseat and after Sarah had pulled out into the street asked, "Would it okay if we talked about my articles while we're on the road?"

Sarah and Martha said they would be happy to listen while she read to them, but instead of discussing her articles, Irene steered the conversation to how Martha and Sarah had met their husbands, and what it was like raising kids in Maple Hill.

As Sarah circled the block in downtown Pittsfield searching for a parking spot, Irene said, "I sometimes wish Chris and I would've had children, and now I just think I'm too old to start. I'm afraid at this point it might be hard on our marriage. Chris doesn't do well with change. Martha, you and Ernie have been married a very long time. How do you two manage to stay so happy?"

"With lots of compromising over the years." Martha shot Sarah a look, and Sarah began to wonder if Irene and Chris were having marital problems. "It hasn't always been easy, but—oh there's a spot." Martha pointed to a minivan with its brake lights on.

Sarah had never been to the The Brew before, a small coffee shop just off Main Street in downtown Pittsfield, but it hadn't been hard to locate. She just hoped Lucas Bach hadn't grown impatient while they searched for parking and left.

"Do you know what Lucas looks like?" Martha asked.

"All I have is a photo from when he was a kid, but Lucas said he'd sit near the front window and he'd be wearing a baseball cap," Sarah said.

"I saw a man at a table when we passed the shop the last time around. I think he had a cap on," Irene said from the backseat.

The minivan finally backed into the street, and Sarah zipped into the space and killed the engine. "Do you two want to come in, or just meet me after?"

Martha turned in her seat to look at Irene. "I feel like getting something cold to drink. How about you?"

"Sounds good to me too," Irene said and they walked in the front door of the small shop. A counter was set toward the back with a glass bakery case and three people lined up, waiting to give their orders to the young woman at the cash register. The place oozed comfort. A couch was backed up against one wall, and magazines and newspapers sprawled over the oval coffee table. Wing chairs created a conversation space. Tall round tables with padded bar stools filled the rest of the interior, and a counter with the same bar stools ran along the large window facing the street.

"We'll find a place in the back, so we don't intimidate Carroll's nephew," Martha said to Sarah with a nod toward a dark-haired man wearing shorts, a sports shirt, and a baseball cap. Judging from when the photo was taken with Dawn, he had to be in his late thirties to early forties. As Sarah approached, he looked up from reading the sports section of a newspaper spread out on the table.

"Mr. Bach?"

"Lucas, please." He moved the newspaper off the table. "Have a seat. Can I get you something to drink?"

"Thank you, but I can get it. In fact, let me get you a refill. I'm sorry I'm late." She glanced at the tall glass in front of him. "What are you drinking?"

"Iced mocha latte, decaf."

"That sounds good. I'll be back in a minute."

Irene and Martha had already ordered and were waiting at the other end of the counter for their drinks. Sarah asked for two iced lattes and two blueberry scones. By the time her bakery treats were ready, Irene and Martha had settled on the couch.

"I hope you like blueberry scones," Sarah said, as she placed the plate on the table.

"One of my favorites here. Thank you," he said.

"Here are your lattes," the blonde barista said and set them on the table.

Sarah thanked her and slid up on the high stool. She reached into her purse and extracted the copy of the photo she had made after she left the Shepherd house.

"Here you go," Sarah said.

Lucas studied the photo for a long moment and then smiled. "That was the last summer Dawn and I got to spend vacation together. We had such fun, considering we were related." His grin lit up his brown eyes. "I appreciate your getting this for me. Did Uncle Carroll give you any problems over it?"

"About the photo? No," Sarah said.

"Well, that's surprising. He must like you." He glanced at the picture again. "I'm not sure if I can be of much help, but since you kept your side of the bargain, I'll try to keep mine. You need family information? Where do you want to begin?"

"Do you mind my asking what happened between your parents and Carroll?"

"I don't mind, but it's just plain stupid." He used his straw to stir his drink and then took a long sip. "This is really good."

Sarah tasted hers and agreed, waiting patiently for Lucas to continue. He broke off a corner of a scone and popped it into his mouth.

"My mother and Aunt Betty were pretty close, so we used to spend a lot of time at each other's homes. Unfortunately, my dad and Uncle Carroll always seemed to be competing with each other, like roosters fighting over their territory.

"It was that same summer after we got back from the lake that Dad decided to buy a new car. Uncle Carroll set him up with a sweet deal because he was family, and I imagine it was his way of showing off. Special order. The works. Then Dad had second thoughts. Didn't want to drive a Cadillac, wanted a Lincoln instead and backed out."

"That's what caused a rift in the family?"

He lifted a shoulder in a shrug. "It was just the straw that broke the camel's back."

"You're right. It sounds stupid," Sarah said.

He smiled. "My mom and Aunt Betty still saw each other, but that was the end of family vacations or holidays together. We started doing more things with my dad's side of the family."

"What about you and Dawn? Were you able to see each other much?"

"Not enough. It hurt to lose her friendship." Lucas sighed. "Thanks for the photo. It's nice to remember the good times." He picked up his scone, and then set it back down without taking a bite. "So, you mentioned you were helping Suzy pack up Uncle Carroll's house?"

"Yes, I've been going through the attic and finding all kinds of interesting things like wedding dresses, quilts, photos, and china. Lots of old papers too."

"I can imagine there must be tons of stuff up there after all those years."

"I've been trying to figure out who owned one of the wedding dresses. Was Dawn ever engaged?"

"Not that I know of. She had a boyfriend in high school, but I think they broke it off when she went off to England for school."

"School?"

"Yeah, the whole family went over to Europe that summer. We weren't invited by then. Story goes that Uncle Carroll got it in his head he wanted her to go to some fancy school that had an international dive team. Did you know she dived in high school?"

"I saw the trophies in her room."

"She stopped after she got back."

"Why?" Sarah asked. "From the number of trophies, it looks like she was good."

"Yep. Could've gotten college scholarships if she hadn't quit."

"So something must've happened to change her mind while she was in England," Sarah mused.

"That's what I figure, or she just decided it wasn't worth it. Sports take a lot of time and discipline. Which reminds me," he glanced at his watch, "my son is in Little League and the All-Stars game is this evening. I need to get going."

"How old is your son?"

"Todd is ten and tall for his age, unlike his father." He stood and Sarah guessed he was probably five foot seven. "It was nice meeting you, Mrs. Hart. Give my regards to my uncle even though he won't appreciate them."

"I will," Sarah said as she added coins to what Lucas had left for a tip on the table. "Lucas, before you go, I just want to ask if your uncle mentioned that someone has been breaking into his house and searching for things. In fact, some of his tools are missing." She carefully watched his reaction.

"Never said a word to me. He really should get an alarm system for that big old house."

"So he's been told," Sarah said with a smile. "One last thing. They still haven't found Dawn's will. Your uncle seems to think that if it isn't found, then you and Suzy may be entitled to some of his assets when the time comes."

"I don't know anything about that," he said, looking at the door. "Thanks for—"

"Then why did you ask about Dawn's will at the funeral?"

"What? How do you know about that?"

"Carroll was upset about it. That was why he brushed you off about the photo."

He nodded. "Uncle Carroll overreacted as usual. I haven't talked to the man in years, and I figured he wouldn't bother to call me if Dawn had left any of her personal belongings to me. I was really hoping for a token of our friendship and family. But then he wouldn't care about stuff like that." He took a step toward the door and Sarah dug in her purse for her business card.

"If you think of anything that might help me figure out what's going on over at your uncle's, can you call me? Suzy's supposed to be back today and the cleanup should go faster." She handed him the card. He shoved it into his pocket and walked out the door without saying good-bye.

She doubted he would call. He would probably toss her phone number the minute he got home, especially if he was the one who had been in the attic. She wrapped the remaining scone in a big napkin and tucked it in her purse. Martha and Irene joined her as she watched Lucas get into a blue pickup across the street.

"You two seemed to be having a good time until the end there," Martha said. "He didn't look happy when he left."

"I just hope I didn't blow it." If Lucas was the one who was poking around Carroll's house, she could have either scared him away or incited him to hurry up and find whatever it was he was looking for.

Irene pushed open the door and as they stepped outside Sarah saw her business card lying crumpled on the sidewalk beside a trash can.

The card hadn't even made it home.

As they reached the outskirts of Pittsfield, Sarah asked Irene and Martha, "Would you mind if we made another stop before we get to the produce stands? I'd like to visit Carroll's dealership."

"I'm not in any rush. What about you, Irene?" Martha asked.

"I have all day. I called Chris and he's just watching a movie. He's turning into a couch potato with this cold."

"It should take only a few minutes. Carroll's talked so much about his old business I want to see it for myself." Also, she was wondering if anyone there might provide a clue to what was going on at his house. Or more information on Eddie. She had never gotten a clear answer about him from Carroll.

Sarah had seen the address for the car dealership on the papers in Carroll's file box and knew it was on Wellington Avenue, not far from the highway.

"There it is," Irene said leaning over the front seat from the back. "See the sign?"

A large sign indicated Shepherd & Stanford Motors. Sarah turned right and motored to the building fronted by ground-to-roof glass walls.

Cool air wafting with new car scent, leather, and lemon floor cleaner greeted them as they entered the showroom. Cubicles lined the back wall and several men wearing suits and ties sat at the desks. They passed two impressive-looking car models with price tags that rivaled the price of a new home.

"May I help you?" A lovely young woman dressed in an ivory suit and a royal blue blouse rose gracefully to her feet and came around the side of a desk that was positioned in front of a black wooden door.

"Yes, I'm Sarah Hart, a friend of Carroll Shepherd, and I was wondering if Mr. Stanford could spare a few minutes to talk with me."

"Ah yes, Mr. Shepherd. How is he?" she asked in a hushed tone.

"Doing as well as can be expected under the circumstances," Sarah answered, although she wasn't sure how to gauge Carroll's behavior.

"I'm Dana Grosset, the receptionist. Mr. Stanford just went on a test-drive with one of our regular customers and should be back in a few minutes. Why don't you wait in his office?"

She opened the door behind her desk and ushered them down a hallway and up a short flight of stairs to a large office.

"This is Mr. Stanford's office. I was hired after Mr. Shepherd retired, but he used to keep a desk in here too. They moved it out after he had . . . well, when we knew he wouldn't be coming back to work." She gestured to a sitting area on one end of the room where a couch and four chairs surrounded a square coffee table. "Please make yourselves comfortable. Can I get you anything to drink? We have coffee, water, juice, and even champagne if you'd like."

"I'm fine, thank you," Sarah glanced at her friends. "We weren't planning on staying long."

Martha and Irene declined beverages also. After Dana closed the door, Martha let out a low whistle. "This is an impressive office."

She settled onto the sofa and ran her hand over the smooth leather.

"I guess if you sell top-of-the-line cars, your office needs to be classy," Irene said.

Sarah wandered across the plush blue carpeting behind a huge mahogany desk to the wall where two portraits hung. One was of a much younger Carroll with lots of wavy blond hair. The other revealed a distinguished-looking man with a receding hairline, warm brown eyes, and an engaging smile. The plaque on the frame stated his name as George Stanford.

The distant sound of machinery caught her attention and she stepped over to look out one of the four windows lining the wall. The service area spread out below her. Some vehicles were balanced high on lifts while overall-clad mechanics maneuvered under them with shiny tools. Other cars rested at ground level with their hoods up.

"I wish Chris were here to see this. He'd never believe a garage could be so clean," Irene said, looking out another window. "Look, they've even gone green and recycle."

Near the wall adjacent to where Sarah stood, a woman was reaching into a white trash can and sorting items into bins labeled paper, metal, aluminum, organic, and cloth.

Martha popped up and hurried over. "Oh, Ernie would love this. He'd think he was in car heaven."

Sarah chuckled. Martha's husband loved to tinker with old cars, fix them, and give them to his grandchildren. "Looks like they've even gotten an award for it." She pointed to a large brass plaque on the wall that indicated the dealership was included in a group called "Best of the Green."

"That's right. Shepherd and Stanford Motors strives to do its very best to help the environment," a male voice said.

All three ladies turned to find a short man dressed in a navy pinstripe suit and burgundy tie. The fluorescent light gleamed off his head, and brown eyes regarded them from behind gold-rimmed glasses.

"No waste goes out of this dealership without being sorted and sent to where it can be utilized again," he continued with enthusiasm. "George Stanford, at your service." He extended his hand and smiled.

"I'm Sarah Hart." Sarah shook his hand and introduced Irene and Martha. "I'm an acquaintance of Carroll Shepherd."

"Welcome. Any friends of Carroll's always get preferential treatment. Were you interested in a particular model that I can show you? Or maybe you'd like to test-drive some of our newest vehicles and see if any of them please you."

"Actually, we're not here about a purchase. It's a personal matter concerning Mr. Shepherd if you have a moment."

"I see. Of course if there is anything I can do ..." He gestured to the couch and chairs. "Please, have a seat."

"Thank you. This won't take much of your time," Sarah said.

Mr. Stanford waited while Sarah and Irene settled on the couch and Martha took a chair, before sitting opposite Sarah. He leaned forward, elbows on his knees. "I was heartbroken when I heard about Dawn. I watched her grow up. Carroll used to bring her here sometimes when she wasn't in school. Nice kid."

"I never knew her, but she took very good care of her father. This has been devastating for Mr. Shepherd." Sarah explained briefly about Carroll having to move.

"I was afraid something like that would happen. As you may know, Carroll's still a silent partner in this dealership, but with the poor economy and people switching to smaller cars, we've had some rough years just as other similar businesses have. We're in recovery, of course, but it will take some time. My retirement is also tied up in this place, but I've made other investments too. I tried to convince Carroll to diversify his savings decades ago. He was a brilliant man, full of ideas, but when it comes to practical matters, well ..." He held his hands out in a futile gesture.

The door opened and Dana leaned her head in. "Mr. Stanford, Mrs. Smith is here."

"Thank you, Dana. Tell her I'll be out in a minute," George said. As Dana shut the door, he asked, "Is there anything I can help you with?"

Sarah nodded. "Mr. Stanford—"

"George, please."

Sarah smiled. "George, would you know of someone named Eddie who Carroll worked with? He mentions him quite frequently."

"Eddie?" He thought for a moment. "I haven't heard that name in years. He might mean Ed Trenton. He came on before I did. Top-notch salesman. Retired now."

"Do you know how we can get in touch with him?"

"I'm afraid not. The last I heard, I think he moved out of state to be near one of his children. Virginia or maybe one of the Carolinas. Why do you ask?"

"Mr. Shepherd talks about him quite frequently."

"Strange. I didn't think he and old Ed were that close," Mr. Stanford said slowly. "Tell you what. I'll have my secretary try to track Eddie down and get you an address. It may take some time though."

"Anything you can do will be appreciated."

"Ladies, it's been a pleasure. I just wish I had time to get to know you all better." He turned a bright smile on Irene and Martha. "We're having a promotion and have some give-aways out in the lobby. I'd really like you to take something home with you." He stood and ushered them out.

Sarah paused by Dana's desk to leave her business card, as George showed Martha and Irene to a table loaded with promotional clock radios, key rings, MP3 players, and travel mugs. As she waited for Dana to get off the phone, Sarah noted some travel brochures near her computer.

"Planning a cruise?" Sarah asked when Dana put down the receiver.

"Oh I wish!" Dana said. "Those are for Mr. Stanford's anniversary. He spoils his wife, the lucky woman." She smiled at her boss, who was introducing Irene and Martha to a salesman.

By the time Sarah had handed over her business card and explained the favor George was doing for her, Irene was sitting in the front passenger seat and Martha was in the back of an impressive black Cadillac.

The tall, well-dressed salesman leaned over the door. "Are you sure you ladies wouldn't like to just take a test-drive?" he asked. "I can promise you it will be a luxurious experience with no obligation. Don't you think this is a magnificent car? Just feel that buttery soft leather."

Irene grinned at Sarah as she approached. "You should feel how wonderful this is."

Sarah smiled. "I better not, or I'll start longing for things I shouldn't have." Just like the person searching Carroll's house. Was she ever going to figure out what they were hunting for?

Sarah set a flat of strawberries on her kitchen counter along with a bag of the first tender lettuces of the season from the produce stand they had stopped at on the way home from Pittsfield. Irene and Martha had purchased strawberries too, and they'd had fun browsing a stand of crafts and homemade pottery.

Sarah had bought Audrey and Amy each an appliquéd tote bag to add to the gifts she was getting for their birthdays. Calico hearts adorned Audrey's bag, and Sarah had chosen one with a baseball, mitt, and bat motif for Amy.

She opened the refrigerator to find a pizza box with a note from Andi saying "Help yourself." Suddenly ravenous, Sarah slid two slices onto a plate and popped them into the microwave.

While she waited for them to heat, she checked the Amish quilt. It had dried thoroughly and Sarah was pleased to see that the white background and the colored fabrics appeared much brighter. The spots she had treated weren't noticeable unless you went looking for them. She would repair the hand-quilting tonight and work on the tear tomorrow. But first she needed to see if Suzy had checked in.

She glanced at her answering machine. No messages. Same with her cell. Maybe Carroll had forgotten to tell Suzy to call Sarah when she got in. She tried Suzy's cell phone number and it went straight to voice mail. Maybe her plane had been delayed and she was still in the air.

She dialed Carroll's number. He answered on the second ring. The six o'clock news chattered in the background.

"Carroll, this is Sarah. Is Suzy there?"

"Nope."

"Has she contacted you? Her plane was supposed to arrive this afternoon."

"Nope."

"Do you have Suzy's home number?"

"Don't think so."

Sarah sighed. "Did you find something to eat for dinner?"

"Yeah."

"I stopped by your dealership in Pittsfield this afternoon."

"Why'd you do that?" His tone sharpened. She had his attention now.

"I wanted to see where you worked all those years. George Stanford was there."

"How is my old partner? Still wooing rich women?"

"I don't know about that, but he seemed charming."

"He's had years of practice," Carroll said.

"You don't seem to like him that much."

"It's mutual, but we complemented each other's strengths and weaknesses well in the business," he said. "Are you coming tomorrow?"

"I will if Suzy doesn't get here."

"Bring a hammer." The connection clicked off.

Carroll and his tools. She still wasn't any closer to finding out who had taken them. He was lucky that she hated to leave mysteries unsolved, or she would have walked long before this.

As she ate her pizza, she looked up the number for Dave Diamond. He should be home now.

Dave's wife Liz answered the phone.

"Hi, this is Sarah Hart. I hear congratulations are in order," Sarah said. "Maggie told me she ran into you at the auction the other day."

"Thank you," Liz gushed. "Yes, we're excited. Davey is going to have a little brother or sister."

They chatted for a bit about little Davey and then Sarah asked, "Is your husband around?"

"He's still at work at the lumber store. I don't expect him home until nine. Is there something I can help you with?"

"I was wondering if he'd know of any handymen who work on the east side of town."

"Dave stopped doing that kind of work, but I'm sure he'd know people who still do. I'll let him know you called."

After Sarah hung up, she went into her office. She powered up her laptop and searched the online white pages for Suzy's home number and came up blank. Maybe her home phone was a private listing. She tried Stephen Carmichael and hit pay dirt with two numbers.

"Carmichael Campaign headquarters," a male voice said. "May I help you?"

"I'm not sure," Sarah said, a bit taken aback. "I'm looking for Suzy Carmichael?"

"Mrs. Carmichael isn't here right now. Can I take a message?"

"Do you know where I can reach her?" Sarah asked. "This is a friend of hers, and I had expected to speak with her today."

"I'm afraid I'm not privy to that information. She left last Friday on a business trip."

"Are you sure?"

"That's what I was told," the man said.

"Is Mr. Carmichael there?"

"No, it's just me right now. He's probably in court doing pro bono work today. He's determined to help the less fortunate in our state, which is why he'll make a great state representative. He's considering everyone's needs in these trying times. May I ask who you'll be voting for this fall?" he asked in an eager tone.

"You can, but I don't live in Arizona."

"Oh," his voice went flat. "I'll just leave a message you called." Sarah gave the man her phone numbers, and then tried the other listing from the computer search. It turned out to be Stephen Carmichael's law office.

The secretary confirmed he was in court and wouldn't give out the Carmichael's home phone number, but said she'd pass the message on that Sarah needed to speak to Mrs. Carmichael.

So where was Suzy? She hadn't mentioned she was going to be traveling before she came back to Maple Hill. Sarah dialed Suzy's cell number once more. It rang several times before going to voice mail again.

Curious now, she typed *Stephen Carmichael* and *Arizona* in a search engine and her page flooded with hits about his campaign. She read a bio of Stephen and his family, which portrayed them as a wholesome American family with good values and the desire to make their state a better place to live.

Why hadn't Suzy mentioned something as big as a campaign for state office? Concern over her daughter and the added burden of Carroll may have distracted her, but Sarah thought that a husband running for state government would be worth mentioning.

She ran a search on Lucas Bach and learned he worked in a real estate office, which explained how he was able to get away in the afternoon to meet her. His occupation might motivate an interest in Dawn's share of the house, but it didn't provide a motive for stealing tools or a baby quilt. What was the significance of all this? Maybe the theft of the tools and the theft of the quilt weren't even related. But that would mean more than one uninvited person had been in the attic.

Sarah's head started to ache from staring at the scrolling screen and she still needed to sew tonight. She shut the machine down and got her big wooden quilting hoop off the shelf.

Carrying the quilt into the living room, Sarah spread it out on the couch and secured the area she wanted to work on in the hoop.

Soft TV sounds drifted down the stairs from her boarder seating area. Andi always seemed to welcome Sarah's company, but tonight Sarah wanted time to relax and think. She'd found that praying or singing praise songs while quilting helped her to settle her thoughts and refocus her attention on what was truly important. With the jumbled mess surrounding the mystery, she hoped it worked tonight.

With a prayer for guidance, she drew white thread through her needle and began.

CHAPTER FIFTEEN

arah walked up Carroll's walk early Tuesday morning, determination in her steps. Neither Suzy nor Dave had phoned her back last night; so while working on the Amish quilt, she had formulated a plan of action beginning with searching for Dawn's will.

As she got out her key, the air shifted and a familiar scent drifted past her. Paint. She had noticed it before but had attributed to it the new eave above her head.

She walked the length of the porch to the far railing. The white paint looked fresh and clean. Someone had embedded shiny new nails in the wood.

The roar of a mower engine starting up behind the house caught her attention. She went down the steps and around to Carroll's shed. Jared pushed the mower through the backyard. She shouted and waved until he looked at her and shut the motor off.

"Jared, I just noticed that someone fixed the railing on part of Mr. Shepherd's front porch and painted it."

"Yeah. So? You asked me about the roof."

"True. Did you see the guy working on the porch?"

"Yeah."

"Do you know his name?"

Jared shrugged. "I don't remember. I only talked to him once."

"What about his car? Or truck? Can you describe that?"

"Old green Ford truck. There was a sign on the door, but some of the letters had worn off, and I can't remember what it said," Jared said. "I think the rear window was missing."

A start of recognition shook Sarah. Jared had just described Dave Diamond's truck, but Liz had said Dave no longer worked as a handyman. Maybe he'd sold the truck and his business to someone else. "Thanks, Jared. You've been more help than you know."

She turned and took a couple of steps toward the backdoor when Jared said, "I'm going to give those coins back to Mr. Shepherd."

Sarah paused and looked at him. A wrinkle appeared between his eyebrows reminding her of Amy.

"He was upset about something, and I don't think he meant to give them to me. He kind of just tossed them at me saying how things don't last, didn't matter, and go ahead and take them."

"If Mr. Shepherd didn't want you to have them, he wouldn't have given them to you. But you can ask him again, and if he lets you keep them, I'd put them somewhere safe. They may be valuable enough that you can sell them when you need money for college."

He nodded, the wrinkle easing.

As she continued on to the door, she wondered what else Carroll might've given away in one of his tempers.

Carroll was in his usual spot in front of the television. Sarah called a hello and charged up the steps to Dawn's old bedroom. She pulled open a few of the boxes to confirm the items she was looking for weren't there and headed downstairs again.

In the living room, she quickly checked the shelves and knelt down by the cabinet where the photo albums were stored. No luck. She turned and something on the floor, almost hidden by Carroll's chair, caught her attention. She picked up a thin white book. She opened the cover and read *In Loving Memory of Dawn Shepherd*. There were three pages of handwritten names along with the city each person had come from. This might prove very useful. Knowing who had attended the funeral might help broaden her list of who had been involved in Dawn's life and had access to this house. She set it on the coffee table to peruse later. Sarah then crossed the room, pressed the TV's Off button, and faced Carroll.

Carroll's eyes widened. "Hey. What do you think—"

"I need to get into Dawn's apartment."

"No."

"Carroll, I need to find some answers about what's going on around here. Do you have a key?"

He twisted up his mouth as if to argue but Sarah quickly added, "If I find what I'm looking for, you won't have to call the police. You might not even need that alarm system I've been bothering you about."

Carroll stared at the blank television screen. "In the kitchen drawer by the sink."

"Good. Get your shoes on." She picked up some loafer-type slippers and handed them to him. "You're coming with me."

She heard him sputter in protest as she marched down the hall to the kitchen. There were only two keys in the drawer and she grabbed both of them. When she returned to the living room, he was still sitting in his chair, but he'd slipped on the shoes.

"I'm sorry," Sarah said. Maybe she was pushing him too hard. "If you don't want to go, that's fine. I'll find someone else. I just don't want to go alone, and it would be quicker if you went."

"Why?"

"I think it's wise to have a witness in case something's missing. I don't want you to accuse me of stealing."

"I wouldn't do that."

She smiled.

"Okay, fine. I might." He rocked forward, grabbed his walker, and got to his feet. "I'm going."

"If you're sure—"

"What are you waiting for? I'm not getting any younger. Let's go."

"Maybe the outing will do you good," Sarah said, hoping it was true. They maneuvered out of the house and down the porch steps. Jared let the mower idle as he watched Sarah help Carroll into the front seat of her car.

With Carroll giving directions, Sarah found Dawn's apartment in a strip of five one-story residences set back on a nice shaded lot. She parked in front of number four and helped Carroll out.

Sarah unlocked the door. "Who's been in here since the accident?"

Carroll sighed, following her through the doorway. "Suzy, and one of Dawn's co-workers brought her stuff over from the office."

Sarah nodded and gazed around the compact living room with a nice matching living room set. A desk shoved in one corner held an impressive desktop computer. The kitchen was set off to one side with an eating area overlooking the backyard. Two doors were open—one leading to a bathroom and the other a bedroom.

Several packing boxes sat on the floor, half-filled. "Looks like Dawn was in the process of moving back to your place. I found the same type of boxes in her old room."

Carroll didn't say anything, but his Adam's apple bobbed. He sat on the couch while Sarah did a quick check of drawers in the bedroom and desk. No doubt Suzy had done the same thing. Nothing that looked official turned up. Chances were Dawn had a safe-deposit box somewhere.

"Dawn didn't say who her lawyer was?"

He shook his head.

"But you know she had one."

"She said she did."

Sarah checked in the packed boxes and then straightened, scanning the room. Her gaze kept going back to the fancy computer. "Okay, this may be a long shot, but assuming I'm Dawn and a paralegal, I'd probably be comfortable drawing up my own will using one of those computer programs."

Carroll sat on Dawn's couch. "She had a copy of her will. I saw it. That's when I offered to put it in the safe at work."

"I'm sure there's a paper copy somewhere, and she could've used one of her co-workers or lawyer friends to look it over and witness it. I'm going to search in her computer if that's all right with you." She turned on the power and the screen popped up. "It's requesting a password."

"Try Studebaker8," he said with a small smile.

"It worked. How did you know it?

"Private joke, and we used the same password at home."

Sarah scanned the files and finally located a will program under "Personal."

"I found it," she said. "I'll print you a copy." She turned on Dawn's printer.

"Here. She handed it to him when the printer had finished. "It's dated 2007, and she lists a law office over in Pittsfield. Alexander Hampton."

His hands trembled slightly as he skimmed the pages. "She still left her half of the house to me." He folded the sheets in half. "I'll have Suzy follow up with the lawyer for the original."

"Why didn't she use a lawyer here?"

"Alexander Hampton is…was a friend of hers. I should've remembered. They dated for a while."

"What if you had…?"

"Passed away first?" He shrugged. "She mentioned once leaving everything to some charity."

"Which one?"

"I don't know. Something to do with children. It doesn't matter now." He stood, grabbing at his walker. "We're finished here."

"Just a minute. I want to see if I can find her yearbooks."

"What for?" he asked.

"Lucas mentioned that she'd gone away for a year to study in Europe."

"So?"

"He said he thought something had happened while she was abroad. I wondered if her friends would have referenced it when they wrote in her yearbooks."

"What does Lucas know? He was just a kid." Carroll shuffled to the front door. "I gave Dawn a shot at being something great, but she blew it. Came back here, barely finished school, and spent her life at a mediocre job."

"What happened to her?"

"Doesn't matter now. You can't change the past." Carroll slammed the door back against the wall. "I don't want to talk about it!"

Sarah sat in Carroll's kitchen, tapping her fingers on the table as she waited for Dave Diamond to come to the phone. No one had answered at his home, so she had tried the lumber store, only to be put on hold.

After they had returned to the Shepherd house, Carroll had lain down on his bed to take a nap. The trip to Dawn's had worn him out physically and emotionally. Sarah probably shouldn't have put him through it, but at least they had found the will.

She decided it was unlikely anyone had been searching for Dawn's will at Carroll's house. The intruder would have looked in Dawn's apartment first, and there were no signs of a break-in. That still didn't mean Lucas Bach or another family member hadn't been searching for something else at Carroll's.

"Dave here," a voice said on the phone.

"Hi, Dave. This is Sarah Hart. Did Liz get a chance to tell you I called?"

There was a moment of silence. "She mentioned it. Sorry I didn't call back. I've been really busy."

"It's fine. I've been helping out over at the Shepherd house on Elm Street and I was wondering if you knew—"

"It was me." He lowered his voice. "I worked on the house. I've been doing part-time work since they cut my hours back here."

"Oh, I'm sorry to hear that."

"I haven't told Liz about it yet. I don't want her to worry in her condition. She's so happy right now."

"I understand," Sarah said. "Maybe you can help me. I'm trying to track down some tools Carroll Shepherd thinks may have been stolen."

"Stolen?"

"Actually, Mr. Shepherd said Dawn sold some of them, but now all of them are missing."

"Mrs. Hart, I made a down payment for those tools. Paid cash. I needed new tools since I was going back to work independently, but I couldn't afford all of them. Mr. Shepherd's daughter took the money and said it could be a down payment for the whole set. Later I changed my mind and called her back. Told her to keep the money for the tools I took, but that I wouldn't need the others."

"Well, I'm glad that mystery is solved. We couldn't find any record of the sale. Do you have the receipt or a canceled check?"

"I have the one for the first set I took. Dawn was going to write up an itemized receipt for the rest. Only, as I said, I decided not to buy the rest."

"I believe you, Dave," Sarah said. "Did you buy any tools from the attic?"

"The attic? The ones I bought were in a tool chest she kept in the kitchen." His voice fell almost to a whisper. "Listen, I have to go. My boss is headed this way. Thanks for letting me know about this. I don't want anyone to think I'm a thief. If I lose my reputation, I won't be able to find work." The phone clicked off.

Sarah sighed. What a mess. At least she knew now where some of Carroll's tools had gone.

Since she hadn't heard Carroll stir yet, she opened one of the two books on the counter. After Carroll had slammed out of Dawn's place, she had done a quick search of the bookshelves in the bedroom and found two high school yearbooks. She had told Carroll what she had grabbed, but he had merely grunted and kept his gaze pinned out the car window.

Sarah decided that the grunt was consent for her to look through them, so she flipped open the first yearbook. A smiling Dawn, in what would have been her sophomore year, stood out in shots with the swimming and dive team. She appeared in numerous other photos, more times than not with the same group of kids. The pages were graffitied with classmates making comments and leaving notes. The second book, her senior year, looked surprisingly blank. There were a few notes from friends, but it didn't have the craziness of her sophomore book.

Sarah retrieved the funeral guest book to compare to the names scrawled in the yearbooks. She ran her finger down the signatures in the funeral book. Lucas Bach was there. She halted when she came to Ed Worth.

Maybe Mr. Worth had been an acquaintance of Dawn's. She flipped through the senior yearbook until she came to the Ws and spied the name Edward Worth under the portrait of a broad-shouldered, tawny-haired, green-eyed young man. He looked familiar. She opened the sophomore book again and searched the group shots. Sure enough, Ed Worth appeared in almost every photo with Dawn, usually standing next to her.

She called information and got the phone number for Edward Worth. She dialed the number and a woman answered who told her Ed was still down at the fire station. His shift didn't end until three.

Sarah continued looking at Dawn's senior yearbook. She was missing from most of the group shots. When she got to the end of the book, she found a stack of graduation cards stuffed between the pages. Most looked to be from relatives. Some still had their original envelopes addressed from the Bach, Morgan, and Shepherd families. But she noted one envelope's return address was from someone named J. Orman with a post office box in Windham, Vermont.

She pulled out a large black and gold card. Inside the sender had written:

Dear Dawn,

Congratulations on your graduation and although I miss your cheerful smile, I wish you a wonderful life full of joy, happiness, and God's blessings.

Love,

Jennifer

Sarah closed the card and turned her attention back to the envelope. Several Polaroid snapshots were stuck inside. Two were goofy face shots of some girls making fun for the camera. The third revealed a pleasant-looking, middle-aged woman sitting at a table covered with bundles of fabric. She held a quilting hoop and needle. Could it be? She got her purse and pulled out the quilt piece in its plastic bag.

The grainy quality of the photograph made it difficult to see the pattern of the fabric, but the square the woman was quilting could belong to a small baby blanket. Was this Jennifer somehow connected to the missing quilt?

Sarah glanced at the kitchen clock. Two thirty. She wanted to catch Ed Worth as he came off his shift at the firehouse. The squawk of the television told her Carroll was awake. She retrieved her purse from the kitchen chair and tucked the quilt piece and Dawn's card inside before heading to the living room.

"I know where some of your tools are." She explained to Carroll about Dave Diamond.

"How do you know he's telling the truth?" he asked.

"I know Dave, and he's a good guy. He was an Eagle Scout and now helps out at a charity for homeless vets. I believe him. Somewhere in this house is the receipt Dawn was writing up. We just haven't found it yet."

"Humph."

"I'm going to go now. I have no idea where Suzy is, or when she might show up. I left you a sandwich in the refrigerator since you missed lunch, and I thought to call in an order of pizza for you for dinner. Is that all right?"

"Would it matter if it wasn't?" he grumbled, flipping through the cable channels with the remote.

"Yes, it matters," Sarah said gently, "but I have some work I need to do today. I'll be back tomorrow unless Suzy arrives." She grabbed the file box that was still sitting by the couch and pulled it over to his chair. "Meanwhile it might be helpful to go through this box again and see if you can figure out what's so valuable in there that someone would break in to find it. We may have figured out who has some of your tools, but we still don't know who's been searching your attic."

Maple Hill's primary fire station was a block off Main Street, and as Sarah entered the front door, she saw Jay Black, one of Jason's high school buddies, standing over a line of beige fire hose.

"Hey, Mrs. H. I haven't seen you in ages." He lumbered over and gave her a hug. "I see Jason around sometimes, but he's busy. I'm busy. Maybe one of these days, things will slow down where we can all sit down and visit."

"That would be fun," Sarah agreed. "Maybe we could all get together for a Sunday picnic this summer."

"Awesome. Get the old gang together." He grinned. "Now what can I help you with?"

"I'm looking for Ed Worth."

"Ed? He's checking the B.A.s. Come this way." He led her around one of the big engines to the back corner where a man sat by an air compressor. He had a hose attached to a gray air tank and was watching a pressure gauge.

"Ed? You about done? Mrs. Hart is here to see you."

"Almost."

"Gotta get back to work on my hoses," Jay said. "Never know when we'll get a call." He strolled away.

"I'll be with you in a minute." Ed shot her a curious look.

"No hurry," Sarah said. Ed resembled his high school photo in Dawn's yearbook, except he had filled out and grown a moustache. He disconnected the hose from the tank and set it beside some others along the wall.

He wiped his hands on a rag and stepped over to where Sarah stood. "What can I do you for?"

"I'm here on a personal matter. I spoke to your wife and she said you got off duty today at three. Is there somewhere we can go and talk in private?"

"Actually, I can't leave the station. One of the guys called in sick so I'm pulling a double shift. Is this important?"

"It's about Dawn Shepherd."

"Oh." He looked around the garage bay. Firefighters were checking gear and chatting with each other. Sarah could see through the door to a lounge area, also occupied by men. "Tell you what. If you can climb up in the engine cab, that should be quiet enough."

Sarah glanced at the big red fire engine. The front seats seemed miles up, but there was a handrail and there were steps as well. She felt like a little kid again. She had always wondered what it would be like to ride in one of these things. This was the probably the closest she would ever get.

"That would be fine," she said. Ed stood behind as she grasped the metal handrail and stepped up. She slid onto the black seat and Ed shut the massive door.

Jay passed the front of the engine. He looked up and caught sight of Sarah. He waved and gave her a thumbs-up.

Ed climbed into the driver's seat and slammed the door shut. "It was a terrible thing that happened to Dawn. I thank the Lord I wasn't on duty the day of the accident. How did you know Dawn?"

Sarah explained how she was helping out with Dawn's father. Then she decided to jump right in. "I wanted to know what happened during high school."

Ed frowned. "That was over twenty years ago. Why are you bringing that up now?"

Sarah chose her words carefully. "Sometimes there are unanswered questions about the past. Although I can't share all the reasons, I'm trying to bring some closure to a situation." And solve a mystery.

"And you think I can help?"

"I don't know. How well did you know Dawn?"

He sighed. "We were friends since fourth grade. Ran in the same group, and both of us were on the swimming team. Then we starting going out in high school."

"Did you two ever talk about getting married?" Sarah asked.

He shrugged and looked away. "We joked around about it. We were young and stupid and in love. Anyway, it doesn't matter. She left."

"That's when she went to England?"

"Yeah, it was supposed to be just a vacation, and the next thing I knew I got a 'Dear John' letter telling me her father thought it best she stay at this fancy school and compete internationally with her diving. Never even got a postcard after that."

He rubbed his moustache with his index finger. "He used to talk about her going to the Olympics, but truthfully, she needed tons of training. She was good, no doubt, but the Olympics are a whole other level, if you know what I mean. I used to think that out of all of us she probably was the only one with enough drive to have a shot at it."

"So why did she quit?"

"I don't know. I asked once, and she just said she wasn't interested in diving anymore. She stopped hanging out with us. I told myself she got stuck up after being at that snooty school and because her father was rich."

"Rich?"

"Yeah, didn't he invent something? Dawn used to talk about her dad being an inventor and how he was going to strike it big."

"Too bad that wasn't true," Sarah mused. If it had been, Carroll wouldn't be in the predicament he was in right now.

"Anyway, her father wanted us to break up, and he got his wish, even though he had to send her to school in another country. Obviously, I wasn't good enough for her. I mean how can you go from being in love to feeling nothing for someone in a week?"

"Good question," Sarah said as a siren blasted through the garage. The firefighters all froze as a voice over the loud-speakers announced a traffic accident on the highway, and then they sprang into action, scrambling into gear.

"Gotta go." Ed leapt out of the cab.

The door yanked opened on her side. "Let me help you down, Mrs. H." Jay gripped his beefy hand around her arm and safely helped her to the ground. "Better wait in the lounge while we pull out. Don't know how I'd explain it to Jason if you got squashed." He winked and escorted her through the organized chaos to the now-empty room.

She heard the giant bay doors slide open and two engines rolled out into the street with red lights flashing and sirens wailing. Then suddenly it was quiet.

She smiled and waved at the twenty-something kid who sat watching a monitor and walked back to her car. Ed had been pretty forthcoming with his answers. It had been over twenty years and she could still hear the teenage angst in his voice when he spoke of his relationship with Dawn.

She didn't believe Dawn had suddenly decided she was too good for her boyfriend and everyone else. What was there to be stuck up about? She had quit diving and her father never struck it rich. So what had made her close herself off from her friends?

Whatever it was, Sarah would find out.

CHAPTER SIXTEEN

A udrey skidded to a stop in Sarah's kitchen and moaned, "Not strawberries again."

Sarah looked up from the stove where she flipped pancakes in one skillet and stirred scrambled eggs in another. She smiled "You don't have to go anywhere near those strawberries. Although I did cut some up to go on your pancakes with some whipped cream."

"Whipped cream?" Amy came around the corner and set her backpack down on the chair. "I'm in. What do I have to do?"

"You can set the table. We'll eat in five minutes."

"Cool."

"Audrey, there's orange juice in the refrigerator. You can use the small glasses that are in the dishwasher," Sarah said, feeling a little out of breath. She had pulled the meal together in less than twenty minutes.

Maggie had called about a half hour ago and asked if Sarah could take the girls to their classes after school since she was going to be extra busy at work today. At least that was the excuse they had used for the girls. In reality, Maggie confessed to Sarah she needed some time at home alone before work to get ready for the girls' birthday. She wanted to make some of their favorite treats and wrap their gifts without fear of them popping in on her.

Always glad to be with her granddaughters, Sarah jumped at the chance to entertain them for the morning. She stacked pancakes onto the plate warming in the oven.

"I was thinking you two might want to enter the strawberry jam contest for the Strawberry Festival, now that you know how to make it. They have a division for teens. The prize is fifty dollars."

"We'll be teens tomorrow!" Audrey said, bouncing into a chair with so much excitement she almost spilled the orange juice. "I can hardly wait. I'm going to be a *teenager*."

"What do we have to do to enter?" Amy asked as she placed forks beside the plates.

"Make your own jam from scratch. I can supervise, but I'm not supposed to do any of the preparation."

"Do we have time to do it today?" Amy asked. Her competitive spirit must be rising to the occasion.

Sarah glanced at the clock. "If you hurry. We only have two hours."

"Hey, I want to try to win fifty dollars too." Audrey jumped up to peer at the now-interesting flat of strawberries.

"There are plenty of strawberries," Sarah pointed out as she put the platter of pancakes on the table and went back for the eggs. "You can enter together or make your own batch."

"Gram, someone's at the backdoor," Amy said.

Irene smiled and waved at them through the glass. Sarah opened the door. "Oh good, I caught you before you went over to Carroll's. I think my checkbook slipped out of my purse and is in your car." Irene peered around Sarah. "Oh hi, girls."

"Let me get my key," Sarah said, turning to go into the office where she had left her purse. When she returned, Irene still lingered in the doorway watching the girls.

"So sorry to drag you way from such a wonderful breakfast."

Sarah paused. "Why don't you join us? We have plenty."

Irene brightened. "Really? I haven't eaten yet. Chris is still sick and sleeping in. I was thinking of going down to The Spotted Dog, but I'd much rather stay here if Audrey and Amy don't mind."

The twins exchanged glances as if surprised to be even considered in the decision. Both shook their heads, and Audrey said, "We don't mind. You'll like it. Gram's an awesome cook."

"We were just going to say the blessing." Sarah pulled out her chair for Irene and retrieved another plate.

After Amy prayed, she turned to Irene who was sipping orange juice. "That's a pretty bracelet."

"Thank you. Would you like to see it?" Irene said, setting the glass down and unclasping the chain.

Amy turned the silver chain over in her hands. "Where'd you get all the charms?"

"Well, my mother gave me the chain for my high school graduation. If you look on the end, you'll see a cap and diploma."

Amy found the little charm. "How cute." She spread the bracelet flat on the table so all the trinkets were visible.

"Most of the charms are from places I've been," Irene said.

Audrey looked over from buttering her pancakes. "Is that a boat?"

"A gondola. Chris and I went to Venice on our honeymoon, and then to Athens." Irene pointed to a rectangular charm. "That one is the Parthenon."

"Cool," Audrey said. "And here is the Capitol for Washington D.C. and oh, I like the Empire State Building."

"The bear?" Amy asked, pointing with her fork.

"Yellowstone Park."

"The cable car must be from San Francisco. We've been there." Audrey lifted a charm shaped like two tiny tubes. "What's this one?"

"Rolled up maps. It has special meaning between my husband and me." Irene ran a finger over the charm. "I love old maps."

Irene smiled and told them stories about her trip to Italy as they finished breakfast and cleaned up.

The morning flew by. Audrey and Amy decided to make separate jam batches with the theory that would double their chances of winning and they would split the money no matter who won.

Irene still lingered. She helped do the dishes and supervised the girls while they made their jam. She smiled and laughed at their antics and jokes, but she seemed on edge, too eager to please.

While the twins were getting their stuff into the car, Irene asked Sarah what she planned for the afternoon.

"I'm heading to Windham."

"Vermont? Why?" Irene asked. "Oh does this have to do with Dawn?"

"Yes. How did you know?"

Irene's face flushed. "I saw the envelope sticking out of your purse." She nodded toward Sarah's bag on the counter. "I didn't mean to be so nosy."

"I can't get mad at you when I'm the queen of nosiness when trying to solve a mystery." Sarah smiled. "Remember when I told you things were missing in the attic? There was a baby quilt that disappeared.

"Really? How intriguing," Irene said.

"Amy found a scrap of it on a nail by the stairs. Carroll doesn't seem to know about the quilt, or at least he's not telling me. But, later I found a photograph of a similar quilt in a card addressed to Dawn. I think I may be able to find out who made the baby quilt, and maybe who took it."

"Do you want company on your trip to Vermont? I'd love to go."

Sarah had planned to go alone, considering what she suspected she might find, but once again the wistfulness in Irene's voice prompted her to say, "Sure, you can come. I have to drop the girls off first."

"Am I dressed okay for where we're going?" Irene glanced down at her olive blouse covered with a denim vest embroidered with delicate roses. Her jeans had a matching design. Supple-looking suede boots adorned her small feet. She wore her shoulder-length hair down today, softening the angular curves of her face, making her appear younger than her forty years.

"You look nice. I'm going to freshen up and then we'll go," Sarah said. She changed her stained work jeans for light-blue slacks and topped them with a yellow print blouse before gently shooing the girls out to her silver Grand Prix.

Irene kept up pleasant chatter with Audrey about her drawing as they made their way across town. After Sarah made sure the twins were safely in their classes, she dropped in on Carroll. He told her Suzy had called that morning and said she would be in Maple Hill on Wednesday. Sarah told him she would be back around seven to fix him dinner then. Meanwhile he had leftover pizza for lunch.

As she was leaving, she noted the file box by Carroll's chair was half-empty. He had actually listened to her. She hoped he would find a clue to why the intruder was interested in the box.

"I hope this is the place." Sarah turned off the country road and drove slowly down a long gravel driveway.

The actual trip to Windham took less time than Sarah had anticipated even with a stop at the county hall of records to get Jennifer Orman's address. Traffic was light and Irene kept the conversation flowing. When she consistently steered the topics to Sarah's childhood and her family, Sarah finally asked, "Are the Draytons going to be the subject of your next article?"

Irene laughed. "Sorry. Historian's occupational habit."

To Sarah's relief they spent the second hour discussing Irene's writing. Irene had brought her revised version of the piece on Patriot Park and read it to Sarah. She had taken Sarah's advice to focus on a human interest angle and had written the article from the point of view of Nathaniel Bradford's bronze statue in the park. This seemed particularly fitting for Irene since she liked to talk about historical figures in the present tense. Irene beamed when Sarah praised the article.

After leaving the hall of records, they had searched for the Orman house. Since displayed house addresses were few and far between, they'd had to backtrack a couple of times.

"It's a big house," Irene said as a rambling two story ranch-style building surrounded by huge oaks came into view.

The closer they got, the shabbier the building appeared. It was badly in need of paint, and a couple of the windows were cracked. The heavy shade cast a desolate air over the property.

"Looks like someone's home," Sarah said, noting an ancient station wagon and a white eighteen-passenger van parked at the side of the house.

Sarah parked by the front door, and they stepped up to a deck that ran the length of the house. Deck chairs and lounges were placed along it, with small round tables. A novel lay open, facedown, on one of the tables. Sarah glanced at the title and saw it was a popular young adult story Liam had displayed prominently in his bookstore.

A row of five or six pairs of flip-flops were lined up by the front door. A small brass plaque on the door stated "Please Ring Bell."

"The place looks like it used to be a bed and breakfast," Irene said.

Sarah agreed, although she already had an idea of what this place was all about. She pressed the glowing white button and a bell sounded. A waif of a young woman opened the door. Despite the late spring warmth, a bulky brown sweater covered her from her neck to below her hips. Her arms and legs appeared toothpick thin, but her round face and cheeks brushed with pink glowed with health.

Her big blue eyes looked them up and down. "Yes?"

"Hi! I'm Sarah Hart and this is Irene Stuart. We're looking for Jennifer Orman."

She looked over at Sarah's car. "Why?"

Irene glanced at Sarah and said, "We were friends of someone she knew in Maple Hill. Dawn Shepherd. Is she in?"

"I'll see." She shut the door with a firm click.

"Well, I certainly do hope they aren't in the hospitality business," Irene tried to joke, shifting from one foot to the other.

"If this place is what I think it is, they have a right to be cautious."

Irene shot her a curious look as the door opened again. This time a plump older woman wearing black denim capris and a maroon sleeveless shirt stood in the doorway. Crinkles radiating from her eyes suggested she smiled a lot.

"Why hello! I'm Jennifer," she said with a big smile. "Come on in. Any friends of Dawn are most welcome." She waved them into a large foyer. Pop music drifted down a large stairway that rose to the second floor.

"Can I get you something to drink? Coffee? Water? Iced tea? I was just having some iced tea out on the sunporch. I made a fresh pitcher this morning."

"Iced tea sounds wonderful," Sarah said and Irene concurred.

Jennifer led them past a spacious living room with worn but attractive furniture where several young ladies were watching TV, a dining room with a long table that could seat at least twelve, and through the kitchen to a glassed-in sunroom overlooking a small pond behind the house.

"Here we are. Make yourselves comfortable. I'll be right back." The sunroom had two white iron patio tables with chairs, and some comfortable rattan furniture with puffy colorful cushions. The windows were open and fans spun overhead.

"Well, this is nice and peaceful," Irene said, moving closer to the window to watch a pair of white ducks float by.

Jennifer strode in carrying a wooden tray with a pitcher of iced tea, glasses, and what looked like lemon pound cake. She set it on the table and after serving them, she asked, "So, what brings you ladies out here in the middle of nowhere? It's rare to have anyone over the age of thirty visit."

"We're trying to get some information about Dawn," Sarah said.

Jennifer's smile faded and her expression became guarded. "I'm afraid I can't divulge anything personal about my girls. Privacy is what this place is all about. A shelter for those who need it. If you want to know something you need to ask Dawn."

"I would but—" Sarah stopped and Irene gazed down at her plate. Jennifer looked from one to the other.

"What? What's happened?"

"I'm sorry, I have terrible news. I didn't realize that you didn't know." Sarah explained about the accident and how Sarah had gotten involved with Carroll.

Tears filled Jennifer's eyes. "Oh that poor, poor girl. And her father. I thought they'd never truly reconcile. Dawn blamed her father for sending her away, but after the complications and Dawn nearly died, she managed to forgive her dad and move on."

Nearly died? "I talked to a high school friend of hers, and he said she'd changed when she got back."

"I suppose it doesn't hurt to divulge what her father could tell you, now that she's gone. Something happened while she was overseas at school. England or France, I think. My memory isn't what it used to be. Apparently she got involved with the wrong kind of guy who took advantage of her. Her dad tried to press charges, but being another country and no proof it wasn't consensual..." She gave a little shrug.

"Anyway, she came here for a few months and we got her counseling. She adjusted, although I don't think she was ever the same. We kept in touch. I'd hear from her at least a couple of times a year."

"So I'm assuming that the quilt this scrap came from belonged to Dawn?" Sarah asked, pulling out the fabric and handing it to Jennifer.

She studied it and let out a little sigh. "I remember this. We made the baby quilt together." She pressed it to her damp cheek. "I was glad she took it with her after..." She swallowed hard and gave the quilt piece back. "I've probably said too much. Please keep this confidential. Even though she's gone, she deserves her privacy."

Sarah and Irene assured her they would. It was obvious Jennifer had revealed all she was going to, so they had a pleasant time chatting about quilting before Jennifer walked Irene and Sarah to the door and said good-bye.

As Sarah started the engine, Jennifer flew down the steps, waving at them to stop. Sarah rolled down the window.

"I just remembered something," Jennifer said taking deep breaths. "Sometimes the girls keep journals while they're here—it's a good way for them to express their emotions—and Dawn accidentally left her journal behind. She always said she'd come by to pick it up but she never did. It's in my attic. I thought her father might like to have it. Tell him I'll mail it if he can call and give me the address. I think he might like to read it. Even though she was angry at him, she wrote some beautiful things about him."

"Thanks, I'll tell him," Sarah said. "One last thing, if you don't mind my asking, did Dawn ever mention an Eddie?"

"It's been so long, but she used to talk about an uncle. There could've been an Uncle Eddie. I think he passed away." Sarah thanked her again. As Jennifer returned to the house, Sarah did a U-turn and rolled down the gravel road.

"I don't remember an Eddie or Edward mentioned in any of the family announcements I found," Irene said with a sigh. "Maybe Eddie is a nickname. I can look again."

"If it's not too much trouble. I really appreciate what you've uncovered so far."

Irene sat quietly watching the fields pass by as they headed south. When they were a few miles from the state line she asked, "What are you doing tonight? I was thinking of seeing a movie. Would you like to go?"

"Thanks for the invite, but Suzy's due back, so I'll probably need to meet with her. And then we'll be celebrating Amy and Audrey's birthday with a party."

"Oh that sounds like so much fun. Do you need any help with the party?"

"I think it's under control. Martha's grandchildren are doing all the work."

"Are you sure? I'd be happy to bake some cookies or clean up. Or maybe help decorate."

Sarah was trying to find a polite way to dissuade her when Irene asked, "Did you see how forlorn some of the girls back at that house looked? Like they'd been abandoned. You'd think that during a time like that, they'd need to be surrounded by people who love them."

"Ideally, that would be the case," Sarah agreed.

"I think Mr. Shepherd was cruel to send Dawn there."

Sarah sighed. Decisions in cases like these couldn't be easy. Years ago it wasn't uncommon to send an unwed mother to stay with other people until the baby could be given up for adoption. "Maybe Mr. Shepherd was hoping Dawn would have a better life if no one in Maple Hill knew what happened."

"Jennifer said Dawn almost died, and it sounded like the baby did. How awful. But then, think how tormenting it would've been for Dawn to wonder her whole life how her baby was being raised by someone else." Irene's voice rose. "Anyone with parental instincts would, right? You think about your kids every day, don't you?"

"Yes, I do."

"Because you love them. If you didn't, you wouldn't care. You wouldn't call. You, you—" Irene took a deep shuddering breath and burst into tears.

Sarah pulled off onto a side road as Irene continued to sob. "I-I'm sorry," Irene sobbed.

"It's all right. Just let it out." Sarah searched in her purse and found a tissue packet. She pulled out several tissues and gave them to Irene.

Irene sniffed and wiped her eyes and nose. "Thank you." She gave Sarah a watery smile. "I suppose you're wondering what this is all about."

Sarah was, but she said, "Only if you want to talk about it, Irene."

She took another shaky breath. "Last week I found out my parents were killed in an accident."

"Oh Irene, I'm so, so sorry."

"It gets worse."

"Worse?"

"They died five years ago, and I didn't even know."

CHAPTER SEVENTEEN

I've never told anyone in Maple Hill about this. Not even Chris." Irene wiped her eyes. "But, I haven't seen or heard from my parents in over twenty years. Not since before Chris and I got married. My parents were fairly strict, but I thought my childhood was pretty good. My father owned a gas station and my mother stayed at home with us. I had a brother Peter, a few years younger than me. He was a good kid, but when he was seventeen, he got into a bad crowd, experimenting with drugs. My parents tried to get him help, counselors, rehab, church.

"When I heard he'd started to deal, I turned him in to the police. He got a year in jail, but he never made it out of prison. Killed by another inmate." She swallowed hard. "My parents blamed me. Said he should never have been there in the first place. That they would've put him in a hospital again."

"Oh Irene, what a terrible burden for them to put on you," Sarah said with tears misting her eyes.

"I realized, years later, how hurt and angry they must've been at what happened. I just thought they'd realize one day that I did the only thing I could do. Pete was hooking young kids and he wouldn't stop. I begged him to. I loved him too, you know?"

Sarah nodded, choked up.

"Every holiday I would spend alone, wondering if my parents ever thought about me all these years. Meanwhile, I married Chris, started my career, and we made a good life. Then on Mother's Day I decided I'd try to call my mom, but the number I had no longer worked. It took me a couple of weeks, but I was finally able to contact an old friend of theirs and found out they'd been killed in a bus accident five years ago."

Irene shook her head. "Five years! I should've tried sooner. I let my pride get in the way." The pain made Sarah's chest ache.

"Oh Irene, I can't even comprehend what you're going through," Sarah said, fighting tears. "I don't know what to say to give you comfort. Can we pray about it?"

Sarah grasped Irene's hands and prayed that Irene would find peace and forgive herself and her parents.

"Thank you." Irene gave Sarah a hug. "I don't know what to do to feel better. How did you get over Gerry passing away?"

"I was brokenhearted. I didn't think I'd ever see a day when I'd wake up happy again. So I just concentrated on my house and business, and over time the sad memories faded some. I started remembering the good times I had with Gerry and the family we made together. Also, good friends helped. At least that's how it worked for me. Everyone's different."

Irene nodded. "I'm just going to keep busy and get out more with people. I appreciated your letting me tag along with you this last week."

"I'm glad we got to know each other better," Sarah said, realizing she meant it. Irene had just needed a friend. Or maybe a mother. This explained all the questions about Sarah's family. Irene was missing her own.

"Ready to head back?" Sarah asked after the sniffles had eased.

Irene sighed. "I think so. I guess I need to face reality, tell Chris what happened with my parents, and try to find a way to deal with this horrible regret."

Sarah pulled the car back out into traffic and Irene went back to gazing out the window, the sniffles and sighs gradually ceasing.

Late afternoon shadows were creeping over Maple Hill when they got to the east side of town. "If you need to stop and check on Mr. Shepherd before we head across town, that's okay with me," Irene said.

"If you're sure. I don't mind dropping you off first."

"No need to have to drive back here. Focusing on someone else who has troubles will help me stop thinking about my own," Irene said. "Chris isn't expecting me back until late. Besides, I like helping out over there."

Sarah's fingers tightened on the steering wheel. Something prompted her to ask, "Irene, you didn't happen to be over there Thursday night, did you?"

"Why, yes," she said. "I couldn't find my cell phone and thought I had left it there."

"Did you go in the back door?"

"Yeah. How did you know?"

"Carroll's neighbor saw someone going around the side of the house."

"Oh, I didn't mean to cause any trouble. I rang the front bell. When Mr. Shepherd didn't answer, I went around to the back thinking he might be in the kitchen. The door was unlocked. I knocked and went in."

"I had locked the door before I left."

"Well, maybe Mr. Shepherd went out back for something. I found my phone on the floor under the table. He was asleep and looked so peaceful. I didn't want to wake him. I tidied up the living room, washed a few dishes, and swept before I left. I hope that wasn't a problem."

"The stealth housekeeper," Sarah commented with a smile. "I don't think anyone would mind that."

Irene smiled. "I've dropped by a couple other times to see if he needed any help, but those times he answered the front door. We even played chess one time, although I'm not very good at it. I thought he would've told you."

"Carroll has not been a fountain of information."

"Yeah, he can be really grumpy. I think he's just afraid to need anyone. He's used to being in control and the breadwinner of the family. Trying to be independent and resisting help now are making him lonely. Poor man."

"That's a good way of thinking about it," Sarah said. Irene's opinion of Carroll's behavior was much more tolerant than hers. Sarah often thought Carroll just enjoyed being a loud, abrasive grump. Old age was no excuse for rudeness.

Sarah braked at the stop sign to turn right onto Elm. As she looked both ways, she spied the brown van rolling away from the curb near Carroll's house. It picked up speed and flew past them. Two men were once again in the cab. Sarah pulled out after it.

"Where are we going?" Irene asked.

"See that van in front of us? Try to get the license plate number. I think it's the same one that's been hanging around the neighborhood. I think they might be burglars."

"Oh my!" Irene leaned forward. "You better step on it if we're going to catch them." The taillights disappeared around another corner, and Sarah tapped down on the accelerator as far as she dared. She was already over the speed limit.

"Hang on." She made the turn faster than she normally would.

Irene braced her hands on the dashboard. "It's stopped at the traffic light."

The light turned green as Sarah rolled up close behind the van and read off the license plate.

Irene grabbed a pen from her purse and wrote it down on the back of a grocery receipt. "Got it! Now what?"

"I'm going to report it to the police just in case, but let's check on Carroll first." The van crossed the street and Sarah made a left to go around the block.

They parked in front of the Shepherd house. Lamps were turned on in the living room, and the TV light flickered against the windows. The front door was locked, so she used her key after ringing the bell.

"Mr. Shepherd, it's Sarah and Irene," she called as they walked down the hall. He wasn't in the living room.

"I'll check the kitchen," she told Irene. The light was on, and lunch meat and cheese had been left on the counter. She checked the backdoor. It was unlocked. She opened it and peered into the dark backyard. The shed door was closed, the padlock in place. No sign of Carroll. She turned and bumped into Irene.

"He's not in his bedroom or the bathroom," she said, her voice tight with concern. "What should we do?"

The last time Carroll was missing, he had walked down the street. But then why hadn't he gone out the front? That door had still been locked.

"Let's check with the neighbors," Sarah said, heading toward the foyer. As she passed the stairs, a faint thud sounded from upstairs.

She froze. "Did you hear that?"

Irene nodded.

Sarah put a foot on the stairs and Irene gasped. "Don't go up there."

"I'm only going to the top of the stairs," Sarah whispered. She told herself she wasn't quite as impetuous as Suzy.

She climbed higher, Irene on her heels, until she was eye level with the second story. Light streamed across the floor from the open attic door. Another thud, and then the sound of something being dragged across the floor. The hairs stood up on the back of Sarah's neck.

Irene clutched Sarah's arm, the charms on her bracelet rattling. "Someone's up there. Do you think they may have hurt Carroll?"

She turned and gently pushed Irene down the stairs in front of her. "Go outside and call the police!"

"Aren't you coming?"

"Yes, but I'm going to check something first," Sarah said as Irene backed out to the porch. Sarah darted to the basement door and yanked it opened. Praying, she flicked on the light. The floor at the base of the stairs was empty.

Thank you, God. She had feared she would find Carroll's body sprawled at the bottom. She went far enough down the stairs to make sure he wasn't in the basement and then joined Irene on the sidewalk to wait for the police.

Sarah paced the sidewalk in front of the Fergusons' where Officer Hopkins had told her to wait. She had knocked on the door, but Jared hadn't answered. Nancy's car wasn't in the driveway, and Sarah just hoped Jared was with his mom or out with friends and not in Carroll's attic.

"What's taking so long?" Irene asked for the third time in five minutes. She sat on Nancy's front steps, twisting her bracelet around her wrist. She jumped to her feet. "Oh, the policeman's on the porch. He's waving at us."

Officer Hopkins was smiling as they approached, which loosened the tight band in Sarah's chest. "Everything's okay."

"But what about Mr. Shepherd?" Sarah asked.

"He's in there. He's—maybe you should just see for yourself." His grin widened. "Follow me." He led the way up the two flights of stairs to the attic. Carroll stood in the middle of the room, wearing his bathrobe and a scowl on his face, the overturned book boxes on the floor around him.

"Carroll Shepherd, what are you doing up here?" Sarah asked. "How did you get up the stairs? Are you trying to break your neck?"

"I can be up here if I want to. This is my attic. My house! And who called the police?" Carroll demanded. "I almost had a heart attack when I saw his gun."

"We did. We thought you might've been kidnapped or something. All this time, I've been working up here and worrying because you couldn't climb the stairs, and now I find out that it's been you moving things around." Anger and a feeling of betrayal washed over her.

Officer Hopkins cleared his throat. "If everything is okay, I'll go write my report."

"Thank you, officer," Irene said as Carroll glowered at them. "I'm sorry you had to come out here."

As Officer Hopkins descended the stairs, Sarah said, "I'm going too." Let Suzy deal with him. She was done.

"Sarah—" Irene started to say when Carroll interrupted. "Wait, Sarah. Please."

The "please" stopped her. She turned. His face dripped sweat, and his knees shook as he lowered himself on a trunk.

"Oh my! Are you okay?" Irene said, stepping toward him, but he waved her away. "Do you want some water?

He nodded.

"Be right back." Irene raced toward the stairs.

Sarah tapped her foot. "Okay, Carroll, what's the game you've been playing?"

"No game," he said, breathing hard. "I was doing what you said and going through the file box, and I realized some things are missing."

"Like what?"

"When I was working on my tool prototypes, I drew some designs, but I can't find them. I also filled out some patent applications. They're missing too. The labeled files are there, but not what was inside. I thought they might be up here somewhere."

That was a distinct possibility, considering how much paper Sarah had found stuffed all over the attic. She gestured to the boxes at his feet. "Why the books?"

"I got distracted and figured while I was up here I'd get some of my books too," he said.

There was a pounding on the stairs, and Irene came in the door carrying a water glass and a handful of orange prescription bottles. "Here you go. I didn't know which meds you needed, so I brought everything on the counter."

He took the water but snapped, "I don't want any pills. Nobody asked you to get them."

Sarah relaxed. Carroll must be okay if he was starting to act his normal abrasive self. "Carroll, just take your blood pressure medication and I won't bother you about the rest. Your face is still flushed, and besides, you're supposed to have them every evening. If you want independence, that's a step in the right direction."

He grumbled but took the bottles from Irene.

"The officer was still down there and I gave him the license plate of the van," Irene said. "I told him you said you'd seen it loitering around the neighborhood. He said that they'd gotten a complaint about the van and were checking it out."

Probably Theresa next door, Sarah thought.

"What van?" Carroll asked, and as Irene explained, Sarah circled the attic.

"If you haven't been up here recently, Carroll, that still leaves the certainty that someone else has." She moved over to the crumpled rug. "This is where I found your tools. The file box was in the corner over there." She walked over to where the Edsel and Studebaker brochures and parts were stacked.

"I haven't seen those in years." Carroll shuffled over and Sarah moved out of his way.

"Sarah, did you take the wedding dress out of here?" Irene asked.

"What?" Sarah turned. Irene stood in front of the armoire.

"I noticed the door was cracked open, so I thought I'd take another look at that beautiful dress. But it's gone."

"What wedding dress?" Carroll asked, lowering himself on a box so he could reach the items on the floor.

"The one I tried to ask you about. There were two wedding dresses up here and that baby quilt." She needed to talk to him about Dawn and the baby, but she would wait until a better time.

Stacks of magazines lay at the bottom of the armoire. Sarah hadn't noticed them before because the skirt of the dress had taken up so much space. *Bride Today* was on the top and similar bridal magazines lay beneath. She glanced at the date and smiled. She knew who the dress belonged to.

Carroll held up two small objects. "Do you know what these are?"

"Looks like toys to me," Irene said.

Carroll sighed. "I meant can you guess what models these cars are?"

Irene shrugged. "Those look before my time."

Carroll made an exasperated sound. "Sarah. Tell her."

"And you think I'm old enough to remember?" Sarah said with a chuckle. She maneuvered closer, trying not to step on the novels scattered across the floor. "One's an Edsel. Looks like my aunt's old car, but I'm not sure what the other is."

"Studebaker. We were making the Studebaker toys for a marketing ploy, and I had the Edsel made as a joke." He handed them to Sarah. "Look inside. Those two people in the front seats are supposed to be Eddie and me."

"Why was it a joke?" Irene stepped closer.

"Eddie started his career selling cars whose production ended that very year. That's how he got his nickname. Eddie for the old Edsels. Our initials are on the trunk."

Sarah turned the car around and found the CTS which stood for Carroll Thomas Shepherd. The other initials sent a shiver from her head to her toes.

"This is Eddie?" she asked, pointing at the letters beneath Carroll's.

"Yes, that's him. We nicknamed him after the Edsel. He spent years trying to shake it but us old-timers remember." Carroll grinned. "He hated that name."

Sarah looked back at the rug where the tools had been. She wasn't sure how the entire puzzle fit together yet, but she had just found the key piece.

"Cat!" Carroll bellowed as he entered the kitchen. Robin, the neighbor's kitty, was on the counter finishing off the turkey lunch meat. "Scat! Get out of here."

Robin turned to stare at Carroll, slowly licked his chops, and with a swish of striped tail, jumped off the counter.

Carroll shook his walker at the feline, but Robin merely shifted his course, curved around the old man, ambled to the backdoor, and waited. Irene opened it and the cat darted outside.

"How does that cat get in?" Sarah asked, gathering up the scraps left on the counter and tossing them in the trash.

"Beats me." Carroll heaved his sweating body into a chair. The trip from the attic had taken thirty minutes as the old man carefully backed down the stairs, resting between each step.

"Mr. Shepherd, are these the tools that were missing?" Irene asked. Sarah stopped cleaning and looked at a pile of tools by the door.

"Yeah, they were on the back step," Carroll said. "The handyman brought them back. He left a note."

Irene reached for the folded notepaper on the floor and read it out loud.

Mr. Shepherd,
Since there has been some confusion about my purchase of your tools, I have returned them until the money I paid, or the receipt, is located.
Dave Diamond

Carroll humphed. "Now why would he do that unless he was guilty?"

"He wants to protect his reputation. I believe him," Sarah said.

"Well, I won't believe it until I see the cash. And XT-9-52 and TR-16-20 are still missing! I told you he was a thief!"

"What's missing?" Irene asked.

"Prototypes for a manufacturing tool I designed that could be used in the assembly line and in the repair shops. The company eventually decided it was too costly to use the system that the tool fit, and so the tool was never made."

Sarah thought about the kitchen gadget Liam had given her with the tools hidden inside. She'd seen something similar in the pile of tools in the attic. "Were they metal rods?"

"Yes, stainless steel on the outside, the components on the inside. I had an embedded electronic chip inserted that could detail any irregularities. It would save lots of time when trying to repair the system." He rattled off more technical details that Sarah didn't understand. "The prototypes were in my workshop downstairs, but Dawn cleaned everything out and put them with the tools."

"I saw them in the attic with those tools, so unless Dave Diamond got into the attic, I would assume he doesn't have them. And even if he did, why would he want some metal rods? Only someone who knew what they were would want them."

"And even then, they're worthless," Carroll grumbled.

"Are you sure? Is there any way that your tool might be modified for use today?" Irene asked.

"They were very specialized for a specific car model, and like I just said, that system wasn't cost-effective even though it cut down on...fuel consumption...oh." Carroll met Sarah's gaze.

"I think I know who has them," Sarah said. "Tomorrow you and I are going to take another outing."

"I should've known you'd figure it out," Suzy said, her hip cocked against the hotel room door. After Sarah dropped Irene off at her car, she had gone to the motel where Suzy had stayed the last time.

"Come on in." Suzy stepped back and Sarah entered the spacious room. The wedding dress lay on a chair. A box with white pumps, a photo album, and other miscellaneous wedding items sat next to it.

"I'm sorry I lied to you," Suzy said. "I've been here since Monday, trying to stay out of sight until I could get into Uncle Carroll's house unseen."

"Why didn't you just tell me you were married before? Why all the secrecy?" Sarah asked.

"Because of Stephen's campaign. And...it's complicated, but I never actually made it to the altar the first time." Suzy plopped down on the bed and patted the spot beside her. "Kick off your shoes and I'll confess." She grinned impishly. "We'll pretend it's the good old days when we stayed up all night talking."

Sarah glanced at her watch. She still had an hour before the birthday dinner with the family. She set her purse down and slipped off her loafers. She scooted back on the bed, and crossed her legs. "I don't think this quite brings back forty years. And I'm mad at you."

"Oh, but wait," Suzy bounced up and dug into a bag and extracted a package of Oreos. "And one more thing."

She opened the small refrigerator tucked into the wall unit and extracted a pint of milk. She grabbed two glasses and returned to the bed. "Will this do it?"

"I haven't had Oreos with milk in ages."

"Then we're in for a treat," Suzy said. "Just don't tell my trainer. Bad enough I haven't been to the gym in over a week."

Sarah twisted open an Oreo and popped a half in her mouth. The chocolate and vanilla flavors were predictably comforting, and with Suzy sitting across from her the combination did bring a flashback of younger days.

Suzy was busy dunking her cookie in the milk when she said, "Okay, let me see if I can explain this without taking all night. When Stephen announced he wanted to run for office, I thought that was big, but a nice, worthy goal. Little did I know how it would take over our lives. We have a campaign manager, a publicist, and an event planner—not to mention his backers—all telling us how to dress, what to eat and drink in public, what we can and can't say. It's suffocating, but … anyway, we're painted as the ideal American wholesome family, which creates a problem."

"How's that?" Sarah reached for another cookie even though it would probably ruin her appetite for dinner with Jason and Maggie.

"How would it look if it came out that the wife of the future state representative was a criminal?"

Sarah nearly choked on her Oreo and took a long swallow of milk. "Criminal? I'm not sure I'm following you. How is a broken engagement a crime?"

"Remember how I was supposed to go to law school right after graduation?"

"I always wondered what happened."

"I lasted a semester and then flipped out. Too much pressure. I wanted to take some time off. So against my parents' wishes I took off for Florida to hang out on the beach."

"I remember. You sent me a post card."

Suzy nodded. "In Miami I met Max. Brilliant, charming, charismatic Max. He owned an investment company, which was doing phenomenally well, or so I thought. He hired and trained me. I helped bring in clients. It was a dream job. I attended parties, art gallery functions, restaurant openings, and charity events, getting to know important people with money.

"And I fell in love with Max. I just wanted a quick wedding at the courthouse, but my mom couldn't stand the thought of her only daughter not getting married in a church. So she flew down and insisted on a wedding dress, a church, and a reception down there. Even china. She pulled it together in less than a week. She was such a nut."

Sarah had always thought Suzy and her mother were two peas in a pod. From the stories Suzy told, her mother had the same mischievous, fun streak. "So what happened?"

"Disaster. I actually never made it to the altar. The day before the wedding, Max got arrested. He was running a Ponzi scheme and had bilked millions from his clients. I was named as an accomplice, but I was able to plea bargain out of it by helping them track down records."

"But you did nothing wrong," Sarah said, taken aback. "Or at least you didn't mean to."

"Luckily the judge gave me the benefit of the doubt. I never told Stephen about this. I mean, I was *good* at my job, which is why so many people lost their money. I didn't realize I was swindling them." She sighed. "If the press gets wind of this, it'll be like living it all over again. I thought I had covered my tracks well. The DA sealed the records, labeling me as a confidential informant. I didn't even know what happened to the wedding dress. I didn't even care until you mentioned you had found it in the attic. Now I realize Mom must've stored things in Aunt Betty's attic when they moved.

"Anyway, I panicked when you mentioned that van. I'm pretty sure reporters or investigators from the opposition have been following me, trying to dig up dirt. Maybe they'd even try to search Uncle Carroll's house. I thought that mom might've left something, like the wedding invitations, that would link me to the case in Florida. Anyway, that's why I lied about my whereabouts."

Sarah chewed on another cookie. "You know, things like this tend to surface. Don't you think the more trustworthy and honest thing to do would be to tell Stephen and let him decide what to do about the campaign?"

"Yeah, after the last horrible week, I was thinking the same thing. Now that I have all that stuff back, I feel calmer. Sorry, old friend. You've done so much for me by helping Uncle Carroll and this is how I repaid you. Do you forgive me?"

Sarah still felt a little angry with her friend, but she thought about Irene and her parents. Sarah didn't want to have any regrets because she hadn't forgiven soon enough. She gave Suzy a smile. "If I could forgive you for taking that horrible photo of me sleeping and posting it in the dorm lobby, I guess I can forgive you for this."

"You're the only one who didn't think it was cute!" Suzy said.

"I was drooling!"

Suzy held up an Oreo. "Cookie toast?"

Sarah laughed. "Sure. Why not?"

"Here's to friendship even when one of us, usually me, okay, *always* me, messes up." They tapped cookies and Suzy gave Sarah a hug.

"One last question," Suzy said. "How did you know it was me?"

"There was a stack of magazines in that armoire."

"So? They weren't addressed to anyone so I wasn't worried."

"One of them was Florida Living, and with the date, I just guessed."

Suzy grinned. "Excellent, Sarah Hart. You always were astute with details. So now, tell me, what's been going on here? Did you ever find Carroll's tools?"

"Oh, wait until you hear."

"Thirteen years old. I still can't believe I have teenagers now," Maggie said from the front seat of their Tahoe.

Audrey giggled. "Thanks for dinner. That was so good." She and Amy sat in the back with Sarah sandwiched between them as Jason drove the family home. He had taken them all out to The Old Mill for a birthday dinner. As he had teased, "a grown-up restaurant for his grown-up daughters."

"Yeah, thank you. I'm stuffed." Amy patted her stomach. For the occasion, even Amy had consented to wear something other than sports clothes. Both girls looked very pretty tonight in colorful dresses and sandals.

"You're welcome. I'm glad you had a good time," Jason said.

"Well, it isn't over yet, we still have cake and presents." Maggie reminded them.

"I can't wait!" Audrey said. "Although we already had a cupcake. The waiters were funny." She giggled again.

Amy glanced at Sarah and shook her head. She had blushed and appeared mortified when their table was surrounded by the waitstaff who sang an off-key "Happy Birthday."

"Don't worry. You don't have to have any of your mother's chocolate-cherry cake," Jason said. "I'll eat it all."

"Dad! Quit teasing," Audrey said.

"Who says I'm teasing?" Jason turned into the drive of their rambling old Victorian. Sarah had texted Martha from the restaurant to give them warning. She felt like she was sitting on pins and needles waiting for the surprise. From the glances Maggie had given her at dinner, she felt the same way too.

The kitchen and backdoor lights were on and they trooped into the kitchen. The girls seemed too excited to notice the rest of the house was dark.

"I'll get the cake out. We can have it after we open presents," Maggie said. "Why don't you go on into the parlor?"

"Cool!" Amy said scampering after Audrey into the hallway. "Coming Gram?"

"Right behind you," Sarah said, following them down the hall. She could hear Jason and Maggie steps behind her. Audrey flipped the light switch.

"Surprise!" A chorus of voices yelled.

Audrey squealed while Amy staggered backward into Sarah. Laughter erupted as the girls stood wide-eyed, staring at the crush of girls and the decorated parlor.

Pink and black streamers lined the ceiling and balloons hung from the chandelier. A tiered pink cake sat on a table surrounded by brightly wrapped gifts. Everyone seemed to be talking at once, filling the room with a happy roar.

Martha came up to Sarah with a huge grin. "Whew! Trying to keep ten teenyboppers quiet even for five minutes stretched my nerves to the limit."

"You did great." Sarah gave Martha a hug. "This is wonderful."

"The girls did most of it, and Irene has been a big help."

Sarah waved at Irene by the table. Her cheeks were flushed and her eyes bright as she supervised the lighting of the candles. Sarah knew she had done the right thing in inviting her. Until yesterday she'd had no idea the burden Irene carried. Suzy, Dawn, and Carroll all had burdens, secrets, to bear also. Maybe everyone did. The cure to help them all get through life a little easier was friendship. Friends who can accept you for who you are and forgive you for your mistakes.

Sarah smiled as Amy and Audrey were ushered over to the couch to open presents. Moving across country and starting a new life had been hard on the girls, but watching them now, surrounded by friends, Sarah knew they were going to be just fine.

CHAPTER EIGHTEEN

T hat blasted cat is in here again," Carroll said, startling Sarah who was cleaning up after a quick breakfast of oatmeal, strawberries, and milk. Robin stared up at them and flicked his tail. Carroll wadded up his napkin and threw it across the room. The cat scampered into the hall and squeezed through the crack between the sliding doors to the family room.

"He has to be getting in here somewhere." Sarah washed the last plate and wiped her hands on a towel. "I'm going to check the family room again." She had inspected the windows in the family room several times over the last week, and they had all been locked. So what were they missing?

She pushed the doors open. "Here, kitty. Here, Robin." She circled the room looking behind furniture and boxes. The cat was nowhere in sight.

She approached the stack of boxes piled by the stone fireplace. Upon closer inspection, Sarah noticed a cutout in the stone about four feet high. Was that light she saw?

"What's back there?" she asked Carroll, who stood in the doorway.

"Wood box."

"Does it open to the outside?"

"Of course, but it's padlocked."

Sarah squeezed behind the boxes and shoved the wooden door. It cracked open several inches. "I'm going to go check the other side."

"It's locked," Carroll insisted. "The padlock must just be too large, and that's how the blasted cat is coming in."

"I'm going to check anyway." Sarah marched out the backdoor and around the corner of the house.

An overgrown bush hid the large wood panel from view. Carroll was right. A large padlock hung on the latch. The lock was long enough that if the cat pulled at the bottom of the door, it would open wide enough to let it squeeze though.

Disappointed, she turned to go inside when a thought occurred to her.

Sometimes things are not what they seem.

She placed her hands on the latch this time and wiggled it. The latch popped off the panel. The screws had been stripped and slid easily in and out of the holes. Sarah pulled the door open and stared into the family room.

She crawled through the opening and walked to the kitchen. Carroll's mouth dropped open.

"I know how your thief got in," she said. "The latch pops off the door out there. Do you want to call the police? Maybe they can dust for fingerprints."

Carroll shook his head. "Do you really think they'll find anything?"

"Probably not," Sarah admitted. If the thief was who she thought he was, then he probably was too smart to leave that kind of evidence.

"What's the point? I'm sure he used gloves," Carroll grumbled, reinforcing her thought as he stood. "He's no dummy. Unfortunately. Let's just go confront the lion in his lair."

"I traveled this road almost every day for thirty years," Carroll said, gazing out of the window from the front seat of Sarah's car. He had dressed in a suit and tie that had to be at least three decades out of style, but he still looked distinguished.

They had decided not to tell Suzy about their trip until after. Subtlety was the name of the game.

Sarah flipped the blinker to turn into Shepherd and Stanford Motors. She parked the car by the showroom door and turned to Carroll. "Now we're going in there and be pleasant, right? Be subtle and lead up to what we want to know."

Carroll nodded. "No problem," he said in a calm, determined voice.

Sarah helped him out of the car and handed him his walker. He shuffled into the showroom, picking up speed as he headed to the back.

Dana looked up and her eyes widened. "Mr. Shepherd?"

Carroll didn't bother acknowledging her, but shuffled past her desk toward George's office. Sarah paused and gave Dana a smile. "Is Mr. Stanford in?"

"Yes, he is." She held up a finger as she picked up the phone and hit a button. "Mr. Stanford, Mr. Shepherd is here." She listened for a moment. "No, I don't know why, but he's on his way back."

Sarah glanced down the hall and noted that Carroll had made it to the stairs. She indicated to Dana she was heading that way.

"Be careful," Sarah called, earning a scowl from Carroll. She took the walker as Carroll used the handrail to ascend the steps, and then placed the walker in front of him as the office door opened.

"Carroll. How nice to see you," George Stanford said heartily.

Carroll pushed his way into the office. "Not so nice to see you. What have you done, Eddie?"

Sarah sighed. She should've known Carroll Shepherd didn't have a subtle bone in his body.

George looked at Sarah and gave a little shrug. "I've always hated that nickname."

"You didn't have to lie," she said.

"I didn't. There was an Ed Trenton who worked here. Only Carroll, here, would think it was cute to name me after a car line that folded. Just what I want to be remembered for. I never—"

"You stole my design." Carroll thumped his walker on the carpet.

George lifted his hands. "Whoa. Wait. Your design, Carroll?"

"Cut the garbage, *Eddie*. You stole the prototype, the designs, and even my patent applications."

"Interesting." He walked around his desk and sat in his leather chair. "Can you prove that I did? Any witnesses?"

Carroll opened his mouth, but no words came out.

"I thought not." George shifted his gaze to Sarah. "Poor Carroll. We know how bad memory can get in old age. Even the police are wondering what's going on with him."

"You moved stuff around in my house and put those candlesticks under my bed to make me look like an idiot." Carroll's face reddened and Sarah placed a hand on his arm.

"Mr. Stanford, I saw the tool prototypes. I'll testify they were there," Sarah interjected quietly.

George smirked. "Really. Are you sure? If I remember right, there was nothing distinctive about them. Just metal cylinders. You probably saw just another tool." He leaned back and steepled his fingers. "The way I see it, Carroll, you're delusional. After the stroke and losing your daughter suddenly, it's understandable. We may have designed some things years ago, but who's around to even remember those obsolete inventions?"

"We?" Carroll sputtered. "How dare you—"

"It's a new world, Carroll," George continued. "You had your time. Let the past go. No one cares what we did or didn't do. Meanwhile, I've come up with an idea for a tool that'll modernize production of the new fuel-saving combustion pistons. Should let me finally retire."

"You're a crook! I'm going to sue."

George shrugged. "Go ahead and try. My word against yours. And we know how good yours is these days."

"Y-You crook!" Carroll swayed, his breathing labored.

Sarah grabbed his arm again. Heat penetrated his jacket sleeve. "Mr. Shepherd, are you okay?"

"Do you think he's having another stroke?" George asked in an eerily calm voice. "Should I call the paramedics?"

"Oh I won't give you the satisfaction. I don't need your help." Carroll spun his walker around and clomped to the door. "You're not going to get away with this."

George gave Sarah another small smile, his expression telling her he already had.

"Now if you'll excuse me, I have a very important client waiting in the showroom." He stood, straightened his suit jacket and marched across the room to the door. "You know the way out."

Quiet descended over the room, the only sounds being Carroll's breathing and an occasional distant air compressor rat-tat-tatting in the service bay.

Carroll joined her by the window. "George is going to win. I'm eighty-nine and don't have the time or the resources to take him to court." He sighed. "It'll be my word against his. Who's going to believe me? There's no proof Eddie was ever in my house."

"Actually there might be." Sarah gazed at the recycling bins below. "I need to get into the service bay."

"Why?"

"I have a hunch," she said, not wanting to raise Carroll's hopes on a long shot.

He opened his mouth as if to argue but then shrugged. "This way."

She followed him into the hallway to a glass door. "Looks like most of the mechanics are on their lunch break," Carroll said as Sarah descended the steep stairs to the garage below. "If anyone bothers you, send them to me."

At the other end of the bay, a woman shoved a push broom along the concrete, and near the stairs a snowy-haired worker in blue coveralls buffed the chrome on a stately looking black sedan. He looked up. "Ma'am, you shouldn't be in here."

Carroll stepped out onto the platform. "It's okay, Al. She's doing me a favor."

"Mr. Shepherd. Long time no see. We've missed you around here." Al gave him a toothy grin.

"Likewise. How's the workload?"

As Al and Carroll conversed, Sarah made her way to the three-foot-high recycle bin, one-quarter full of greasy towels and rags. A quick search proved what she was looking for wasn't there.

She caught Carroll's attention and pointed to the other end of the room. He nodded and she walked, looking under the cars on the lifts and into the pits. What rags had been left beside the toolboxes were either white or gray.

Oh, please, dear God, if it's here let me find it.

The woman with the broom gave her a curious look as Sarah reached the far wall. Sarah turned back, her footsteps heavy. She'd have to find another way to help Carroll. She was about to give up her search when a thought occurred to her. What if...?

Her gaze scanned past Al to shelves of shiny chrome parts. On the bottom was a stack of folded rags. Most of them were white, but there were a few gray and blue rags mixed in.

Her heart pounded. She looked up to see the platform empty and that Al had resumed buffing the sedan. "Where did Mr. Shepherd go?"

"He's coming in the customer entrance. No stairs." Al paused, dangling a spotted cloth. "Can I be of assistance?"

"You recycle rags here, don't you?"

He blinked. "Yeah, if they can be cleaned."

"I bet you like to use extrasoft ones for doing the chrome."

"It helps."

"I know this may seem strange, but would you mind if I took a look at your shelf over there?"

"Lady—," Al began in an exasperated tone but then caught sight of something behind her. Carroll was clomping his way into the bay through another door at floor level. Al shrugged. "Sure, go ahead."

Sarah sidled past the sedan and walked to the shelf. She carefully lifted the top rags and gazed at the treasure beneath.

"What are you doing?" Carroll stopped at the base of the stairs, his chest heaving.

Sarah backed away from the evidence and hurried over to him. "I found your proof, Mr. Shepherd," she said softly, aware Al was still scrutinizing her. "I want to call the police."

"But—"

Sarah held up a hand, and Carroll snapped his mouth shut. She stepped through the doorway that Carroll had just come through. She pulled her cell phone from her purse and requested police assistance on a theft.

Sarah returned to Carroll, who seemed to be breathing easier now. "They said a car was nearby and will be here in a few minutes."

He glowered at her. "What's going on?" Al had gone back to work, but kept shooting glances at them.

"Remember I told you about the missing baby quilt in the attic?"

"I'm tired of hearing about the stupid quilt."

Sarah sighed. She needed to discuss her trip to Windham and the significance of the baby quilt soon, but first she had to try to secure Carroll's future.

"I think Eddie's been sneaking into the house through the firewood door. He took the file box, found your designs, and then replaced the box. He probably assumed you'd never notice that the paperwork and the prototypes were missing."

"So? What good does that do me now?"

"The prototypes were mixed up in the pile of tools under the rug in the attic, correct? Suppose Eddie saw them, and maybe something spooked him or he didn't have time to sort through them all, so he grabbed something to carry them all out."

Comprehension dawned in Carroll's blue eyes. "You think he grabbed the quilt."

Sarah rummaged in her purse and pulled out the scrap. "See this dark spot? I'm pretty sure it's grease. I had a spot of it on my blouse after I handled those tools the first time. I'm thinking that Eddie wrapped your tools in the quilt and it caught on the nail on the way down. The quilt, or what's left of it, is on the shelf back there. I'm assuming Eddie, er, George, must've stopped by here with the prototypes and tossed the quilt, which was retrieved by the cleaning crew."

"We have our proof he was in the attic." Carroll started toward the shelf, but Sarah grabbed his arm.

"Wait for the police. We don't want to disturb the evidence. It might not be enough to convict George of any crime, but it's enough to create doubt about his being the inventor of that tool of yours."

"Well, we can't have that."

Sarah jumped and turned as George rounded the corner of the customer door.

"I should've guessed you were the type to skulk around corners." Carroll glowered at his old partner.

"Yes, and in my case eavesdropping has proved valuable."

"Hey boss," Al called in a nervous tone. "Mr. Shepherd said it was okay if she was down here."

"Don't worry about it, Al. Why don't you take a break? I have something private to discuss with Mr. Shepherd and Mrs. Hart."

"You know he's still a witness."

"Not if there isn't anything to be a witness of." George shoved past Sarah and headed for the shelf.

"Al, stop him. He's committing a crime," Carroll said.

George glanced at his employee. "Mr. Shepherd has been ill and doesn't know what he's talking about."

Al looked from one to the other and held up his hands. "I don't want to get involved. I need this job."

"Then I suggest you get back to work," George said. Al stepped to the car, his hands shaking as he resumed polishing.

"George, other people have seen the quilt pieces," Sarah said, trying to stall him. *Oh, where were the police?*

"What quilt? I just see rags." George grabbed the pile and hurried toward the customer door. Sounds of laughter and people talking sounded in the hallway. George veered toward the stairs. Carroll planted himself in front of the landing, hunched over his walker.

"Move, Carroll!"

"Not on your life."

George hurtled forward, knocking the walker out from under Carroll. Carroll grabbed George as he tried to get past him. They tumbled to the ground as Dana and two uniformed policeman appeared at the top of the stairs and workers swarmed in the other door.

Sarah rushed over to Carroll. George was pinned under him. "Are you okay?"

Carroll lifted his head. "Well, don't just stand there gawking. Get me up so the police can do their job. Looks like I have to come out of retirement for a while. First order of business is to sell my invention. What are you staring at? Get me up!"

Sarah shook her head in exasperation, but a big smile tugged the corners of her lips as she helped the old grouch stand.

Epilogue

The morning of the Strawberry Festival dawned with a brief shower, but as Sarah and Martha walked across the wet grass in Patriot Park, the sun tried hard to make an entrance, its rays turning the raindrops into tiny diamonds.

Brilliant white open-air tents had been set up around Patriot Park. Sarah and Martha had already stopped by Maggie's tent and sampled the white chocolate-dipped strawberries and were now headed for the tent where Audrey's and Amy's strawberry jam was being judged.

"Sarah!" someone called.

She stopped and turned to see Irene, her husband Chris, and, surprisingly, Carroll heading across the grass toward them. Irene broke into a light jog leaving the men behind.

It had been a hectic two and a half weeks since their visit to the dealership. George had been taken into custody and immediately went to work striking a deal to keep out of jail. He agreed to return the prototypes, drawings, and patent applications to Carroll, and to perform community service in exchange for Carroll's not pressing charges.

Carroll began negotiations with one of the big automobile manufacturers. The times had finally caught up with Carroll's invention, and with more fuel-efficient engines, Carroll's modified tool design was going to be in hot demand. This also meant Carroll would be able to afford to hire live-in help and stay in his home. Meanwhile, Irene had volunteered to take over Sarah's daily visits. She said she liked caring for the gruff old man.

Suzy flew back to Arizona to deal with her own past issues and her husband's campaign. It turned out that the people in the brown van were not reporters, but movie location scouts trying to keep a low profile while scoping out neighborhoods for a small town TV drama. Suzy promised she would be back to visit in July for Maple Hill's 225*th* anniversary celebration and fair.

"Guess what?" Irene said, rather breathlessly "I called your writer friend Chester Winslow, as you suggested, and he referred me to someone at *Living History Magazine*. They're going to look at my articles. Chester thought they were good enough to publish, so we'll see."

"That's so exciting!" Sarah said giving Irene a hug.

Martha smiled. "Congratulations. There's going to be another published author in our midst."

Irene spun around as Carroll and Chris reached them. "Oh, and we have some more big news, don't we, Carroll? Tell her about your phone call to Jennifer Orman."

"Oh good, you talked to her," Sarah said with relief. "How did that go?" Sarah had sat down with Carroll and told him about her trip to Windham and that the quilt George stole was actually one Dawn had made during the time she was pregnant. Tears had welled up in his eyes. That had been a difficult time for all of them. Dawn had never told him about the quilt and Sarah had promised she would do her best to restore it.

"Well? Are you going to say something?" Irene said.

Carroll humphed. "I have a grandson out there. Somewhere."

"What?" Sarah and Martha said at the same time.

"Dawn never gave me any details about the baby, and I didn't ask," Carroll said. "We'd already decided that adoption was the best option, but I'd just assumed the baby died during childbirth because Dawn almost did. She was all tore up over the ordeal, so we never talked about it."

"Jennifer was shocked that we all thought the baby didn't make it," Irene added. "Dawn must've felt it was better that way. Jennifer gave Carroll some databases he can put his name in just in case his grandson is looking for family."

"Carroll, that's wonderful," Sarah said. "Maybe someday you'll get a chance to meet him."

Carroll nodded, a smile twitching his lips. "I'd like that. Very much."

Chris tugged his wife's sleeve. "Tell Sarah about the ice cream."

"Ice cream?" Sarah looked at Irene.

"Oh, you were right about Dave Diamond. Wasn't she, Carroll?" Irene nudged him with her elbow. "Tell her."

He looked skyward and shook his head slightly, but it was obvious Irene had been good for him.

"You were right," he said to Sarah.

Sarah chuckled. "In what regard?"

He sighed heavily. "When I was pulling the ice cream carton out of the freezer, money fell on the floor."

"And?" Irene prodded.

"And there was the receipt," he said grumpily. "Happy?"

"Dawn was apparently stressed those last few weeks before the accident, so we think that when she put the ice cream away she accidentally stuck Mr. Diamond's money in there too," Chris said.

Sarah smiled. "Well, I'm glad that mystery is solved."

"Gram, Gram! Come see!" Audrey called, running toward her. Amy waited by one of the tents, but she was waving too.

Sarah excused herself and hurried toward her grandchildren. "What is it?"

Audrey grabbed Sarah's hand and tugged her over to the white tent. "They finished judging the jam."

"Oh! How did you do?"

"Come look!"

Sarah ducked under the opening of the tent to see rows of pint jars full of bright red jam sitting on white tablecloths. Jason and Maggie were standing by one jar that had a red second place ribbon lying in front of it.

"We got second place!" Audrey said. "When I saw all the jam that was entered, I didn't think we stood a chance."

"Congratulations!" Sarah gave them each a hug. "I'm proud of you."

Jason had his arm around Maggie, with a big grin on his face. "I think it's very appropriate. A red ribbon for red jam."

Sarah looked from the jar to the girls. "So...which one of you won?"

Amy glanced at Audrey and they giggled. "We don't know," Amy said. "We accidentally mixed the jars up at home and just decided to enter this one together."

"Sarah, sorry to interrupt," Irene called from the tent doorway. "But before I forget, I have something for you."

Sarah stepped outside into the sunshine as Irene pulled out a small velvet drawstring bag. Sarah opened it and a sparkly silver charm bracelet slid into her hand.

"It's not much considering how you've helped me."

"Oh, Irene. You didn't have to get me anything. But it's beautiful." Sarah held up the chain and examined the charms. "What's this bee clutching a blanket?"

"A quilting bee." Irene clapped her hands together with delight. Sarah grinned. Other charms on the bracelet included a thimble, an inkwell and a feather pen, an enchanting Victorian house, a puppy that held an uncanny resemblance to Murphy, a quilting hoop, and the head of a man smoking a pipe.

"Sherlock Holmes. I tried to find Agatha Christie since you like her books, but this was the closest I could get. I figured you and Sherlock have a lot in common solving mysteries," Irene said with a little laugh. "I know it may seem a little silly—"

"Oh, Irene, I love it! I'm touched by your thoughtfulness. I've enjoyed our times together."

"Sarah Hart, you did more for me than you'll ever know. I still have a way to go to get over the past, but I realize now that with friends like you I have all the family I need." Irene glanced over her shoulder at her husband and Carroll who were still talking with Martha.

She gave Sarah a quick hug. "Now go have a great time with your family, and I will with mine. I'll see you later." She turned and walked away with a bounce in her step.

Sarah slipped on the bracelet and spotted Liam and Murphy strolling across the park to where The Spotted Dog was sponsoring a tent. He lifted a hand in greeting and her heart fluttered.

"Dad! Are you serious?" Audrey cried out. Sarah ducked back into the tent. It appeared Jason was going down the line taste testing every jar of jam in the place. Maggie and the girls were following him, laughing.

Sarah smiled, breathing in the sweet scent of strawberries, and let out a deep contented sigh.

ABOUT THE AUTHOR

From her first introduction to the beginner readers with Dick and Jane, award-winning author Kelly Ann Riley has wanted to be a writer. She started penning stories at an early age, and received special recognition for her short stories. Later, she became a reporter and the editor for her high school newspaper.

Now Kelly Ann enjoys penning romantic suspense and cozy mysteries. Her past hobbies of quilting, cross-stitching, and crocheting make the *Patchwork Mysteries* particularly fun to write. She loves watching fabric, string, and yarn transform into art. She is a member of American Christian Fiction Writers and Romance Writers of America, and lives in Alabama with her family. You can contact her through her Web site at KellyAnnRiley.com.

SQUARED AWAY

BY CARA PUTMAN

 CHAPTER ONE

Sarah Hart stepped into Wild Goose Chase and sucked in a breath. The place was packed. Crowds of ladies worked their way through the aisles of fabric. Bolts of muslins and silks and wools unspooled on the shelves, the small notions section was hopping, and even the yarn and embroidery aisle was crammed with people. While Vanessa usually reserved the cutting table for cutting fabric to the right length, today there were piles of fat quarters strewn across its surface. Saturday morning light shone through the plate glass windows, the sun filtered through soft white clouds. Sarah let her eyes adjust to the light inside the store and then glanced up at the mural of a lone gosling trying to keep up with a flock of Canada geese, but the cacophony of women's voices brought her gaze back down to eye level. Sarah couldn't imagine how Vanessa Sawyer's first fabric swap could be more successful.

Sarah worked her way across the store, looking for her friend's dark hair. She saw dozens of women clutching fat quarters, browsing through the stacks of fabric on the tables, but she didn't see Vanessa.

Sarah smiled at several women she recognized and many women she'd never seen in the shop before. Maybe they would be new converts to the art of quilting after this. That would make the day even more successful for Vanessa's business. A new quilter would make numerous return trips to the store.

Sarah stood on tiptoe to look over a freestanding fabric display and the rack of patterns, notions, and trims that stood next to it. Many of Maple Hill's regular quilters were here, but she was surprised Janet Stevens wasn't among them. Janet might be Maple Hill's most talented quilter. She usually focused on replicas of antique quilts, so maybe a fabric swap didn't interest her. Allie Turnquist wasn't here either, though she was really more of a quilt collector.

But Sarah did see Alison Vanter, owner of the Copy Shop, next to the tea station. She was wearing a simple pair of tailored jeans and a striped oxford shirt and was chatting with a few women. Sarah also recognized Cate Goodman looking through the stacks of fat quarters, her blonde hair pulled back in a low ponytail. The young woman had grown up in town and had come back to Maple Hill to care for an elderly aunt. She had stayed on after the aunt died a few years back. Cate glanced up and waved.

"Hi, Cate," Sarah said. She moved toward the girl and rummaged through her large canvas quilting bag to pull out a stack of fabric she'd brought from home. The swap was the perfect opportunity to get some of the larger remnants out of her closet and replenish her own stash with new fabric.

"Hello, Mrs. Hart. There's a lot of fabric here."

"With more on the way," Sarah said as she added her offerings to the table. Flannels, velvets, and muslins landed on the overflowing surface.

"It's a little overwhelming!" Cate said, reaching out for a floral print Sarah had used in a baby quilt years ago. "But I've been here awhile, and I've got plenty. I should probably head home. Nice to see you."

"You too." Sarah turned to the kaleidoscope of options in front of her. The table overflowed with a mix of calicoes, dotted swiss, muslins, and wool blends. Sarah rubbed her fingers over a soft flannel piece decorated with dancing Christmas trees and candy canes. Though she'd been a quilter most of her life, Sarah never tired of fabric swaps, places where quilters could explore and exchange the scraps and leftovers from their miscellaneous projects. It was also an opportunity to observe what kinds of quilts and fabrics were popular among casual quilters. Though the hodgepodge offerings made it a challenge to find pieces that would work for her, Sarah had learned that if she was patient and dug deep enough, she could usually find at least a few pieces to take home and integrate into her projects. Not knowing who brought each fat quarter was part of the allure.

"Sarah Hart, I wondered when you'd show up." Sarah looked up to find her old friend Hannah Grace smiling broadly, her lips painted a bright magenta. "I'm thrilled for Vanessa that so many people came."

Sarah smiled back. "Why, Hannah Grace, I haven't seen you in almost a year now! What have you been up to?"

"I've been in Virginia a lot of the past twelve months or so, where my daughter lives," Hannah replied.

"Oh, that's right. How is she?" Sarah asked. Hannah's daughter was married with young children, and she was also fighting a serious illness. Sarah remembered she had heard that Hannah was going away for a while to spend time helping her daughter with the kids and the house.

"Two rounds of chemo later, they say she's cancer-free."

"That's wonderful," Sarah said.

"Thank you," Hannah said, sorting through the fabric. "If you see any holiday prints, let me know. I'm working on a Christmas quilt for my daughter."

"Absolutely. In fact, I saw one over there that had candy canes." Sarah pointed to the other end of the table. Hannah nodded and moved toward the pile of remnants. Sarah, on the other hand, was looking for a fabric for the center block of the quilt she was working on for Maple Hill's 225th anniversary celebration. The town was planning a huge festival. As part of the festivities, the volunteer fire department had planned a silent auction and benefit to raise funds for badly needed equipment. One of the volunteer coordinators, Irene Stuart, had asked Sarah to contribute a quilt for

the cause, so Sarah had been working on a quilt that show-
cased the area's history and seasons.

With only eight days left until the auction, Sarah still
hadn't found a fabric that looked right for the center square.
Vanessa didn't have anything in stock that worked, and although Sarah had driven to a lot of the fabric stores in the
area over the past few weeks, she hadn't found anything with
the perfect fall colors. But with so many quilters bringing
pieces from their own stashes, perhaps she would find something here today that would work. Sarah shuffled through a
pile of vintage material that looked like former flour sacks,
and then moved on to a stack of juvenile and holiday prints.

"Hannah, there are some holiday quarters here," Sarah
called.

Hannah looked up from the fabric she was examining
and moved closer to Sarah. "Ooh, let me see."

Sarah handed over a few red and green florals as a print
covered with tiny Christmas trees caught her attention. She
held up the fabric. "This would be nice in a Christmas quilt."

Hannah nodded her head, gray curls bouncing. "Thanks,
that's nice." She rummaged through the pile and pulled out a
few more fabrics. "This is exhausting work. Maybe I'll break
for some tea."

Sarah handed her the Christmas tree fabric and kept
hunting. Surely somewhere in this disorganized mess there
would be the one fat quarter that met her needs. She moved
on to the next table. This one had several stacks of brightly
flowered prints and a couple of elegant toiles. Maybe there

was something she could use buried underneath. She moved to the left a bit, and bumped into a petite woman.

"Excuse me," Sarah said, sticking out her hand. "I'm sorry. I'm Sarah Hart."

"Hello." The young woman squinted a bit as she glanced at Sarah and then back down at the fabric. "I'm Rachel Taylor. I've seen you at Bridge Street Church. You have granddaughters in my daughter's class at school, too, I think."

"Of course." Sarah remembered seeing the woman toward the back of the sanctuary last Sunday. "I didn't recognize you without the kids."

Rachel held out her empty arms. "I barely recognize myself without them. My youngest is in preschool so it's rare that I get a moment like this to myself. Except for my spinning class every day."

"I didn't know you were a quilter," Sarah said.

"I try, but I'm pretty new at the whole thing. I think it will be fun, though. I don't know why I even got into it ... it's not like my kids don't keep me plenty busy! What kind of fabrics are you looking for?"

"The impossible. A pattern that gives the illusion of the vibrant colors our leaves turn in the fall. I've about decided I'm asking too much of one piece."

"Let me help." Rachel circled to the other side of the table. "Between the two of us, we'll find the perfect thing."

"I like your optimism." Several women Sarah didn't know poked around the piles of fabric. Grace Fletcher, a nurse at the nursing home, grabbed a fat quarter and added it to her personal stack, which was quite large. Rachel made short work of flipping through piles, but Sarah didn't find a swatch with the right colors. She had the rest of the quilt ready to piece together, but without fabric for the center square, she was stuck.

Sarah flipped through another stack and paused. She fingered a calico with a small swirled pattern of red, gold, and green. The colors matched those of fall leaves. "This could work."

"Hmm?" Rachel looked up from a pile. "Oh, that's pretty."

"It is, isn't it?" Sarah picked up the fabric. When she cut it into the tiny squares and triangles she needed for the center square, it would create the impression of a beautiful Massachusetts fall. "I could use this."

Sarah picked through a few more stacks, but nothing else caught her eye, and she moved to the back of the store to get a mug of tea, still scanning the store for Vanessa. Sarah finally spotted her at the cash register. A young woman she didn't know studied the assorted teas in the basket Vanessa had laid out. The woman selected an Earl Gray, and Sarah grabbed a mug and a chai tea bag. She doctored it with a bit of sugar and cream, settled down in a chair next to Hannah, and watched as the other swap participants steadily worked through the piles. There were lots of new faces here, and many of the women weren't here just to look at the free fabric. Several of them had picked up bolts of new fabric and were moving toward the front counter to make their purchases. Vanessa chatted with the customers, and the line moved quickly. Sarah was glad for Vanessa. She would do well today.

A woman collapsed into the vacant chair next to Sarah, leaning her wildly painted cane against the chair. Sarah looked up and recognized Vivian Banks, who lived near Jason and Maggie. "So much fabric, so little time." Vivian rubbed her knee. "Glad I found a few things I like quickly." She held out a stack of childish prints that made Sarah think of colorful nurseries.

"Making some baby quilts?"

"Yes. Our church ladies are making some for a crisis pregnancy center."

"What a wonderful way to use your quilting." Sarah eyed her. "Knee acting up?"

Vivian nodded. "These old bones aren't quite what they used to be. Wouldn't be surprised if a storm blew through tonight. It's like having my own weather station." She rubbed her knee again and nodded toward the fabrics in Sarah's lap. "Find something good?"

"A few pieces. Though I'm here mostly because it's fun to catch up with quilters I don't get to see enough, like you and Hannah."

Vivian stifled a yawn. "Well, I guess I'd best head home before the storm blows in." The woman stood and walked gracefully across the floor despite the small hitch in her step, the colorful cane tapping the way in front of her. Sarah waved to her old friend and said a prayer that she would be safe.

Over the next half hour, the rest of the swappers drifted out slowly, but Sarah remained, hoping to catch up with Vanessa.

"Need another cup of tea?" Vanessa asked her, but the lines around her eyes showed her weariness.

"Not unless I want to float out of here." Sarah joined Vanessa at the counter. "Just wanted to say thank you."

"For what?" Vanessa asked.

"Hosting the swap. What a great idea. People really got into it."

"My pleasure," Vanessa said. She moved to the front door and turned the open sign to the closed side. She leaned against the door. "It went really well . . . and looks like it was worth all the extra time and effort. I sold some fabric and notions, and if half the new ladies become frequent customers, I'll be thrilled."

"Everyone had a great time and seemed to find what they wanted, including me." Sarah got up and set her fabric finds on the now-vacant chair. "Can I help you clean things up? I'm sure you're ready to get home to the kids."

"I'd love the help. Kathy's away for the weekend. I should never have planned this without my assistant around!" Vanessa looked around the store. "Would you mind sweeping and straightening the tea area? I'll tackle the area around the cutting table and then get to work on the cash register."

Sarah accepted the broom Vanessa handed her. "Sure. What are the kids up to? Saturday morning cartoons?"

Vanessa laughed. "They don't really have time for those, much as they'd like to. Lena's busy as ever with her dance classes. I have to pick her up in half an hour. And Terence had soccer practice this morning. Fortunately, a friend's mom could take him home with them, so he gets time playing with a friend."

Vanessa held up a couple of fat quarters. "Would you like any of these leftovers?"

Sarah studied the fabrics, one an eggplant-colored paisley, the other a cherry red check. "I don't think I can use either."

Vanessa tossed them in a box. "I might as well save them. I think after today's receipts, I'll host more swaps." She arched her back and twisted from side to side, then swiped the table one more time. "That'll do. Now for the money."

She perched on the stool behind the counter and punched buttons on the cash register. It churned out a strip of paper that looked like it belonged in a ticker tape parade. Vanessa flipped through receipts as the paper spooled out. Then she turned to the drawer and counted out bills. "I could use a fraction of Terence's energy right now. He's always bouncing off the walls after school or practice."

Sarah chuckled, remembering days like that with her own kids. "Trust me, one day you'll miss that little ball of energy. He'll be a teen, then off at college, and you'll wish for these days."

"I know." Vanessa grinned. "I really just think the boy needs a strong male influence at home. He doesn't say so, but he misses his daddy. I've been praying so hard for Drew to ... to come back." Vanessa and her husband had been separated for over a year now. They had opened the store together almost ten years ago, fallen in love, then had Lena and Terence, their two lovely children, and ...

"I'll pray too." Sarah had never really understood what had happened between Vanessa and Drew, and Vanessa rarely spoke about her husband. But she'd been content to pray for Vanessa as her way of helping out over the past year.

The cash register quit its clicking. Vanessa turned back to it while Sarah finished the sweeping and then tidied the tea area. The tea nook, with its soft chairs and warm lighting, gave the store a bright, welcoming feeling, inviting people to stay even if they didn't find what they sought.

The cash register drawer snapped shut. Sarah leaned the broom against the counter and walked around to Vanessa. "Are you okay?"

"Yep, just ready to go get my kids. Everything else can wait until Monday. I'm ready to be home. And if I leave now, I might have time to drop off the deposit at the bank before it closes."

"Give your kids a hug for me."

Vanessa nodded and followed Sarah out the front door and locked it behind them. Sarah watched a minute and then climbed into her car. She couldn't wait to get home and see how the fabric looked in the anniversary quilt.

When Sarah got home, the windows were dark. Andi McCormack, her current boarder, had moved in more than a month before, but she attended community college and worked at the Miss Maple diner so she wasn't around much. She must not be home now.

She plopped her bag on the kitchen counter and flipped on the lights, illuminating the white cabinets set against her cranberry walls. She filled the teakettle with water, set it to boil, and then took her new fat quarters to the sewing room. The 225th anniversary quilt blocks lay on a length of muslin stretched across her table. She arranged the shapes she had already cut for the center square on the new piece of fabric to see how it looked. She stepped back and tried to picture the finished square.

The teakettle whistled, and Sarah started and walked to the kitchen. As she filled a mug with water, the phone rang, and her hand jerked, sloshing water across the counter. She grabbed a towel and mopped up the mess with one hand while she grabbed the phone with the other.

"Hello?"

"Sarah, it's so awful. You'll never guess what the bank told me."

Sarah stopped wiping the counter. "Vanessa?"

"Yes." Vanessa sounded harried, and Sarah could hear Terence's and Lena's voices in the background. "I managed to make it to the bank before it closed, so I swung in. The teller took one look at the money I brought and started asking questions."

"About what?"

"Where I'd gotten the money. Who'd brought it in. Odd questions like that. Then he disappeared behind a closed door. It was the strangest thing."

"I've never had that happen." Sarah had been going to Maple Hill Community Bank her whole life, and they had always treated her kindly.

"I know! He came back and asked another bunch of questions. Then he said the bank couldn't accept the money."

"Why not?"

"The bills are counterfeit. He said they wouldn't be able to deposit them in my account. Said they weren't worth the paper they were printed on." Vanessa's voice shook as she continued. "It's a hundred dollars, Sarah. And to top it off, he told me to stay available in case the police need to contact me."

A NOTE FROM THE EDITORS

Patchwork Mysteries was created by the Books and Inspirational Media Division of Guideposts, a nonprofit organization that touches millions of lives every day through products and services that inspire, encourage and uplift. Our magazines, books, prayer network (OurPrayer.org), and other outreach programs help people connect their faith-filled values to daily life.

Your purchase of Patchwork Mysteries makes a difference. When you buy Guideposts products, you're helping fund our work, which includes ministry to military personnel, prisons, hospitals, nursing homes and educational institutions. To learn more, visit GuidepostsFoundation.org.

To find out about our other publications and to enjoy free online resources such as inspirational newsletters, blogs, videos, Facebook and Twitter links, visit us at Guideposts.org.